UNDER THE MOON

Kelthorne looked into her eyes, glittering as they had that first night, beneath the scattered moonbeams piercing the orchard. "I believe I must agree quite wholeheartedly with you," he said, surprised a little that his voice had fallen to little more than a murmur. A breeze swept a dangling curl over her cheek and instinctively he brushed it back toward her ear, his fingers touching her skin. He heard her sigh softly.

He met Judith's gaze fully once more. He had never, throughout their slow walk through the orchard, considered kissing her, but the thought entered his head now with such force that before he could consider what he was about, he slid his hand behind her neck, leaned forward and placed his lips gently on hers.

BOOK YOUR PLACE ON OUR WEBSITE AND MAKE THE READING CONNECTION!

We've created a customized website just for our very special readers, where you can get the inside scoop on everything that's going on with Zebra, Pinnacle and Kensington books.

When you come online, you'll have the exciting opportunity to:

- View covers of upcoming books
- Read sample chapters
- Learn about our future publishing schedule (listed by publication month *and author*)
- Find out when your favorite authors will be visiting a city near you
- Search for and order backlist books from our online catalog
- Check out author bios and background information
- Send e-mail to your favorite authors
- Meet the Kensington staff online
- Join us in weekly chats with authors, readers and other guests
- Get writing guidelines
- AND MUCH MORE!

**Visit our website at
http://www.kensingtonbooks.com**

WICKED
AND
WONDERFUL

VALERIE KING

ZEBRA BOOKS
KENSINGTON PUBLISHING CORP.
www.kensingtonbooks.com

ZEBRA BOOKS are published by

Kensington Publishing Corp.
850 Third Avenue
New York, NY 10022

All Kensington titles, imprints, and distributed lines are available at special quantity discounts for bulk purchases for sales promotion, premiums, fund-raising, educational or institutional use.

Special book excerpts or customized printings can also be created to fit specific needs. For details, write or phone the office of the Kensington Special Sales Manager: Attn. Special Sales Department. Kensington Publishing Corp., 850 Third Avenue, New York, NY 10022. Phone: 1-800-221-2647.

Zebra and the Z logo Reg. U.S. Pat. & TM Off.

ISBN 0-8217-7847-1

First Printing: September 2005
10 9 8 7 6 5 4 3 2 1

Printed in the United States of America

ONE

Somerset, England 1818

"Foolish, foolish dare!" Judith Lovington whispered in agony.

She had just caught sight of a man on horseback at the far end of the orchard and now realized she had erred wretchedly. She knew quite well that if she could see him, even though only leaf-shaped bits of moonlight were scattered on the ground, then he could most certainly see her. What rotten luck that this man had chosen to ride his horse at so late an hour, and at that in an orchard!

She watched his head rise. She stood very still hoping that perhaps the dark, boy's clothing she was wearing, borrowed from the troupe's vast store of costumes, would make her but a shadow in the orchard. Her heart pounded as she waited. Suddenly, he spurred his horse in her direction. He had seen her!

She groaned, pushed her hat down hard about her ears and, turning around abruptly, began to run. All the while, stolen apples dropped to the ground in dull thuds from the shawl clutched to her chest. How could she have allowed herself to be persuaded to enter the Earl of Kelthorne's orchard in the first place!

She stumbled more than once but managed to right herself and keep running.

From behind, the man yelled after her—none too politely. "Stay a moment, young halfling!" he taunted. "A word with you, and then my riding crop, for I promise you I mean to beat you within an inch of your life! At the very least, 'twill mean the stocks for you and I believe I will only now be made content by throwing half a dozen cabbages at your head!"

The man, whose diction bespoke the gentleman, was clearly outraged by her crime. She should never have allowed Charles Hemyock to provoke her to the deed. From his first joining the troupe nearly a year past, he had barely had a civil word for her. He was arrogant and cruel, and she did not like him above half, but when he had called her a worthless female with little wit and no bottom at all, just like all the other females of the dramatic troupe, she felt obligated to vindicate herself and her sex.

So he had dared her to collect a dozen apples from Kelthorne's orchard and she had accepted his challenge, although she now thought he may have been right about her lack of wit—or certainly her lack of sense—for here she was, being chased by a man intent on doing her serious injury and in some danger of being brought before a magistrate. Thievery was not looked upon kindly by the king's law and visions of dangling from Tyburn Tree pressed her to move faster still.

She glanced back again. He would be on her in a trice for she could hardly outrun his horse. Still, she ran, slipping through the orchard sideways, moving from row to row of thickly leafed trees in hopes of forcing him from his horse. She might then have a chance to escape, for the nearby hill was thick with growth and she knew how to hide. She had at the very least some practice in that skill.

As she neared the edge of the orchard, she glanced again and saw that she had made some progress. He was having difficulty, just as she had hoped, navigating his horse after her. She felt a sudden rush of exhilaration believing she now had a chance to escape when she heard a terrible sound, the deep bark of a large dog, not too far distant.

Glancing once more over her shoulder, she saw moonlight glint off the dusky coat of a bounding dog heading in her direction. Her heart sank, fear engulfed her chest as she ran faster still. She dropped her shawl and the rest of the apples as she raced for the woods. She did not know how she might escape now, but she meant to make every effort.

She held to the last vestige of hope until she heard the wheezing of the dog behind her and suddenly found herself shoved forward landing, fortunately, on a patch of grassy turf at the very edge of the orchard.

"Rufus!" the man shouted from a distance. "Desist!"

Judith found herself pressed to the ground. The big dog was standing on her back. At the same time, she covered her face with her arms fearing that she would soon feel the creature's teeth tearing away at her flesh. Her heart pounded in her chest so that the top of her head hurt. She felt dizzy and more frightened than she had in her entire life, even more than on the day she had run away from home some eight years earlier. Had death come to her at last?

The dog sniffed her neck and throat. Judith prepared for the worst, then she suddenly felt the wet lick of his long tongue.

"Oh-h-h!" she cried in disgust. "I believe I would rather you had bit me, you abominable creature! Do get off. How heavy you are!"

The beast, having appeared to understand her, leaped aside, forcing the breath from her once more. She turned to face him and only barely avoided another wet assault by turning away from him and pressing her hand against his muzzle. He licked her fingers instead, then began to whine. His friendly nature became more apparent with each whimper so that there was nothing for it. She sat up and began to rub his ears.

She could not help but smile as she spoke to him in a soft voice. "I had a dog like you once—the same shaggy fur, of that I am certain. A delightful mongrel."

The dog whined a little more.

"There's a good boy, Rufus," she said. "And what a horrible but very sweet dog you are! However, I do not hesitate to say that your master will most certainly be most displeased with this performance." She glanced up and watched as the horseman approached. Rufus whined again in response to her speech as though trying to offer a reasonable explanation for his conduct. At the same time, he laid a paw on her arm. "Well, I am in the basket now. See what you have done and I was so close to the making my escape!"

Rufus tossed his head and barked.

Judith remained on the ground and felt for the sheathed dagger she wore strapped to her leg beneath her clothing. The voluminous breeches she wore would allow her to reach the dagger quite easily, but she would not do so unless the situation became desperate. She was well able to defend herself if need be, but she would hardly serve the troupe well were she to do injury to a gentleman who must have some relationship with Portislow Castle, thereby possibly incurring the wrath of the owner. The troupe was presently indebted to the Earl of Kelthorne who was permitting them to camp in his field near the orchard.

The stranger dismounted and tied his reins to a nearby apple tree. The orchard was quite dark in shadow, but moonlight served to reveal three things: he was quite tall, his hair was wavy and longer than most, and his face appeared to be a collection of very strong planes indicating a rather determined disposition—if she did not much mistake the matter. Beyond that, details were quite lost to her. She could, however, sense his present sentiments even if she was unable to decipher them by the expression on his face, for he walked with a brisk gait, he clenched his fingers into fists and hunched his shoulders ever so slightly.

"Rufus," he called stridently. "What a ridiculous dog you are! Come!"

Only when Judith ceased kneading his ears, however, did Rufus slink toward the tall gentleman.

When he had his dog sitting obediently beside him, he looked down at her. "Do I apprehend correctly that you are not a boy after all?"

"You are correct," she stated, staring up at him.

Lord Kelthorne looked down in bewilderment at the figure sitting on the ground. How greatly shocked he had been to hear not only the voice of a young woman, but a quite genteel voice as well. How very promising! A breeze caused moonlight to flicker over a shiny wave of dark curls that hung down her back. Somewhere in her flight, or perhaps Rufus's assault, her hat had fallen away.

Despite all his newly formed good intentions toward womankind in general—truly he did mean to reform since he would soon take a wife—a smile slowly overtook his lips. "You have given me a shock, my little thief. I thought you were a lad." As he watched her gain her feet, a warm, familiar sensation set a quick fire in his veins. Her legs were encased in snug boots over white stockings and the oversized breeches she wore did not quite meet her knees. She was in that sense shockingly underdressed and he was frightfully glad of it.

From years of experience, he knew precisely how to orchestrate the next several minutes in order to bring the young lady to just the right tilt of romantic inclination. He would kiss her. Yes, at the very least he would kiss her. Such a lady in this disguise would probably allow him to do more. He looked her up and down once more. How odd to think that a ride at nearly midnight for the sole purpose of relieving some of his present frustrations would have resulted in this.

She straightened her shoulders. "What do you mean to do with me, sir?" she asked coldly.

He stepped close to her and caught her chin with the tips of his fingers. "I have not yet decided." The scent of lavender rose in the air. How intriguing. A perfumed thief in boots and breeches, a lady of quality by speech, a daring young miss by dress—better and better.

She batted his hand away, but he would have none of that. He caught her chin again and said, "Have you forgotten so soon that I have captured you, my dear? If you do not prove, at the very least, obliging, then I shall have no choice but to deliver you to the constable in Portislow."

She took hold of his hand and very firmly pressed it away from her face. "I beg you will do so at once, sir!" she cried.

"You would prefer to hang than to permit me to simply look at you?"

He leaned close to her and moonlight struck his eye. He heard her gasp and he smiled quite fully. He had, for many years, understood his charms and he meant to employ them to advantage now.

Rufus, apparently growing bored, cocked his ears and scarcely a breath later took off suddenly to the left, his nose strafing the rich orchard ground.

"I know who you are," she said suddenly. "Why, you must be Kelthorne! Of all the odious luck!" Even in the darkness of the night he could see the disgust on her face.

"I am," he returned, amused that she would express such disapprobation. "Though I cannot see how such a circumstance would offend a lady of your stamp." He suddenly wondered just what she was doing traipsing about the countryside in boy's clothing and stealing apples from his orchard. She did not look deprived and in need of sustenance. Here was a mystery that intrigued him even more.

"Oh, la, me lord," she returned, feigning the coarse accents of a tavern wench. "Oy suppose ye be thinking oy ought to be fully compleemented by yer addresses. Well, ain't I the daft un!"

He narrowed his eyes trying to make her out. What game was she at, how was it she knew how to speak in that coarse voice and why did she seem so disinclined to flirt with him? "Are you with the acting troupe that has just camped in my fields?" he asked, certain he had uncovered the mystery.

She gasped. "How could you even think such a thing!" she cried, now speaking in her proper accents. She was obviously offended by such a remark.

"Because I cannot explain your presence here otherwise."

"Well, I am not with such a troupe and though I did notice a great deal of tents in your pasture, I supposed that a band of gypsies were taking advantage of you."

He narrowed his eyes at her. Clearly, she was a lady of quality. He was fully and completely mystified. "Then you take a great deal of pleasure in practicing the accents of the lowly born?" he inquired.

"As it happens, I do. My, er, uncle is quite amused by them."

"Your uncle. You live nearby then?"

"I suppose you will learn the truth regardless, but as it happens, yes, I do."

He smiled rather slowly. "This is most promising. Though I wonder why I have not met you before."

"My uncle is rather shy of his neighbors. We do not go out in company much."

"That is a great pity."

He leaned down to take a kiss, but she recoiled in apparent horror.

"I beg you will let me go, my lord. I . . . am not such a female as you seem to think me to be!"

In his rather vast experience of young ladies, it was a rarity indeed that his lures would be repulsed so quickly and so firmly and especially not when he made his identity as a peer known. The lady, it would seem, was full of surprises. But neither was he in the least discouraged by her repulse. He was fully confident of his powers and decided not to waste another moment.

He took her in his arms abruptly and held her tightly against his chest. "Let me make my intentions plain," he murmured. "I shall only keep you from the constable by having a kiss from you."

"A kiss you shall not have!" she cried. Much to his surprise, she began to struggle. She was the first woman he had ever known to do so. Even the most properly well-bred young ladies he decided to torment tended to swoon rather than kick up a dust.

She aimed the hard toes of her boots and struck his legs forcefully. He would have been injured had his own boots not offered ample protection. At the same time, she swung her elbows and her arms, twisting back and forth. He was not impervious to a sharp elbow now and then and he knew he would sport more than one bruise on the morrow for she was rather skilled in her maneuvers. Still, he held her firmly, if loosely, and began matching each of her assaults with subtle shifts of his hands and body. He was well muscled from hunting, boxing and fencing and quite able to disarm the majority of the mischief she aimed at him, but he had never thought his expertise would have benefited him in such a way.

"Let me go, you horrid rake!" she cried.

She was a wild thing in his arms. He could only laugh, which served to increase her wrenching, pulling, and kicking.

He forced her to stop at last by wrapping one leg about both of hers and clamping her so tightly against him that he doubted she could breathe. "A kiss!" he cried, "Or I shall never let you go and if you think for a moment to wear me down, let me just say that I took part in a wager once in which I stood on a fence post, on one leg, for two-and-a-half hours. I know how to stay the course! And right now, you are my course!"

At that, she relaxed though breathing hard from her exertions as she stared up at him. Moonlight filtered through the apple trees, breached an opening among the leaves and revealed her features in milky perfection. He was dumbstruck. She was an absolute beauty. Her eyes, perhaps dark brown, though he could not be certain in the dim light, were almond-shaped, her brows sculpted in gentle arches that gave her a patrician appearance. Her nose was straight and perfect, her cheekbones high and pronounced in the prettiest manner, her lips full, her chin faintly dimpled. "Sweet Aphrodite," he murmured softly. She was perhaps the loveliest female he had ever seen. "I had thought you pretty, but I now see that you are utterly enchanting. Good God! What the devil are you doing out so late at night when any adventurer might have found you?"

"What?" she cried, obviously stunned, but she had begun to smile. "Do you know what an absurd thing it is you have just said to me, when you, my lord, are the adventurer? Or am I mistaken and 'tis someone else who is holding me captive and insisting on a kiss before I am to be released?"

"Well," he said, feeling amused once more, for she was very right, "that is a very different thing entirely for if you do not know already, I promise you that though I am an adventurer, you may trust me."

She laughed anew.

"Upon my honor!" he continued. "'Tis true! You may inquire of my friends and acquaintances and only one answer will return to you—Kelthorne is a man of his word! I do not hesitate to say that there are a hundred more who would have used you very ill in this moment!"

She laughed more heartily still, or at least as well as she was able given how tightly he held her. "Yet, you hold me in your arms quite against my will. Besides, have you not the smallest notion, my lord, as to the wretched extent of your reputation?"

"As to that," he returned piously, "I have never injured an innocent nor advanced my interest beyond the desires of the lady." He lifted a brow.

"I hardly know what to say. You seem to abide by your own peculiar code of conduct. And since you are profoundly stronger than I, and I have grown fatigued, there is nothing left, I suppose, but to allow you the kiss you are so insistent upon having."

"Much better," he said, feeling very pleased with her acquiescence. He lessened his grip.

"I only beg that you will be quick about the business. My, er, uncle will be missing me sorely."

Kelthorne glanced about the ground. "Will he be overset that you have failed in your object of collecting my apples for his kitchen?"

"Abominably so. He will probably beat me."

He laughed. "Yet I do not sense the smallest fear in you on that score. What are you about, miss?"

"If I tell you, will you permit me to depart in peace?"

"Without a kiss?" he asked.

"Aye."

He shook his head. "I would rather have my kiss than a hundred explanations."

She sighed heavily as though having grown quite weary of his conversation. "Then have done with it." She closed her eyes and tilted her head back so that once more the moonlight grazed her face.

He withheld another surprised gasp for he vowed even in London, whether consorting with the pretty in the drawing rooms of Mayfair or with the petticoat brigade in the East End, he had never seen so beautiful a face. He wondered precisely how old she was. Glancing at her youthful manner of presenting her lips for kissing, puckered as they were, he rather thought she was quite young as well as lacking in any significant experience, twenty at least, perhaps one or two, but not much more so.

Well, after tonight, he hoped she would have a new measure by which to judge all future kisses. He slid his hand behind her neck and leaned very close. Although, if she thought he would kiss a pair of lips that presently resembled a prune, she was greatly mistaken. As he readied himself, he could only imagine what her thoughts might be at this moment.

Judith did not comprehend in the least why he did not tend to business. She waited and waited and was about to demand of him to take what it was he required that she might

be on her way, when she sudd
on her cheek, followed by a ver
spot. She ceased her pursing and wou
he was doing, but another whisper of air w
along with another kiss. A shiver raced from
her side and her breath caught again. A series of s
whispers and kisses followed until it was as though a con
uous stream of shivers slid over her neck and side, sometimes even down her right leg.

She began to smile, for the whole experience seemed
rather silly and yet exceedingly pleasing. What a strange
man Kelthorne was. She wondered if this was how a rogue
tended to his victims. She should have objected, but she
could not seem to open her throat to begin a protest. When,
however, the little puffs of air and small kisses reached her
ear, her smiles gave way to a string of gasps. What on earth
was the fellow doing?

She lifted her hand and caught his arm awkwardly, trying
to fend off this strange new assault, but he took her hand in
his and held it firmly cradled against his arm. Again, she felt
the need to protest, but she found she could not form a single
word on her lips. She felt confused, every rational thought
obliterated by whispers of air. Really, it was quite extraordinary! An odd sound trembled in her throat, but still no
sound emerged to halt the rogue in his progress, for now he
was kissing her neck and whispering air over it all at the
same time. More shivers, lightning-like this time, raced one
after the other down her back.

"Kelthorne," she finally managed, but so hoarsely she
sounded liked a frog. Whatever he was about, he should
most definitely cease at once.

Her use of his name had an effect. The whispery air
ceased, but without warning his mouth was on hers, very
hard and deliberate, so different from all the other migrating
whispers. At the same time, he released her hand and she
found she was grateful that he was still holding her tightly,
now about the waist, for both her arms simply dangled to her

...re floating in a
...p as a doll made

...ended and he drew
...t, one arm still firmly
...r back. She found she
...ves of the trees. Wispy
...easing the moon. "I be-
...to my bed," she said. She
...ad cleared and panic rolled
throu... in heaven! Had she actually
spoken the... e had thought them, of course,
but had she actua... pass her lips?

His hoarse laughter... poke the truth and as he drew her
toward him so that she was once more upright and looking
into his eyes, she felt a hot blush instantly over her entire
face. What must he think of her?

"I am so sorry!" she cried. "To have said such a thing! I
never meant . . . that is, I should never think to do anything
so . . . that is, I cannot imagine why it is I said such a . . . and
of course I do not have any chains at all!" She gasped anew.
Tears of mortification brimmed in her eyes.

Kelthorne began to laugh, throwing his head back. "What
a darling you are!" he cried, gathering her up once more.
"And I should let you keep me chained to your bed, at least
part of each day." His smile nearly made her swoon. So this
was what it was to be seduced by a rogue! How dreadful!
How dreadful and how wonderful all at the same time!

She spoke rapidly. "No, no! Pray forget that I said such a
wicked thing. I did not mean to. I spoke my thoughts aloud
and never should have done so for I fear I will have given
you such notions of me but I promise you, my lord, I am not
such a female!"

"In that I believe you either to be greatly mistaken or
used to telling whiskers about your true nature. Regardless,
you shall not hear a single reproach from me. Your apologies
are not in the least necessary!"

At that, Judith stiffened. This must end! She spoke hastily. "I beg you will release me as you promised. You told me earlier I could trust you. Will you now make a mockery of your honor?"

"Tell me your name first?"

She hesitated, but saw little harm in it. "Judith."

"Well, *Judith*, go home to your uncle, only do not imagine for a moment that I shall rest until I have found you again . . . and brought you a gift of the chains you say you do not have in your possession!"

"How vile you are!" she cried.

He merely laughed in response, but he was as good as his word and released her. Judith turned and hurried away.

"Until we meet again!" he called after her.

She ran into the woods, not looking back as he began calling his dog.

She had not advanced far, however, when she remembered her shawl, her hat, and the apples. She stopped and returned to the edge of the beech wood where she could not be seen. She saw the earl walking his horse slowly in the direction of the town.

"Kelthorne," she murmured, her fingers touching her lips quite unwittingly.

Rufus bounded along beside the now trotting horse. She remained watching him for several minutes until he disappeared into the lane that led to the castle. She glanced up at the turreted outer wall visible in the moonlight, wondering what it was like to live in such an evocative dwelling. The castle stood in strong relief, outlined by a bright moon, which now descended over the Bristol Channel not a mile from the vale. The breeze freshened from the west and the smell of the sea was strong in her nostrils. She felt changed and frightened. The awful truth came to her that a rogue had breached the careful order of her world.

Long after he had disappeared, Judith at last ventured slowly back into the orchard. She recovered her hat and shawl but retrieved only two of the apples. One of them she would give to Charles, for she still needed proof that she had accomplished at least a portion of the dare. The other she meant to keep for herself as a memento. The remaining fruit, however, she left in the orchard. She simply could not bring herself to take it.

Laurence sat on a sofa in the billiard room, squinting his eyes at Kelthorne. "Was she very beautiful?" he asked. His speech was slurred, his eyes red-rimmed and he waved a brandy snifter about as though it were a flag. "And I wish you would stop moving about! Making me dizzy."

Aubrey Watchfield, fourth Earl of Kelthorne, who had been standing in one spot while he revealed his most recent encounter with his *Judith*, pointed his cue at his friend. "Just how foxed are you?"

"Excessively so but not so very much that I should be disinclined to hear about this apple lady of yours."

Kelthorne sighed, leaning the cue on the edge of the pool table, preparing for his first shot. "She was exquisite. I have never seen the like in all my days."

"That is saying something, indeed!" He weaved and squinted his eyes anew.

Laurence Doulting, a year Kelthorne's junior, had been his closest friend since time out of mind. He was a man of intelligence, a great deal of humor and in possession of an interesting face. He was broad in the cheek upon which a few freckles had chosen to make their home, had a somewhat pointed chin and an excellent smile. He also had a great deal of curly brown hair which, it appeared to Kelthorne, he had been pulling at for his locks looked like a cloud about his head. His shirt points had wilted and his coat had been removed as well as his shoes. The big toe on his left foot stuck out of a hole in his black stocking.

Pulling at his hair again, he asked, "Did you kiss her?"

Kelthorne chuckled and moved about the table in search

of a better position from which to break up the neatly grouped balls. "That is none of your concern," he stated firmly.

"How is this?" his friend inquired, clearly surprised. "You always tell me of your conquests."

"Well, not on this occasion."

"That is quite sin . . . gu . . . lar," he said leaning back and stretching his legs. "Good God, I must be foxed. Could hardly get that word out. And you, why must you be moving about in that manner and why are there two of you!"

"Good God, Laurence, I have only been absent an hour or two. How much brandy have you imbibed since I left?" Rufus appeared in the doorway then bounded over to him. He rubbed his ears. "Was your trip to the kitchens successful?" Rufus sat back on his haunches and panted happily, staring up at him in his adoring manner. The presence of his dog put him forcibly in mind of Judith sitting on the ground and rubbing his ears. Yes, *Judith*. He liked knowing her name and hearing it in his head. He liked that she had treated Rufus so sweetly when he had so disobligingly knocked her to the ground.

"I have only had a bottle," Laurence said, answering his question but completely disrupting his happy reverie. "Well, not the entire bottle but a great deal of it. I hope you do not mean to complain, for, if you must know, I find I am quite miserable tonight. Wretchedly so. The lowest wretch on earth." He sighed heavily and sipped his brandy.

Kelthorne patted Rufus on the head and attended once more to the pool table. He bent over slightly, aligned his shot and scattered the balls. "You do this every summer, you know," he said, addressing Laurence's complaints. "I had thought we would finally escape your melancholia this year."

"But you do not understand. You never did. Fanny was my entire world."

"'Twas fifteen years ago," Kelthorne stated reasonably. "You cannot possibly still be in love with her. Besides, she has probably given birth to a dozen brats, orders her husband like a slave, and now speaks in a shrill voice even when tending her babes."

Laurence reclined carefully on the sofa and stared up at the ceiling, balancing the snifter on his chest. "You are probably right and perhaps my love is not so passionate as it once was. I can't even remember the precise shade of her hair though I believe it was a very light brown, though sometimes blond in the summer months." His words were still abominably lazy. "But her marriage serves to remind me of my lot, the eldest son of an impoverished vicar—no property, no prospects, no profession, no chance at love. Fanny loved me, but she married the squire's son. He had prospects." He frowned. "And the devil of a temper. I have always wondered how she fared."

"Undoubtedly very well since I am persuaded she is become a fishwife."

"You are horridly cruel to my memories. I refuse to listen to you."

"Have you written an ode in her honor yet?"

"No, not yet."

"How many do you have in your possession now? You must have enough for a volume. Perhaps you should see them published."

"I do not have sufficient genius to be in print. I have always known it."

Kelthorne moved around the table, ordering his shots. "But I hope you do not mean to despair of love."

"I have never despaired of love," Laurence responded, "but I have of marrying for love, or marrying at all. You, on the other hand, will probably be wed before the year is out."

"So it would seem."

Kelthorne had known Laurence since schooldays at Eton. He was the eldest of seven children, the son of an impoverished vicar and wholly lacking in ambition. He was a mixture of romanticism and pragmatism and the best friend a fellow could ever have. His sole interest was in the poetry he wrote and since Kelthorne rarely had the privilege of reading his scribblings, he had not the smallest notion whether or not he was a man of talent. Together, they had had many adventures; all of which had come to an end in recent months when the death of Kelthorne's uncle had forced him to take up his new life as heir to an earldom. Laurence had born the change nobly, but he did seem more inclined of late to empty whichever bottle happened to be at his elbow. Laurence was not happy.

As he slung his cue again and cracked as many billiard balls as he could, he smiled. "You may be easy, you know, since both Radsbury and Newnott are coming with my sisters. Radsbury, at the very least, will be content to lose a hundred or so pounds at cards or even hazard. He is equally fond of both."

"Don't know what the deuce your sister was thinking in marrying the old goat. Good God, he must be twenty years her senior."

"You are too severe," Aubrey stated. "Radsbury dotes on Mary. He is a good husband to her."

Laurence shuddered, his eyelids drooping. "Do you know that his teeth are made of rhinoceros tusk? I can only imagine what it must be like to kiss him. How does Mary bear it?"

"Just as a *viscountess* should, I imagine."

"I would never marry to get a handle to my name."

Kelthorne glanced at him and smiled. He was very foxed, indeed. "No, I do not think you would."

Laurence turned to squint at him again. "You know very well what I mean. I mean *if* I were a female."

"Of course."

Laurence lifted his brows. "All I know is that Mary was deuced pretty when she was young. Now she has a pinch between her brows which never goes away."

"She has five daughters," he said, moving around the table and as he spoke, striking ball after ball with his cue. "The eldest thirteen and the youngest nine, all of whom she intends to marry off to wealthy young men. And as for her three sons—and did I tell you she is increasing again—she spends every waking moment cultivating her connections and planning for each of their futures. Stephen will inherit, of course; Marcus is for the church; Sylvester apparently shows all the proper qualities to make a most excellent solicitor though he is but four and as for this next brat, should the darling prove to be a boy, I would expect him to be born with a sword in his hand."

"I am grown fatigued from listening to your story. Though I must say it is no wonder she has the look of a merchant on market day. I would advise her to stop kissing Lord Goat."

"You may tell her yourself when she arrives in a sennight's time."

At that, and even in his state of inebriation, Laurence sat up quickly, if unevenly, and just barely kept the snifter from rolling off his chest. "They are coming so soon? When did you learn of this?"

"A few minutes ago. I knew I had a letter from my sister, but I could not bring myself to read it until just now." He sighed heavily. "It would seem my sisters are bringing a young lady who I believe they hope will become my bride, a Miss Currivard, a very great heiress."

"What the deuce do you need an heiress for?" Laurence cried.

"I have no need of an heiress," he said, working his cue again. "It is as much a mystery to me why they have chosen this lady except that Amy says she is uncommonly pretty with a profusion of blonde ringlets." Of the moment, he preferred dark hair, masses of it.

"Sounds like an angel," Laurence observed.

Kelthorne laughed suddenly as he slung his cue once more. "Then she will hardly do for me."

"Or for me," Laurence cried laughing heartily. His melancholy descended once more and he said, "So, I suppose you will be married before the winter."

He sounded so sad that Kelthorne regarded him steadily

for a moment. "I suppose I shall," he murmured unhappily as well.

For several minutes he stood in this manner with his friend, each in a pitiable state and no longer a drop of brandy to be had between them by which to soothe their joint sadness.

"Well," he said at last. "We still have one week and there is some consolation for both of us yet."

"What is that?" Laurence asked.

"Have you forgotten the delights to be found in my pasture not a mile away?"

At that, Laurence's red-rimmed eyes brightened. "By God, I did forget, only . . ."

"What is it now?"

"Aubrey, I dislike to mention it, but I feel I ought to remind you of the awful truth that you quite recently made a vow to mend your ways."

Kelthorne felt a familiar stubbornness take hold of him. "And so I shall, the moment my sisters and my hopeful bride-to-be darken my doorstep. Until then, my dear friend, I mean to have a little fun!"

TWO

Judith brushed out her long chestnut curls slowly. She was taking far too long on her toilette this morning, but she found she could not force herself to hurry. The camp was fully awake but an argument was already in progress, one that made ample use of her name, so much so that she rather suspected what had happened. She was far too mortified to find out just who had discovered that Lord Kelthorne had caught her in his orchard last night and forced a kiss upon her.

She set her brush down on her small dressing table and rose from her chair. She picked up one of the two apples she had in her possession and turned it around and around in her hands. She still could not credit she had actually been kissed by so infamous a rogue nor that she had enjoyed the experience so much as she had. Of these two thoughts, the latter caused her the greater distress. She felt vulnerable, wretchedly so. The thought that she would be living for the next month in the relative shadows of his windows was nearly more than she could bear. And if he kept his resolve, he would find her sooner or later.

When the arguing turned to shouting, she realized she could hardly remain hidden in her tent forever. She tossed the apple on her bed and slipped on her underdress, a gown she had made from a pale shade of blue calico, then quickly donned the overdress of Swiss muslin, closing the embroidered band in front. The quarreling grew louder still and the voices of John Ash, Henry Thurloxton and Charles Hemyock could be heard echoing through the narrow valley from one hillock to the next.

"We ought to be leaving at once!" Henry cried.

"I'll not give up a promising engagement fer her supposed *virtue*!" Charles shouted.

"Enough, Charles!" John cried. "Ye as well, Henry!"

"But Judy is in danger," Henry returned hotly. "We should never ha' come here, not with that rake ready to pounce! I saw him riding his horse last night, not far from the camp."

"Why is it that only Judy be in danger?" Angelique asked. "Why not the likes of me, fer instance."

Freddy cried out. "More like Kelthorne ought to be warned of ye!"

A burst of laughter followed, which Judith knew from experience would have something of a calming influence on the situation.

Silence followed for a few seconds, after which Charles began to speak, pressing the troupe yet again to be rid of her, once and for all, that her presence hindered their opportunities and shortened their earnings. "I'll be damned before I pull up stakes on 'er account again!"

For the past year, Charles had been the troupe's principal and quite superior actor. He was greatly talented and even more ambitious. Judith understood his complaints perfectly and believed he was not without cause to be out of reason cross that Henry was demanding the troupe leave Somerset.

More than one of the actresses as well, of which there were five including Margaret, echoed his sentiments. Generally, both John and Margaret Ash, who had the management of the troupe, ignored his ranting, but this particular engagement had been anticipated greatly by the entire troupe for it meant residing in one place for nearly a month. Given the large size of the market town not a quarter mile from the castle, they were guaranteed a sizeable audience each night. There was money to be made in Portislow and Kelthorne's unexpected but quite pleasing generosity in allowing the troupe to pasture in his field made the situation absolutely ideal. To ask the troupe to leave the vicinity on her account, therefore, was beyond imagining. She shuddered faintly thinking just how many times they had been required to do so, and always because some "gentleman" or other had become insistent on possessing her. Far too many times, she thought.

Margaret bid entrance just as she had picked up her brush anew. "Come," she called out softly. When her friend entered rolling her eyes, Judith said, "There seems to be quite a to-do this morning."

"Aye," Margaret said, taking up her habitual seat on the stool by the tent door. She was a tall young woman, four years Judith's senior, and her dearest friend in all the world. Her hair was a brilliant shade of red, which she wore in an absolute riot of curls atop her head. Her eyes were a brilliant blue and her face was shaped like a perfect heart. She was adorable without quite being a beauty. Margaret continued, "Henry be like the knights of old this morning, on a crusade as it were, he is that intent on our leaving. Would ye be knowing why?"

Judith now understood that Margaret must have somehow learned what had happened on the evening prior. She began to suspect that Henry had seen her with Kelthorne. "Aye," Judith responded.

When the shouting increased, both ladies stopped to listen, afterward sighing heavily together. Henry was proclaiming in his actor's voice the absolute necessity of leaving immediately while Charles continued pontificating equally as loudly on the harm such a move would do to the troupe.

"I imagine by now Charlie is pacing to and fro."

"Aye," Margaret said, nodding, "and throwing his arms

this way an' that as though he's speaking the bard's words and not his own."

Judith sat down carefully on her bed. Although four posts supported the narrow low frame, the corner at the foot of the bed was weak and tended to collapse without warning. "Poor Charlie," Judith said. "He will not be content until he is roaring like a lion on the London stages."

"Ye can scarce blame him."

"No, of course not, but I do grow weary of hearing of his ambitions."

"We all do. O' course, this morning he has reason to be upset. Do ye not think so?"

She met Margaret's gaze. "What is it you know?" she asked forthrightly.

Margaret grimaced. "Oh, Judy, is it true? Did ye kiss Kelthorne last night in the orchard?"

Judith closed her eyes. "I fear it is so."

Margaret gasped. "I had no reason to doubt Henry, o' course, but I was that shocked, I was."

"He did see us then? And he told you?"

"Aye."

"I should have never gone to the orchard. I would wish that stupid dare undone a thousand times. How came I to be so foolish?"

"I canna say," she responded, "only how did it happen that ye let Kelthorne kiss ye? 'Tis not like ye."

"He caught me stealing his apples and once he discovered that I was a young woman, he demanded a kiss before he would release me. I struggled for a very long time but he is quite strong. In the end, there was nothing for it. So, I permitted the kiss, or, rather, he took it. He would not have released me otherwise."

Margaret stared at her, a frown pinching her brow. "And ye were aware 'twas Kelthorne ye were kissing?"

"Aye," Judith returned. "He spoke of the apples as his and then I guessed at his name. He had no reason to deny who he was and I had no reason to doubt him particularly since there was something so commanding in his address."

Margaret shook her head. "All these years, we was so careful to take care of ye . . . so many blackguards wat called themselves gentl'men all ready to, well, to not serve ye a good turn as well ye know. Wat? Wat is it? Wat be ye thinking?" She gasped. "Judy, why be ye smiling in that odd way?"

Judith had no desire at all to reveal her thoughts for she had suddenly recalled in brilliant detail all the little whispery kisses of the night before. Her cheeks grew quite warm. "Nothing to signify," she said hastily.

"What a whisker—fer yer eyes are as bright as one of Mrs. Marnhull's copper pots, all polished and gleaming! La, don't tell me that ye've taken a fancy to an earl!"

Judith put her hands on her cheeks as though by doing so she might cool them. "No, of course not! It is just that, well, I had never been kissed before and I had no notion that a man would . . ." She could not finish her thoughts.

"Wat?"

"Well," Judith said quietly, grateful for someone to confide in, "as it happens, he blew these little puffs of air against my cheeks and . . . and elsewhere . . . and, indeed, I did not know what he was about. Then he kissed me. Is that how it is usually done?"

Margaret's eyes grew very wide. "I never had such kisses before. La, Judy, but he is a rogue!" She then fell to contemplating the notion for a brief moment then suddenly shook herself like a duck emerging from water. "But pay no heed, a rogue's trick, only. All I wish to know is that ye are not injured. Tell me he did not do ye harm in any way."

Judith remembered his odd comment that she had been unwise to be abroad since others of less refined and careful notions about ladies would have hurt her. She could not help but smile recalling he had said as much while holding her captive in his arms. "No," she said. "Not really. He may have a shocking reputation, and he may be a rogue, but he apparently has a set of careful rules by which he conducts himself. He did not hurt me nor do I believe he would ever do so."

Margaret shook her head in bewilderment. "Ye trust him then?"

"Yes, I suppose I do though I cannot explain it. I believe him to be more a man of art in his conquests than force which I suppose for me was a very good thing, indeed."

Margaret rose from her seat. "Well, ye had best come. The troupe will want to be hearing from ye. And no matter wat Master Hemyock says, we make our decisions together." With that, Margaret quit the tent.

Judith tied a blue ribbon around her mass of curls, picked up her portable sewing stand and followed in her wake. By the time she drew close to the fire, upon which Mrs. Marnhull's largest pot had been set to boil, Charles and Henry were nearly at daggers-drawn. Henry caught sight of her and instantly his demeanor changed. He stood straighter, even turning away from Charles.

Charles, however, addressed her with all the force of his acting voice, each word trembling with emotion. "Ye . . . would do this to us . . . again!" He even gestured with a wide sweep of his arm encompassing the entire troupe.

"Oh, do stubble it, Charlie," she responded evenly. She took up a seat near John and far enough away from the fire to keep from scorching either her skirts or her workbox. "Save your breath to cool your porridge or at the very least for your next performance." This address of course brought a flame of rage to his face and a round of laughter passing through the ranks. "Now, what is all the fuss?" she added before he could begin another tirade. From her box, she withdrew the boy's shirt she was presently embroidering with neat, even stitches, took up her needle and continued her work.

"Ye know very well wat this is about," Henry cried. Glancing up at him, Judith could see that he was very angry. "I think ye know precisely wat 'the fuss' is."

She saw that he was restraining himself with some effort. "You must be referring to the Earl of Kelthorne and his reputation." She lowered her gaze and set another stitch.

"O' course."

"But I thought the matter was already settled particularly when we were given permission to stay on his lands." She smoothed out part of the shirt on her legs and plied her needle anew.

"Aye, but I began to think mebbe he had a purpose in letting us stay on his land and now I think 'tis true!"

"Humbug," she declared, meeting his gaze.

He ground his teeth. Everyone was watching him. Little Shelly, Margaret's daughter of five, sitting on her papa's lap, pointed at Henry. "Why is Henry mad at Judy?"

John took hold of her little fist and the accusing finger and gently returned her arm to her side. "He wants Judy to be safe is all."

Shelly turned to look at Judith. "Are ye not safe?"

Judith, near enough to touch Shelly, reached over and tickled her. "I am perfectly safe as Henry well knows."

John glanced at Judith and smiled in his kind manner, "Are ye certain?"

"Quite," she responded firmly and set another stitch.

Charles, however, refused to be satisfied with this. "'Tis the outside of enough!" he cried. "Judy is naught but a songstress who we use between the real meat of our performances and yet we are required to arrange our lives around her safety!" He addressed Judith directly. "Ye are scarcely more than a lady of the chorus and no better than an opera dancer, whatever ye pretend to be!"

John intervened. "That's enough, Charles!" he cried sharply. "Judy's voice has brought in the shillings when our best tragedy could not, so I will hear no more from ye on that head. But there is something else." Without warning, he jerked the shirt from Judith's hands and waved it in the air. "There is not a village where we perform that she does not leave clothes fer the poor. And yes, I know that some of the ladies help as well but do ye have even a speck of an idea how kindly we are looked upon fer that? Most gentlefolk scorn troupes like ours, but Judy has opened doors we otherwise could not."

Judith had never heard John so vehement on the subject before, but now she felt a little embarrassed. She had never meant to have her one little effort at charity to be paraded before the troupe in such a manner. She was certain the effect would only be to increase the resentment toward her. There was nothing to be done, however.

"I believe you make too much of the matter," she said firmly, taking the shirt from him. "And if you have lost my needle, I shall insist you purchase another one for me."

She met John's gaze and shook her head. Even Margaret understood the delicacy of the situation and laid a hand on her husband's arm.

Charles grew sullen, turning to sit on a log beside Horace who scooted away from him. He picked up a stick and poked angrily at the fire so that sparks rose in the air.

"Wat do we do then?" Betty called out.

Freddy sitting next to her groaned loudly and exclaimed, "Zeus, Betty! Do ye never eat anything but onions?"

Betty laughed heartily at this, slapped Freddy on the back and blew her breath on his face. "Oy am particularly fond a' onions and Mrs. Marnhull says I may eat as many o' them as I like." She rose and moved to stand near Charles. Lifting a challenging brow to Judith, she said, "I quite agree with Charlie. We should stay. And if proper Miss Judith can't manage the gentlemen, I shall be happy to do so for her." She swung her hips, clucked her tongue and rolled her eyes.

Margaret covered Shelly's eyes. "Betty!" she complained.

"Aw, she'll learn soon enough!" Betty responded. She sat down at the long bench next to the table and this time blew her breath on Bobby.

In response, he gave her a strong pinch. A row might have

erupted had Henry not suddenly cried, "I will help take every tent down, I am that convinced we should leave. John, will ye not agree with me?

John tilted his head. "Our camp is all but settled, as ye can plainly see, and Judy is not troubled, not by half. I am that sorry, Henry, but I believe we should stay."

The majority of the actors added their agreement to John's pronouncement.

Henry grimaced a little more, breathing hard through his nostrils.

John, always ready to navigate swiftly the shoals of troupe tensions, added, "Since I can see that ye are overset, wat do ye say to three days? If Kelthorne has bothered any of the ladies during that time, then we shall follow yer bidding and move on to Devonshire."

"Oy wouldna mind if Kelthorne bothered *me*," Betty called out. "Judy, if he sets to pestering ye, give him a nudge in my direction."

Bobby jumped to his feet stepping several feet away from Betty. "I agree, Judy. If ye need protection, send Betty. Her dragon's breath would slay a thousand rogues."

Laughter passed round the troupe. After a moment, John reverted to the subject at hand. "Henry, will ye agree to that?"

"I don't see as I have been given a choice."

"What say ye, troupe?" John asked. "All those fer three days, say aye."

The resounding collection of *ayes* silenced Henry. He cast one last rather fierce glance at Judith then turned to set up his tent anew.

Charles, on the other hand, moved in Judith's direction and with a well-aimed blow, overset her worktable. She caught it before it fell to the ground but cast him a scathing glance. She was not surprised at his antics. Charles Hemyock had been angry with her nearly from the first. There was nothing to be done, however. Only when she had saved enough money to purchase her cottage, a dream she had had from the first, would she be free of such troublesome moments. For now, she must endure.

Three days later, Kelthorne sat in the front row of the King's Theatre in Portislow, tapping his foot in frustration. He crossed his arms over his chest and sighed heavily. "I knew I should not have come tonight. I have traveled twenty miles today and I had rather be at home."

"Yes, but I had rather be here. 'Tis not my fault you must spend your days searching for your bewitching *Judith* but I, after all, am your guest," Laurence said. "Your first duty should be to me. Besides, I have been given to understand that this particular troupe is superior in every manner. There will be a few dramatic presentations, a farce or two, a demonstration of swordplay and perhaps a song. I also heard they have excellent jugglers."

"Oh, well, then," Kelthorne responded facetiously. "If there are to be jugglers, then I will cease my complaining on the instant!"

"I refuse to feel sorry for you."

"I cannot credit that she seems to have disappeared into the earth. Not a single family has owned to the possession of a daughter of such a description. And I went to countless neighboring villages and hamlets, conferring with the admiral of the blue in each location and the vicar in many more but came away with nothing. Nothing! It is as though she never existed, that I only dreamt her!"

"Perhaps she is with the troupe."

He shook his head. "If you had heard her speech, in every nuance that of a lady of quality, you would dismiss the notion as readily as I did. Besides, she was especially offended when I asked her the very same question."

His gaze drifted to the chairs stationed near them. "Do you know that lady? The one whose face is nearly white from powder?"

Kelthorne also glanced at her. She was smiling and waving at him. He lifted his hand and smiled in acknowledgement. "One of the local gentry, but I do not know her name."

"And she does not have a daughter with dark wavy hair?"

"She tried to tell me she did," he whispered. "She is the fixture beside her."

Laurence glanced askance. "Good God," he muttered. "Platter-faced with a nose even Rufus would envy."

Kelthorne choked his laughter. A lad of perhaps thirteen or fourteen emerged from the wings and set the limelight to blazing at the very front of the stage.

"You will enjoy the performance," he whispered, elbowing him. "I have seen several of the actresses—quite pretty."

"Well, there are always the actresses." With such a thought, his blue-devils began to dispel.

The curtain parted. "Ah," Laurence murmured. "And so it begins."

A smattering of applause ensued as a tall and rather fit man approached the center of the stage. He greeted the crowd in very warm, enthusiastic terms, gave a brief history of what would soon follow, flourished a low bow by doffing his hat, and the next moment the stage was alive with players engaged in a fierce swordfight, all staged, of course, but Kelthorne found himself quite impressed.

He was proficient at fencing and noted the form was excellent among the actors. But what made the entire display enjoyable were all the outrageous moves, the use of hats, gloves, and woolen scarves to thwart another's weapon or to steal it away completely. All the while, the banter was bawdy, comical and so engaging that he forgot completely about his own disappointment in not having discovered his darling Judith among his neighbors.

Judith sat quietly in a corner backstage, setting her stitches in the little boy's shirt. She was almost finished with this task and thought that next she might do a girl's gown and embroider a few bluebells along the bodice or perhaps the high waist.

As she plied her needle, she listened to the familiar commotion on stage and was not surprised when at the end of the swordfight, after Henry had tumbled dramatically off the front of the stage, that a round of applause filled the theater. She smiled, for the swordfight was always a favorite.

Another town, another engagement.

For eight years this had been her life. She knew how to prepare her songs and how to deliver them on stage. From her first faltering performances at the tender age of fourteen, she had accepted the troupe's criticisms and had developed into, she supposed, a mature songstress, even though she was but two and twenty. That she could be sitting as she was, sewing without so much as a butterfly in her stomach was telling of just how long she had been with the troupe. There was only one circumstance that could possibly overset her equanimity—if Kelthorne actually attended a performance. Since he had been absent for the first two, she suspected he had little interest in the theater.

She was just weaving her needle into the sturdy cloth, when the ladies of the troupe excepting Margaret approached like a flock of geese after a morsel of bread.

"Ye must come see!" Kitty cried.

"Indeed, ye must!" Betty exclaimed.

"He is here!" Angelique whispered excitedly.

"Who is here?" Judith asked, although she thought she already knew the answer.

"Kelthorne! He is that handsome!" Lydia cried.

"Oy mean to work me wiles tonight!" Betty added. "But ye must come see."

Angelique took the shirt from her, Kitty took strong hold of her arm and, before she could protest, she was fairly dragged to the curtain where a peephole had been constructed. Lydia lifted the flap of heavy velvet and through a discreet webbing of black lace fixed over a small hole in the curtain she was able to see the audience.

"He is to the right and sitting with a man with curly brown hair. To the right! The right!"

Judith was grateful that Bobby and Freddy spoke uncommonly loud while performing their juggling. When her gaze landed upon Kelthorne, she nearly swooned.

Oh, dear God, she thought. Was there never a man so dashing, so striking in face and figure! She had known he was handsome, the moonlight had told her as much three nights past. But in the glow of the stage his face was fully exposed. She now understood why the ladies had been so insistent. He possessed a strong nose, almost aquiline in appearance, his jaw line was firm, his smile infectious, his brows pronounced but not too much so. But it was his eyes that dominated his face: they were large, almost exotic in appearance and very blue.

"La, but don't she seem ready to faint!" Betty hissed, her onion breath quite bringing Judith back to her senses.

"Did we not tell ye he was that splendid? I think 'tis his blond hair, wavy and sitting on his shoulders, that gives him the look of a rogue," Angelique said.

"He is quite uncommon," Judith murmured, striving to feel her feet as she turned to make her way back to her stool.

The ladies followed after her. Lydia whispered, "I would keep my tent door untied for such a man."

"As would I," Kitty agreed on a heavy sigh.

John appeared and ushered them back to their positions for the four ladies performed a farce next.

Judith resumed her stool, severely shaken.

Now, as she plied her needle with trembling fingers, she struggled to compose her mind and heart. How was she ever going to be able to bring sufficient air to her lungs to swell her song? She did not know.

And so the minutes rattled on, the audience obviously enjoying the various performances. Her fingers trembled more and more and her throat grew tight. Kelthorne would know her at once, then she would be in the basket, indeed.

Finally, she ceased sewing and stared unseeing and unhearing in the direction of the stage. When Margaret approached and laid a hand on her shoulder, she jumped.

"What be the matter?" she asked.

She could hardly speak.

"So ye have seen him?" Margaret queried, guessing at the truth.

"Aye," she whispered in return. "Margaret, I am having a fit of the nerves. I have never felt so frightened in my entire life. Perhaps I ought not to sing tonight?"

Margaret chuckled. "Well, that would make Charlie quite happy."

"That it would."

"So ye must perform."

"Of course I must only my mouth is so dry, my throat hurts and I am having trouble breathing."

"All this because of a man? But why? Is he not like all the others?"

Judith shook her head. "That night, I saw him only in the deepest shadows. Now, to have really seen him! Margaret, is he not the handsomest creature you have ever seen?"

Margaret smiled. "Not especially. I like John's looks a great deal better, his long interesting face, his crooked nose and a smile that, though his teeth be somewhat twisted-like, makes me think of spring." She sighed warmly.

At these words, revealing so eloquently her love for her husband, Judith began to relax. "I have always envied you, Margaret. You cannot know how very much."

Margaret laughed and tears filled her eyes. "That you should envy me . . . ! Ye must be mad as Bedlam."

"But you have John and Shelly. What more could a woman truly desire than the affection and company of those she loves?"

"Well, when ye speak of it like that, maybe you ought to envy me, a little. But as fer his lordship, remember he is just a man, like all the rest of 'em, handsome or not!"

"Of course you are right. Thank you. I shall do better now . . . at least, I hope I shall."

"Try not to look at him, and instead, think of yer cottage fer ye know there be a lot of gentry in the hall tonight and ye will probably be asked to perform at a party or two."

From the beginning, Judith had been invited to give private concerts in the homes of the local aristocracy and gentry. She knew the invitations came to her in large part because there was nothing in even the smallest degree offensive about her songs, demeanor or gowns. Having come from their world, she knew how to dress and behave properly for them. Even now, she wore a typical half-robe of apple green satin over an underdress she had embroidered with little red cherries. Pearls—not real, of course—adorned her earlobes and were draped several times about her neck. Her hair, however, she wore hanging to her waist in heavy waves and caught up by a single green ribbon which matched her gown. She had learned quite early on that her appearance of innocence and youth somehow affected the audience as much as her voice and choice of song.

"I see the pianoforte is being moved onto the stage. Are ye ready, Judy?"

Judith took a deep breath, put the shirt, needle and thread into her workbox stationed beside her stool, and rose from her seat. Margaret slipped her arm about hers and together they made their way forward waiting in the wings until John completed their introduction.

Margaret crossed the stage first, taking up her seat at the pianoforte. When John spoke her name and flourished his arm in her direction, Judith found her confidence had returned in full measure. She walked to center stage and took up her place. The initial response to just her presence tended to unnerve her, for there was always a strange gasping sound that came from the audience as though she gave them a shock, and then silence would ensue. However, since this was very familiar to her, her confidence increased. She nodded to Margaret and the first notes from the pianoforte drifted into the expansive theater. From the corner of her eye she could see that Lord Kelthorne's mouth was agape and somehow his shock sufficed to relieve her of the rest of her fears and thus she began to sing one of her favorite songs, "My Mother Bids Me Bind My Hair."

Kelthorne stared and listened and stared a little more. Good God, the young woman he had kissed three nights past was now standing on the stage before him. And her voice! How completely such sounds could charm any ear. Such purity, such feeling, such ease of delivery, such gentleness of gesture! Her gaze swept over the audience, back and forth like the gentle rocking of a boat. The effect was mesmerizing. The audience around him sighed and sighed again.

Was this truly the young woman he had kissed? Of course, he recognized her, but the darkness of the night had not done her the smallest justice. She was absolute perfection, to the lovely oval of her face, to the cream of her complexion, to the magnificent cascade of chestnut waves, and the soulful gaze of her warm brown eyes. How his heart hammered in his chest as he gazed upon her. Was this truly the creature he had held in his arms? Was she truly a songstress, an actress, traveling with the troupe?

Suddenly, he realized he had been duped. She had denied being with the troupe and he had believed her. Did she know, therefore, that he had spent three days searching the West Country for her? Undoubtedly!

So she was essentially an actress, a lady of the stage. Better and better! Well, he had known a number in his career and they were all relatively the same: talented, lovely, scintillating to kiss, but as avaricious as a child before a sweet shop. Oh, yes, he had known a few but never had he been so tricked.

Judith Lovington's accent had been perfection when he had caught her in the orchard and heard her speaking to Rufus. He had never considered for a moment that she was anything but a gentlewoman out for a lark.

Now, however, his blood began to burn within him. All that he could see presently was the absolute necessity of taking another kiss, and hopefully much more, from the lady now singing with every effort to create a portrait of complete innocence.

When Judith—for she would never be *Miss Lovington* to

him—had sung the last note, a silence held the air for several remarkable seconds followed by a pounding of applause that rose to the rafters.

He and Laurence were both on their feet at once.

"Extraordinary!" he said, nudging Kelthorne.

"She is the one."

"What?" Laurence cried, the applause in the hall still deafening. He leaned close.

"She is the one," Kelthorne repeated.

"The one what?"

Kelthorne just looked at him with a cocked brow.

"Good God? Do you mean the one in the orchard?"

Kelthorne nodded.

"Well, don't you have the devil's own luck!" he cried, grimacing.

THREE

"I must see her," Kelthorne said, the moment the entire troupe took their final bows.

Laurence clapped him on the shoulder. "I would have supposed no less of you, my good man!"

Kelthorne made his way to the stage entrance and found a throng in high gig milling about.

Finally, he reached the front of the crowd intending to do what he usually did in such situations—slip a sovereign into the hand of whatever burly fellow had been assigned the task of keeping undesirables from the premises.

Instead, however, he found two of the actors, standing shoulder to shoulder, refusing admittance even to the most exalted of persons. He was told that the ladies of the troupe could only be seen by permission of the requested lady.

Kelthorne smiled and proffered his card with a practiced flip of his wrist. The taller of the two eyed him in some hostility while the shorter snatched his card and said hastily, "We are that grateful fer the use of yer pasture, m'lord. Isn't that right, Henry?"

"Fer use of the pasture, aye," Henry said, but he breathed fire through his nostrils.

"I will return forthwith," the shorter fellow cried cheerfully, flourishing a grand bow.

Judith was standing near her stool and workbox, untangling a long piece of thread when she saw Freddy hurrying in her direction.

She turned toward him. "What is it?" she asked.

"Kelthorne," he cried dramatically, waving in the air what she could clearly see was a calling card. "He wishes to meet ye."

Judith had been expecting something of this nature but seeing his name printed on the white card set her fingers to trembling again. She spoke the words she had been rehearsing from the moment her performance on stage ended. "I beg you will offer my apologies, but I do not wish to see Lord Kelthorne. You may tell him, if you like, that I have the headache."

"He seemed quite anxious to see ye, Judy," he said, frowning. "And we are staying on his lands. Maybe ye ought not to refuse him."

John was quickly beside her. "Treat him as we do all the gentlemen," he stated firmly. "Judy has said, no. 'Tis enough." When Freddy hesitated, he added, "And should his lordship dare to require Judy or any of the ladies as payment fer the use of his land then we will leave Somerset. Fer now, though, we took a vote this morning. 'Tis all settled. We stay in Somerset."

Freddy lowered his voice. "'Tis your own fault, Judy," he said, but he was smiling. "Were ye not so pretty, there would not be half the trouble."

Betty came running up. "Oy just heard that Kelthorne is asking fer ye, Judy. Ye do mean to go to him. Are ye not excited?"

"I have no intention of doing so," she said quietly. John smiled his encouragement but moved away to help Horace tend to the removal of some of the props.

Betty's eyes seemed to pop in her head. "Oh, la, Judy, what a fool ye be! I heard he was worth nine thousand a year.

Think o' the diamonds and pearls he could buy fer ye! He could even pay fer yer cottage."

"Thank you very much, but I had greatly prefer to purchase my cottage myself."

"Well," she said, breathing a heavy sigh. "I think ye be daft!" The smell of onions hung heavily in the air.

Judith wished she would chew the fresh mint leaves Mrs. Marnhull was in the habit of giving her each morning, but the lively actress rarely remembered to do so. Inspiration suddenly struck. "Betty," she cried. "I have just had such a notion." She took the card from Freddy and extended it to her. "How would you feel about tending to Lord Kelthorne in my stead?"

Betty grabbed the card, her eyes popping once more. "Oh, la, would I not!" she cried, expanding her breath over both Judith and Freddy.

Freddy took a step backward, turned away from her and groaned.

Judith's eyes began to water. "May I suggest that you pretend to be me? Freddy can tell him that I have decided to meet with him and since you and I are of a size, and if you wore a shawl over your head, he would not know 'twas you."

Betty's eyes gleamed. "Ye intend fer me to play him a trick?"

"I do, indeed, after which I have little doubt you will be able to take full advantage of the situation. Are you willing?"

"By Aphrodite's eyelashes, Oy am!"

Judith turned to Freddy. "Pray tell his lordship that I will meet him beneath the large oak near his drive in an hour when all the crowds have dispersed."

An hour later, Kelthorne waited alone by the great oak just east of his property just past his drive. The camp was visible in the distance where many of the actors and actresses had already retired. The wagon that carried the numerous props and costumes was just turning into the pasture. He marveled at the skill, execution and pleasure the troupe took in all its efforts. There was a masterly organization to the endeavor that was visible even in the careful arrangement of the tents, wagons and horses that attended the troupe. These folk worked quite hard to earn their bread. He had no small admiration for them.

His thoughts slipped to Judith. His heart was heavy with desire. She was an actress and used to a certain sort of attention and tonight he meant to be very *attentive*. But how clever of her to have incited his interest with all her protests of innocence, all her struggling in his arms. The kiss had betrayed her true nature, however. He chuckled thinking how she had puckered her lips, an actress's trick, of course. He was intrigued, vastly so. The best part, though, was the incontrovertible truth that no lady attached to such a troupe could be innocent and he would have his amusement before his proposed bride-to-be arrived to change the course of his life forever.

But what a beauty Judith Lovington was! Almost he could feel his arms around her, as they had been not so very long ago. Would she be shy tonight or as eager as he?

His gaze was drawn away from the camp by movement to his left. The desire he was feeling sharpened for she was approaching. The moonlight revealed her shapely figure but she had covered her head modestly in a lace shawl. How very discreet!

When she reached him, she extended her hand and he took it, kissing her fingers lightly. "Good evening, Miss Lovington," he said politely.

"And you," she responded, drawling her words together.

Her voice sounded a little odd as though she was perhaps a trifle foxed. Better and better! Most of the actresses he had known enjoyed their wine very much.

He did not release her fingers but gave a strong tug and drew her suddenly against him. She giggled, lifted her face and laughed a little more.

The odor that followed, swirling over, around and through him nearly caused him to stumble backward. Good God! What had the child been eating? Rotten eels? For his own protection he quickly caught her head to his shoulder and breathed in fresh air. "My dear Miss Lovington, I was not prepared . . . that is, I suppose you must be fond of certain vegetables."

She giggled some more and wrapped her arms about his waist. "Oy am . . . er . . . that is, *my lord,* I am very fond of onions."

Drunk, full of onions, and feigning her coarse accent once more.

"Most gent'men don't mind." She lifted her face.

He held his breath lest he take another deadly whiff of the fire coming from her mouth and leaned to kiss her on the lips. But it was too much. He could not bear it.

Releasing her, he backed away. "I am very sorry, my dear, but this will not do."

She slipped the lace shawl from off her curls and even in the moonlight he could see her hair was darker and curlier than it should be. He realized with a start that the lady he had held in his arms was not Judith at all. "What is the meaning of this?" he cried, taking her chin, turning her toward the moon and staring into a lovely face but one which belonged to the actress who had played a milkmaid in the last farce. "What the deuce is going forward and what is your name?"

"Betty, m'lord." She dipped a curtsy, smiled and giggled a little more. "We was funning you, we was—Judy and me." She then reached into her pocket and withdrew something that she popped into her mouth. Very soon the redolence of mint filled the air, thank the gods! "Judith, er, had the headache and begs yer apologies, but she could not oblige ye. Now that ye are here, m'lord, why do ye not show me yer castle? Oy am very friendly and as it happens, Oy am very fond of castles." She moved to slip her arm about his and he decided to permit her to do so. However, he had no intention of taking Betty to his house, far from it. He had a completely different notion entirely!

"In other circumstances, I should probably have agreed quite happily, your enjoyment of onions not withstanding, but I have different quarry tonight. However, if you are interested in earning a sovereign, there is one particular task you might perform for me."

Even in the moonlight he could see her eyes glittering. "A sovereign?" she inquired. "Wat would the task be?"

"That you accompany me to your camp and show me, though at some distance, the precise location of Miss Lovington's tent."

Betty smiled broadly. "Oy should be delighted, me lord."

She proved to be delightfully garrulous, chatting the entire distance. He found himself grateful for her disarming discourse for then he was able to ponder quite at his leisure the trick Judith had played upon him this evening. More particularly, he spent many minutes deciding just how he should go about punishing her for what proved to be an odiferous prank.

At the outskirts of the camp, where the shadows were dark and deep, Betty quietly explained that Judith's tent was at the edge near Mrs. Marnhull's wagon. "She be our cook," she explained. "The tent to the right of Judy's belongs to John and Margaret Ash, so ye must take great care not to let them hear ye else John will run ye through with his sword, he is that protective of her. Judy came to the troupe as a girl of fourteen so he thinks on her quite as his little sister, so take care." She then held out her greedy palm.

He withdrew the sovereign from his vest pocket and placed it firmly in her hand. He was not surprised when she bit it, afterward smiling broadly once more, dipping a lively curtsy, and swishing her way into the camp.

When she had disappeared, and he knew even she could not see him, he crept closer to the edge of the camp that he might steal into Judith's tent. In the center of the half circle of tents was a log fire, blazing and crackling in the cool night air. The sound of a lute being plucked and the harmonies of two male voices held an almost melancholy note. Taking another step, suddenly Judith came into his range of sight. She was seated facing the fire so that her profile was perfectly visible. He drew in a soft breath. His heart seemed to constrict in his chest. Even at this angle she was lovely. What was it about a beautiful woman's face that so enchanted the senses of man?

After a moment, when his head cleared, he realized she was holding a child on her lap. He recalled once in passing the camp he had seen a girl playing in the distance and there she was, of perhaps four or five and obviously content being held by Judith.

The scene was so tender that an odd pain passed through his chest. A longing pierced him so deeply that he had some difficulty drawing breath. He felt as though his ribs had been bruised, so profound was the sensation.

He drew back into the shadows fearing discovery. His original intention of stealing into her tent took a hard turn. He had been knocked out of stride and now he must recover. Only how to proceed? Frustration began working in him. This was not how he had meant to conclude his evening. He had been in pursuit of another kiss and much more, but there she sat with a child on her lap smiling at the troubadors, whispering into the girl's ear, bouncing her on her knees.

Now he was angry. How dare she sit as a mother might sit, pretending to be honorable and pure when he had kissed her and he knew that she was no different from Betty? How dare she in her present attitude make him long for a family, for a wife, for children racing up and down his halls and she just an actress?

He knew but one desire in this moment, to punish Judith Lovington for her hypocrisy, for rejecting his attentions and for sending Betty and her dragon's breath instead, for having sent him all over the county of Somerset in search of her when all the while she was in a tent in his pasture!

He determined then and there that Miss Judith Lovington

would soon feel the soft sting of his revenge. If she wished to play at her games, he knew quite well how to play. The scent of the hunt filled his nostrils, but this quarry, he instinctively knew, would not easily be run to earth. He turned around and crept quietly away from the camp. He would soon visit her tent, but not tonight. Instead, there were plans to be made.

On the following morning, Judith lifted her head from her labors, stretching her back a little. An unwelcome sight met her eyes.

"Oh, no," she moaned. Her hands were sunk to the wrist in bread dough, kneading, flipping, and turning. But her gaze had become fixed upon Lord Kelthorne who had just come into view. He was astride his horse and sporting hunting gear. A wagon, driven by one of his servants, followed behind him.

She knew she was not readily visible, situated as she was behind a rack of copper pots. Today, she was helping Mrs. Marnhull make several loaves of bread, but presently her fingers had stopped kneading since the sight of Kelthorne had stunned her completely.

"Wat is it, Miss Judy?" Mrs. Marnhull rose up from cleaning her largest pot.

"'Tis Kelthorne."

"So it is and such a handsome man. Look how he carries his hunting rifle as though it were but a feather in his hand. La, do but look in the wagon! He's brought down a young stag."

Kelthorne caught sight of Mrs. Marnhull and guided his horse in her direction, signaling for the driver and wagon to follow. He did not look at Judith.

"You must be Mrs. Marnhull," he called out. "My bailiff has had many kind words to say of you and by the looks of the camp I would say you run an orderly ship."

"I do at that!" she cried. "Thank ye fer saying as much."

He smiled at Mrs. Marnhull and Judith's breath caught. In the strong light of day, in hunting gear and his heavy rifle now resting on his forearm, he had all the appearance of a soldier returning from war. Sweat beaded his face, dust marred his clothing and blood stained his neckcloth. She felt very strange of a sudden, almost queasy, as though she might swoon.

"I have venison which I should like to offer to you and to the troupe. Would a haunch be of use to you?"

Mrs. Marnhull's eyes bulged. "'Twould, indeed, m'lord!"

"Send your man," he gestured to Horace who turned bright red at being acknowledged, "to the butcher's this afternoon."

"I will," she responded.

He tipped his hat to her then to Judith. "Miss Lovington." He met and held her gaze quite firmly, even deliberately. Then he smiled anew and in his look was the hunter. She suddenly felt as vulnerable as a rabbit in a crate. With that, he called sharply to his horse, wheeled about and loped away.

"What did he want?" John called from behind Judith.

She turned and saw that he had just emerged from his tent, soap still on his cleanly shaven face and wiping his hands on a strip of linen. "He had been hunting and was kind enough to share a little venison with the troupe."

"A little!" Mrs. Marnhull cried. "A haunch! A whole haunch!" She turned to Horace, a lad of fourteen whose duties ranged from feeding the cattle to hauling water and to tending fires in camp. "Build a spit for us, a good sturdy un!"

"Aye, Mrs. Marnhull," he returned with a smile. He was adept at constructing things and one of the most useful members of camp even though he was so young. He immediately went to the second wagon in which the camp tools and equipment were kept.

As for Mrs. Marnhull, she clapped her hands together. "Roast venison! Tend to the dough, Miss Judy," she called sharply, "'tis rising already and that won't do!"

"Yes, Mrs. Marnhull." Judy resumed her task and immediately plunged her hands back into the dough kneading strongly as Mrs. Marnhull had taught her so many years ago.

Judith knew she had grown quite strong since joining the troupe from all the bread she had made over the past eight years. She punched, folded, kneaded and punched again. The problem with bread making of the moment was that her mind was left to wander and very soon Kelthorne took up residence in her head.

What did he mean, for instance, by bringing venison to camp? Was he merely being a considerate neighbor or was it possible he had some other more sinister motive in mind, something that had more to do with the kiss they had shared in the orchard than with generosity of temperament? Was it possible this was his way of trying to put himself in her good graces or was he trying to ingratiate himself with all the ladies of the troupe by so doing? Betty had said he had treated her with great kindness, that he had been a real gentleman and escorted her back to camp but that she had not been able to tease even one kiss from him. Was he, therefore, working his wiles on all the ladies?

This thought made her hit the dough harder still. She knew her thoughts were ridiculous. No good could possibly come from such idle speculations. She did not truly know Kelthorne so how could she make a meaningful evaluation of his conduct? He had brought venison to the camp. He had shown kindness, therefore, to the troupe. Beyond that, she refused to make any other judgments. Time would prove his character. "The truth," as Shakespeare said, "will out."

Several hours later, with the venison roasting on the spit and fresh-baked bread teasing the nostrils of all the hungry actors gathering about the savory meat, a castle servant arrived in camp with a wagon laden with properly chopped firewood. As though never before having seen such a sight, all fourteen members of the troupe gathered about the wagon and stared at the tall piles of wood.

"This be fer Mrs. Marnhull, with his lordship's compliments," the servant said.

Freddy slung his arm about Mrs. Marnhull's ample waist. "I do believe Lord Kelthorne has taken a fancy to ye."

"Aw, go on with ye!" But she was blushing and smiling, her expression joyful yet queer with three missing teeth.

Judith felt stunned once more, just as she had earlier. The image of being a rabbit caught in a cage came back to her. Her heart pounded in her chest. She felt like running, as hard and as fast as she could.

"He's an excellent host," Charles said, glancing at Judith. "Are ye not glad that we have decided to remain?"

Judith saw his expression of triumph, but she chose to smile. "I am very glad, Charles, as well you know."

He was not well satisfied with such a pleasant response and merely glared at her.

Margaret drew Judith aside. "Wat think ye? First venison and now firewood. Kelthorne seems to be a good sort after all." When Judith did not respond, she added, "Why so silent? Wat be ye thinking?"

"I do not know," Judith admitted. "I feel very anxious. I do not trust these acts of kindness."

"Ah," Margaret murmured then laughed aloud. Drawing Judith further away from the ears of the troupe, she said, "'Tis not as though he's sent ye jewels or the like. Do ye really think he is trying to win yer affections with firewood?"

Judith laughed. "It sounds horribly vain of me, I know, but I cannot be easy. Had he not kissed me already and sought me out at the theater, I would think nothing of the matter. As it is, I do not trust his generosity."

"And I might agree with ye had he sent flowers, but a haunch of deer meat 'tisn't precisely romantic-like." She turned sharply away. "Shelly! Leave the biscuits, now, or I shall make ye feel it quite painfully!"

Shelly, who was a terrible if charming little sneak, withdrew her hand from the laden plate of macaroons, and instead nibbled on the end of her finger. She appeared like a little angel in that moment, her expression completely innocent.

"How are you ever able to discipline her?" Judy whispered.

"A thankless task when my heart swells so just by looking at her."

Judy glanced at Margaret. Margaret never spoke of her life in the East End and no one asked but Judith had come to believe that in one sense she and Margaret were sisters, in that they had both left intolerable situations, having struck out into the unknown with nothing but their wits to guide them.

Perhaps it was for that reason they had become the dearest of friends. Judith had even been present at Shelly's birth.

As she looked at Margaret now, she suddenly slipped her arm about her waist. "How happy I am for you. I believe you have everything even the most privileged of ladies desire."

Margaret glanced at her husband who was holding Shelly and kissing her forehead. "I would only wish the same fer ye."

That evening at the theater, Judith took her turn looking through the peep hole in the curtain and saw that Kelthorne was sitting as he had the night before, in the front row on the left. Was he playing at a deep game or was it possible he was merely a kind and generous man? Somehow she believed he was the former, only what was he about?

After the performance, she lingered longer than usual at her sewing. She kept waiting for Henry or Freddy to bring her Kelthorne's card, but no such event occurred. She wished she could feel gladdened by the circumstance instead she found she was oddly piqued.

The next day, while she had been closeted in her tent and bathing in privacy, she heard rather than saw Kelthorne's arrival. He was greeted warmly by several of the actors and a moment later by Mrs. Marnhull who exclaimed over several brace of pheasant, thanking him profusely.

"Horace!" she called loudly. "We'll be needing several spits this time! Thank ye, m'lord. Ye are a good man."

Worse followed when, as she was washing her neck and arms, she heard John actually invite him to dine with them.

"With pleasure," Kelthorne responded warmly.

"And Mr. Doulting, too, o' course," John added.

"He will be much gratified. And if it pleases you, Mr. Ash, I shall bring a keg of small beer."

The actors who had followed him to Mrs. Marnhull's wagon, all cheered him with several rousing, "Huzzas!"

"Ye have yer answer, m'lord."

Judith was horrified. Had he now so insinuated himself into the troupe that she must endure his presence at nuncheon? So it would seem.

The real question, however, she could not yet answer— was this by design?

Judith sat down on her bed, only this time a little too hard for the corner gave way and she landed with a bounce on the canvas floor.

"What was that?" she heard Kelthorne ask.

"Judy, did yer bed fall again?" John called to her. In this moment, her tent was far too close to Mrs. Marnhull's wagon for her to be in the least content. She wore only her shift and her corset and even though she could not be seen, she felt quite exposed. "Aye," she responded. "But 'tis no matter."

"Miss Lovington's bed has a weak post," she heard John explain.

She felt her cheeks grow warm. How could he be speaking to Kelthorne about the state of her bed?

"How unfortunate," Kelthorne said. "Perhaps someone should tell her to stop jumping about on it."

The men laughed at his joke. She rolled her eyes and pulled a face, an expression no one could see, of course, but which afforded her some consolation.

"I must go," Kelthorne said, "but I shall return with Mr. Doulting. At what hour?"

"Nuncheon be served at one," Mrs. Marnhull stated firmly.

"We shall not be late."

Judith spent the next several hours wishing some evil would befall Kelthorne to prevent his coming. No such misfortune, however, occurred, for five minutes before the hour, both gentlemen arrived, dashing in their riding clothes and top boots and astride two very fine horses, which Horace immediately took charge of.

As it was, nuncheon set her nerves on fire. With Lord Kelthorne sitting at her table she felt more vulnerable than she had in a very long time though, given his conduct, she did not feel particularly justified in her feelings. He held a pheasant drumstick and complimented Mrs. Marnhull on her culinary skills. He slipped peas into his mouth and flirted audaciously with Betty who in turn had taken to chewing her mint leaves more frequently than was usual for her. He ate the potato and cheese dish that was a favorite with the troupe but only once deigned to look at her. He did not even smile. Instead, he asked Bobby to pass the small beer and winked wickedly at Angelique who trilled her laughter so delightfully that Judith had the strongest urge to pull hard on long, curly locks.

Fortunately, Judith sat beside Mr. Doulting who proved to be a very good sort of man and an excellent companion at table. He kept a small flow of conversation going throughout the meal and in the end she realized he had learned quite a lot about her: that the red rose was her favorite flower, that she favored pearls over diamonds and that Byron did not hold so much pleasure for her as Wordsworth.

A wonderful discussion of poetry followed and very soon she culled from him the information that he was a hopeful poet.

"Perhaps not *hopeful*," Mr. Doulting cried, taking a long

pull on his tankard. "I have no expectation of finding my efforts in print, but I am excessively fond of scribbling."

"I should love to read your work some day." Only then did Kelthorne speak to her.

"He will never permit you to do so, Miss Lovington," he said. "No one is allowed to read his poems."

"Have we a poet among us?" John asked.

Mr. Doulting was obviously embarrassed and said, "A poor amateur at best."

Judith knew that a score of questions would follow, so she said hastily, "I have been noticing your waistcoat. Do you perchance have your clothes fashioned by Weston? I am in the habit of making use of a needle, as most of the troupe is, and cannot help but admire the stitchery. Quite perfect!"

She watched him breathe a sigh of relief as he said, "Weston, absolutely. He is the very best tailor in London."

"Henry, you should look at the embroidery work," Judith said. "I think it might suit the Richard II cape you have been working on." She turned back to Mr. Doulting, "Henry, if you must know, designs the costumes but we all share in the labor of fashioning them."

Mr. Doulting was indeed very impressed and so followed a lively discussion of the various costumes he had already seen on stage and after nuncheon requested a tour of the designs for forthcoming performances.

Judith removed herself from the lively group clustered about the earl and his friend choosing to help Mrs. Marnhull clear the table. She had an opportunity, therefore, to watch Kelthorne among his inferiors. He seemed quite comfortable with them, perfectly at ease. He had a congenial manner that thwarted either condescension or defensiveness from those around him. Nor was his language bawdy in the presence of the ladies and he turned every such comment aside as lightly as though he were fencing with great skill. She found much to her dismay that she actually approved of him.

And yet, particularly after living in such a wild, insecure

manner for eight years, her instincts had been carefully honed, and she sensed rather than saw that he had begun a determined, careful assault on her innocence.

"I think him a good man," Margaret whispered, as the pair of them began preparing to wash the dishes. "He is my idea of wat a gentleman ought to be."

"He does appear to have some rather fine qualities," she agreed, glancing at him over her shoulder. He met her gaze briefly and nodded to her. The smile reached her lips before she could stop it. His smile broadened in a manner she could only think appeared rather triumphant. With a lift of her chin, she turned back to the duty at hand. Thus she and Margaret worked quietly side by side for several minutes. Her friend glanced back more than once but Judith refused to do so, not after such a smile as Kelthorne had given her, at least not until Margaret said, "Do look, Judy! La, but has he just won me heart!"

At such a warm statement, Judith could not help but turn around. She saw a sight that melted her heart as much as it had Margaret's. Shelly was sitting on Kelthorne's lap and feeding him a biscuit, his arm protectively about her waist.

Judith quickly averted her gaze from the tender scene and concentrated instead on scrubbing the plates, sinking her hands once more into the hot water. Unexpected tears bit at her eyes. How wretched of Kelthorne to do something so sweet for now the deepest longings of her heart rose up like a fiery dragon from the hidden places of her soul. She felt as though her heart was being burned within her chest.

She rarely thought of what she had left behind in Sussex, the day she had run away from home. Yet somehow, seeing Kelthorne holding little Shelly as he was brought a dozen memories swelling in her mind all at once, of her invalid father whom she had adored, of a beloved uncle and cousins, of all her girlhood hopes and dreams, that one day she would have a family of her own. She had been a proper Miss Pensbury, her father a respected baronet, Sir Christopher

Pensbury. On the heels of these precious reveries, however, came the awful reasons for her escape.

The memory returned to her sharply in this moment, of the vile attentions of the Marquess of Stolford. He had been introduced to her in a bookshop in Brighton by her stepmother during the summer of 1810. He was afterwards a frequent visitor, by her stepmother's invitation, to her home. She had not understood why she had been so often summoned to the drawing room, always, of course, when her father was resting in his bedchamber. She had been so young, just fourteen, and it was highly unusual to be in company, nonetheless with a Peer of the Realm.

When the marquess took to kissing her hand upon his departure, she grew uneasy, though she could not say why for he was always kind in his attentions. Her governess, Miss Holywell, however, had understood precisely what was going forward but had said nothing until she overheard Stolford suggesting to Lady Pensbury that they take Judith on a tour of the West Country, perhaps spending the autumn at his country house.

How innocent she had been at the time for she had not in the least comprehended her governess's extreme disquiet. Miss Holywell had been forced to explain in horrifying detail both the nature of Stolford's reputation as well as precisely what would happen to her once he had her captive in his home. How quickly her childhood had disappeared in that moment.

She had fled her home with but a note left for her father. Little had she known she would never see him again, for he perished that Christmas. Her intention had been to reach her uncle to seek his protection. Fearing that Stolford would overtake her were she to use the most direct route, she had traveled in a circuitous manner. But by the time she reached her uncle's house, the marquess's coach had been in the drive. Only then did she understand that she would never be safe.

Tears now trickled down her cheek.

The memory of Stolford still haunted her. In securing her safety from him by disappearing she had forsaken her girlish dreams. To dwell on her former life, however, was to break her heart anew so she was in the habit of avoiding such thoughts. But how could she not be reminded today, with Kelthorne in the camp and holding Shelly so tenderly, putting her forcibly in mind of the life she had been taught would one day be hers—a gentleman to take as husband, a comfortable home, and, of course, a dozen children all racing down the halls and playing and squabbling.

Kelthorne had done this to her, with his kisses that had affected her so powerfully, whose mere presence caused her heart to flutter, and whose character was more complex than she would have thought possible. How much she wished such a man did not exist.

"Judy," Margaret called to her softly. "Ye have washed that un fer the last five minutes."

She felt a blush rise on her cheeks. "I fear I was thinking of other things."

Margaret, who was drying the dishes, reached up and wiped a tear from her cheek. "So I see," she murmured gently.

FOUR

"We would not press you, Aubrey, but she is absolutely perfect, you can have no notion, though you shall see for yourself when she arrives with the rest of the party shortly."

Kelthorne regarded his elder sister quite coolly, his arms folded over his chest. Mary and Amy had arrived much to his surprise only this morning. Upon returning from another hunting expedition—brought short by a sudden downpour—in which he had still been able to provide Mrs. Marnhull with several rabbits, he returned to the stables only to find Mary's carriage on the drive. They had arrived several days earlier than expected and the disappointment he felt was profound since he not only had been enjoying himself enormously with the troupe but he was right in the middle of his most precious scheme to tear down Judith's defenses. He felt as though a bucket of ice water had just been dumped over his head. Worse still, his prospective bride-to-be was due to arrive within the hour.

"You know I do not like to be surprised," he said coldly. "Why did you not stay with your original plan?"

"I fear it is Radsbury. He has been required to go to London in three weeks time rather than six and we felt we should step up our plans. I do apologize for not informing you sooner, but a letter sent post would not have arrived before us."

"Where are Radsbury and the others?"

"One of the wheels in the third coach was loose," Amy explained. "Radsbury and Newnott stayed behind to see the task accomplished. He begged us to go on that you might be given fair warning of our change of plans."

"Well, it is most inconvenient," he said, thinking how Judith had looked this morning. When he had left the rabbits with Mrs. Marnhull, he had caught sight of her in a gown of pink muslin, her chestnut hair hanging to her waist and swinging little Shelly in circles. At the time, he had known the strongest impulse to leave his horse and even if she protested violently, to gather her up in his arms and kiss her. What fortitude it had required to merely tip his hat to her and ride away.

"Aubrey!" Mary snapped.

He turned to look at her and saw that her eyes had narrowed suspiciously. "What is it?" he inquired.

"Have you got up a tryst with one of those actresses? I have already been given to understand by your most exceptional butler that you have permitted an entire troupe of actors to camp in your pasture beyond the orchard. We saw them as we drove by. I was never more shocked to learn you had done so."

"It seemed a harmless request to oblige, particularly since the troupe has promised us an entire month's entertainment and so far their performances in the local theater have exceeded our expectations. Have they not, Laurence?"

"Very much so," Laurence said. He was seated by the fire reading a newspaper and did not bother to look up as he spoke.

Mary rolled her eyes at both of them. She was but three years Kelthorne's senior yet had always treated him as though she was a great deal older. She had large hazel eyes, sharp features and light brown hair looped in several very tight narrow braids. She would have been accounted a beauty had she not been in the habit of keeping her lips pinched tightly together as though to keep her thoughts and feelings from streaming out of her all at once.

He wished she would hold them back now only she seemed incapable of doing so where his future was concerned, in this case, his choice of bride. "I had rather choose the next countess of Kelthorne myself," he stated firmly.

"And so you shall," Amy said. She was a year younger than Mary but at least did not treat him in the same officious manner as her sister. She was taller than Mary but had a sweeter countenance. "Perhaps Mary has spoken too stridently." When he barked his laughter, Amy continued hastily, "But even I have hopes that you might find this young woman quite to your taste. She is refined, elegant, in possession of more poise than any young lady ought to be, and very, very beautiful."

At this, he turned and frowned at Amy. "Indeed?"

She nodded.

"Exceptionally so," Mary said.

Laurence folded his newspaper and rose from his seat by the hearth. "I confess that now even I am grown intrigued."

Amy turned to smile upon him. "So you should be, Laurence, for not only is she quite the most beautiful lady I have ever laid eyes upon, she is also a considerable heiress. If my brother will not have her, she might just do for you!"

"What is her name?" he asked.

"Abigail Currivard."

"And why have we not heard of her or seen her in London? We are there quite often as you very well know," Kelthorne inquired.

The sisters glanced at one another.

"Oh, ho!" Laurence cried. "Do I apprehend the stench of *trade* in the air?" He was laughing as he spoke.

Mary lifted her chin. "The spice trade and you will not call it a stench when you hear that her dowry alone is eighty thousand pounds. Upon the death of her father, she will inherit more."

Kelthorne was astonished.

"Good God," Laurence cried. "I believe I may swoon. And where did you discover this creature?"

Mary left the small circle they had made and took up a seat on a sofa opposite the chair Laurence had just vacated. "We shall tell you everything you wish to know, but not before I have had a glass of sherry."

Kelthorne moved to the table behind the sofa. "Of course." He ought to have tended to her sooner, he realized, for when she was increasing, she was easily fatigued.

Mary looked about her. "I approve very much of the changes you have made. Uncle was such a nipcheese but these fabrics—and such a pretty shade of green—are of the first quality. I am so glad that you have inherited Portislow for a finer house one may not find in many counties." She was puffed up with pleasure. "And it is so fortunate that the house proper is not part of the castle, otherwise, given how cold and damp as castles are wont to be, you probably would never be at home."

"You have the right of it," he said. He poured two glasses of sherry. "And it has become a very comfortable house, I must say. Of course, I relied entirely upon the expertise of the woman you sent me. Do I apprehend that since she resided in Bath, you had a hand in choosing and sending the fabrics?"

Amy laughed. "Of course we did!"

"Well, you did rightly. The result is very pleasing. Of course, with so much excellent wainscoting, the refitting of the main rooms was done with little inconvenience to myself. But do you think Miss Currivard will approve?" He brought a glass to Amy and the second to Mary.

Amy sat down as well, settling her sherry on the table at her elbow. She removed her bonnet and patted her blond curls, even working to fix one that had become twisted from its long imprisonment under her bonnet. Of his two sisters, Amy was more in Kelthorne's likeness, sharing with him the color of her hair and the blue of his eyes.

"How could she not? And the companion yellow is just soft enough not to be too jarring to the nerves."

The drawing room of Portislow Castle was a well-lit chamber overlooking a narrow valley that ran between the hill upon which the castle was perched, and an opposite series of hills that ran from east to west meeting the Bristol Channel not a mile farther on. The décor was pleasing now, Kelthorne admitted.

Initially, he had taken little interest in it, but his sisters had been right to give him a push. When his uncle died during the prior year, the rooms were dirty and the old brocades—so popular a half-century past—had grown threadbare. Some of the rooms had suffered from mildew and more than one piece of furniture had been damaged from the excessive dripping of cheap tallow candles. Nothing but the finest beeswax was present now and his housekeeper, given permission to hire an appropriate number of servants for the size of the house, had set even the darkest corners to glowing with her zeal and expertise.

He moved to the window that overlooked the vale. In the distance, to the west, he saw the camp, probably soggy from the earlier drenching. The tents, however, were now rippling happily in a fine breeze. He could even espy Mrs. Marnhull hanging laundry.

Suddenly, he wished he was there and not in his refined drawing room, awaiting the arrival of his sisters' *chosen one*. Irrationally, he disliked her already—Miss Currivard of the spice trade. He disliked that he must marry. He did not require an heiress, for he had a very comfortable nine thousand a year. He was a little surprised to think that his sisters had become so grossly avaricious on his behalf.

"I am confused on one point," Kelthorne said. "How is it you arrived before noon? You cannot have traveled directly from Bath."

"Indeed not," Amy said. "We have made a new acquaintance if you must know. The Marquess of Stolford has purchased a house in Bath and is now quite accepted in the first circles. We broke our journey at his home which is but four hours drive from Portislow."

"Good God!" he cried. "The Marquess of Stolford! You account him a proper acquaintance? How is that possible when he has one of the worst reputations in all of England?"

Mary shrugged. "'Tis all forgot," she said. "He has been redeeming himself in polite society, at least in Bath, by making very great contributions to our local charities and has promised to provide new draperies for the assembly rooms."

When footsteps were heard on the stairs, indeed, a profound trampling of feet, it appeared that the remainder of the Bath party had arrived all at once. Any further questions either he or Laurence had concerning Miss Currivard must now wait.

Kelthorne turned to await his doom. Would that he could fly from the chamber down to the camp and settle his gaze on the beautiful Judith and, instead of doing the pretty in his drawing room, envelope his mind in scheme after scheme of seducing her.

The first to cross the threshold was Lord Radsbury. He was a vibrant man who crossed to him immediately, his hand outstretched "How do you go on, Kelthorne! Damme, but am I glad to see you ensconced here. Portislow has been in need of you these thirty years and more."

"Hallo, Radsbury," he shook his hand warmly. "I am happy to hear you say as much."

Lord Radsbury turned and waved his arm in the direction of the doorway. As if on cue, two ladies appeared on the threshold. "But let me make the introductions. Miss Banwell and Miss Upton, both lately of Bath."

The young women were pretty enough in their way but on no account the beauty he had been promised. They offered their curtsies at which time Laurence was introduced.

Kelthorne glanced at the doorway. He could hear voices beyond. A young man appeared, tall, lean with curly black hair, brown eyes and a quite good-natured expression.

"Mr. Emborough, allow me to present Lord Kelthorne."

He bowed properly. "How do you?"

"Quite well, thank you."

"Mr. Doulting."

"And how do you do, sir?"

"Exceedingly well," Laurence responded, then lowered his voice. "Only tell me, is Miss Currivard a beauty, indeed?"

He pressed a hand to his chest and lifted his gaze to the ceiling. "Venus incarnate."

"Well, then!" Laurence cried, clapping his hands together.

Kelthorne laughed at his friend for he was being ridiculous.

A lovely feminine voice could be heard just beyond the doorway. "Are you certain you are all right, Mr. Newnott? Indeed, I am sure you are not!"

And so Miss Currivard appeared on the threshold, supporting Amy's husband by the arm. He was limping badly.

"Good God, Sylvester," Amy cried. "What happened this time?"

"I am sorry, dearest, but I twisted my foot on the bottom step. I can hardly put my weight upon it."

She shook her head in some disgust. "Well, do come sit down and elevate it. Aubrey, would you fetch a footstool?"

"Of course."

Miss Currivard guided Mr. Newnott to the chair at which Amy now stood like a sentinel. Kelthorne sought a footstool but had to cross to the library in order to find one. By the time, he returned, Mr. Newnott was sitting but still in apparent pain. "Shall I fetch the doctor, Newnott?"

"No, no," he cried bitterly. "I am sure it is only a sprain but, why do these things, as absurd as they are, always happen to me? I should like to know! Do I bring them down on my own head? All I did was offer Miss Currivard my arm then I missed my step and now, I am persuaded the deuced thing is swelling! The devil take it!"

"Mind your words, Mr. Newnott," Mary murmured. "The ladies will not like to hear you speak in such a manner."

Miss Currivard intervened quickly, offering a glass of sherry. "Will this do, Mr. Newnott?"

"Dear God, yes," he cried. "What a darling you are! Heaven sent. Heaven sent." He took the proffered drink and swallowed it at once.

"Shall I fetch another?" she asked, an amused smile on her lips.

"Yes, my dear. Thank you. Thank you."

Miss Currivard went readily about the business. For the first time, Kelthorne was at liberty to look at her. He liked the amused expression in her eyes. She certainly did not take Mr. Newnott seriously but he rather thought her conduct both admirable and kind. He liked that without the smallest ceremony or begging of permission she poured out his sherry. He found he liked her.

The rest of what had been said about her proved very true. She was a great beauty, indeed, with thick golden curls and a pair of large, almost mesmerizing green eyes. There was a look of intelligence about her as well and he believed he saw in her the qualities that had made her forebears successful merchants.

She is perfect, he thought—beautiful, discerning, kind and wealthy. Did any gentleman require more?

Judith Lovington came sharply to mind and a war began in his heart. Judith was beautiful, even more so than the exquisite Miss Currivard. She had the voice of an entire choir of angels mingled into one, resonant tone. Kissing her had been like holding the moon in his hand. She had inspired in him the hunt, as he had never been inspired before, even to the use of great calculation and trickery.

Yet here was Miss Currivard, embodying all that would prosper the house of Kelthorne. She represented his intent to relinquish his roguery, to do what was right by his birth and breeding, even his desire to create a family of his own as his sisters wished him to.

But how could he leave off pursuing Judith when she was the moon in his hand? How could he possibly settle into the life played out almost in dramatic form before him, with Amy tending to her husband and his injured foot, with Radsbury already engaged in a heated discussion with Laurence and Mr. Emborough about political concerns, with the younger ladies gathered about the pianoforte searching through the music Mary had weeks ago sent to Portislow. This would be his life, he thought in some horror. He ought to have found at least a measure of satisfaction in it, but for whatever reason, his heart bolted within him. Not for him this insipidity day after day.

His attention was drawn at last to Miss Currivard. She was watching him intently and there was but the faintest smile on her lips. She appeared to be in some thought as though perhaps she was trying to make him out. He met her gaze fully and it seemed to him in that moment he was understood. She gave the smallest shrug of her shoulders, a helpless, resigned gesture that funneled his vision of her into an understanding of the equal pressures of her own life. He wondered suddenly if she was here as much by the design of other well-intentioned family and friends as by his sisters. He decided to honor what he assessed to be her integrity and goodness and crossed the room to her.

Three days later, Judith hummed in her tent, laying out her pattern papers on a length of beautiful violet patterned silk, which she had spread out carefully on her bed. She was content. Of course, she was. Indeed, she was.

The castle gentlemen had not visited the camp since Kelthorne brought several brace of rabbits to Mrs. Marnhull, although at least one hamper of peach preserves, fresh bread, and olives had been sent to the troupe in the intervening time. Of course it was well known that a large party had arrived at the castle, that Kelthorne's sisters and their husbands were now in residence along with three young ladies and a young gentleman.

She was relieved. Of course she was relieved. Quite relieved since it would seem Kelthorne had given up his pursuit of her, or at least what she had supposed was his pursuit of her. She moved the patterns again and hummed a little more, this time standing over the silk looking down upon the arrangements of the patterns and tapping her foot. She felt foolish, of course she felt foolish, quite foolish since she had all but persuaded John and Margaret that Kelthorne's generosity had had only one purpose, to break down the defenses of her heart. Now it would seem he had had no interest in her, none whatsoever!

Not that it mattered. Of course it did not matter. Not one whit. After all, she was quite relieved that his pursuit was at an end, if he had ever really pursued her. And she was very content!

She sank down on her bed, sitting on the patterns and the silk and not precisely caring. The door to the tent was tied back. The summery day was lovely.

She was engaged in one of her favorite occupations, making a new gown, which she would wear during her performances. She had several in her possession, but the nature of a performance, the limelights, and the dirt backstage quickly took its toll so that from the first she had found it necessary to continuously replenish her gowns. Nor was there an aspect to the creation of her costumes that she did not enjoy.

She loved the process of hunting for just the right fabric, and in this instance she had found some lovely gold braid to embellish the ribbon about the waist and in Portislow only this morning she had purchased a length of crocheted lace, which she would use to adorn the bodice. Laying out the pattern on the fabric was always a point of real gamesmanship—to make the most of the fabric, not waste one inch if she could possibly help it. The setting of her stitches she looked forward to as much as she did the beauty of the day outside.

So why it was then that she was presently sitting on her bed, creasing the fabric and patterns, was a complete mystery to her.

Margaret appeared in the doorway. "Did ye send a missive to the castle?" she asked sharply, a hard frown between her brows.

Judith sat up a little straighter. She did not have the smallest notion of what she was speaking. "No. Was I to have done so?"

"O' course not," she snapped. Folding her arms over her chest, she huffed a sigh. "Well, then, did ye see him in recent days when no one was about? Did ye say something awful to him?"

Judith was all at sea. "To whom?"

Margaret's eyes bulged. "To his lordship! To Kelthorne! Wat have ye done, Judy, that sent him away like this?"

Judith was quite shocked by Margaret's demeanor and accusing tone. She could only presume that the loss of the meat every day had become a great concern to her but she could not understand why. The troupe rarely received such beneficence. Surely Mrs. Marnhull had not come to depend upon Kelthorne. "I have not spoken or seen him since he dined with us the day he brought the pheasants. Why? Whatever is the matter?"

"Oh, very well, then," she returned grumpily. "I suppose 'tis not yer fault!"

Before Judith could inquire what was troubling her, Margaret stalked away.

Judith was utterly mystified by Margaret's behavior. Why was *she* so overset that Kelthorne had ceased calling? What was it to her unless she truly was dismayed that he was no longer hunting and providing meat—but that seemed quite unlikely. No, she could not account for Margaret's conduct in the least.

She rose from the bed and turned to look at the fabric. She had crumpled it wretchedly. She could only wonder how she had come to be so daft. She could not even remember precisely how it had come about she had sat down.

Outside, the camp rattled about noisily. She could hear John and Charles arguing as they often did when they were in the midst of adding something new to the repertoire. Both were highly creative individuals with great dramatic ability. More than once she had been completely mesmerized by one or the other during a dramatic portrayal on stage. This was the part of troupe life that she enjoyed the very best. She would always feel desperately sad that her life had taken such a difficult turn, but at the same time she believed she would be forever grateful for the richness of the experiences she had had in the eight years since she first joined the troupe.

From her doorway, she could see Freddy, Henry and Bobby practicing their juggling routine. They were both remarkably expert even doing a little tumbling in the midst of tossing every item imaginable back and forth to one another. Yes, she loved the troupe so why it was she had suddenly come to feel so blue-devilled she could not say.

At least there would be a performance in the evening. She could swell her song, a circumstance that always served to ease her heart. Perhaps Kelthorne would attend this evening. Not that it mattered. Of course it did not matter. It did not matter one whit.

The evening proved very fine, indeed. Kelthorne walked beside Miss Currivard, a very peaceful sensation having taken strong hold of him from the time of her arrival. She had done this to him, he thought, smiling warmly down upon her. "The walk is quite steep," he said. "Will you take my arm?"

"Gratefully," she responded. "For I have the worst fear that I shall trip in these lovely but quite impractical shoes I am wearing, and then I shall tumble down the hill and completely disgrace myself."

He chuckled. "I must say, though I have known you only three days, I would find myself utterly shocked were such a circumstance to happen. You seem so capable and in command at every moment, it is hard to believe that even in *impractical shoes* you would ever lose your balance."

She frowned up at him slightly. "I fear there is something in your remark that disturbs me."

"How is that possible? I am certain I have just complimented you."

"I suppose you have but I believe you may also have struck a chord that sounds dissonant to me. You see, I have striven to perfect all the teachings of my most proper, most educated, most genteel governess but I have always feared the results might be rather . . . stilted."

"Ah," he murmured, turning this over in his mind. Was this true about her? He glanced down at her. She was staring ahead, minding her steps, her fingers clutching her gown in just the right place to keep the skirt an infinitesimal degree above her slippers so that she would not slip on the steep terrain, but nor would she reveal her ankles.

"Then it is true," she said, sighing heavily. "Just as I feared."

"I said nothing!" he cried.

"Your thoughts were shouting at me."

He sighed. "You are very proper. There can be no fault in that. And I have every certainty that given your background as a daughter of *trade,* as it were, the Tabbies are always looking for the smallest opportunity to rain criticism down on your head."

"You can have no notion," she said. But she turned at the same time and smiled up at him, her large green eyes luminous in the fading light of the summer evening. She wore a shawl draped casually over her elbows, as was also quite proper. Yes, she was very proper, but she was something more, something he admired very much. She was overcoming a difficult situation with all the appearance of ease and confidence. Of course, having eighty thousand pounds would lend confidence to even a troll, but he felt certain she was revealing to him in this moment the best of her character and he admired her.

"Your critics be hanged," he whispered.

At that she laughed quite warmly, even perhaps crossing

the bounds of a proper lady's laugh. He gave her arm a squeeze.

His sisters had chosen well. He admitted as much to himself. After three days of coming to know Miss Currivard, of understanding her nature, something of her character and her general disposition, he found himself quite comfortable in her company. She did not lack for conversation and though his station was very far above hers, she was not in the least obsequious. Yes, his sisters had chosen well.

"Is this not a fine evening, Kelthorne?" Laurence called to him from behind.

Kelthorne turned back to glance at his friend. He had the adorable Miss Banwell on one arm and the sweet-tempered Miss Upton on the other. He seemed quite content. Mr. Emborough had gone on before to secure the best seats for them.

"I love the theater!" Miss Banwell cried.

"I understand there are jugglers," Miss Upton stated. "I think it fascinating how they can keep so many things in the air all at once."

"Neither of you will be disappointed tonight," Kelthorne said. "The troupe excels at every form of entertainment."

"The swordfighting is superb," Laurence said.

"Are there any singers among the troupe?" Miss Currivard asked. "I am especially fond of music."

Kelthorne nearly stumbled as thoughts of Judith rushed over him like an unexpected wave in otherwise calm surf. "Yes," he said evenly, or as evenly as he could manage.

"How can you be so mild?" Laurence cried. "You must tell them of Miss Lovington! You must! Otherwise they will all swoon for hearing her sing."

"Now we are utterly intrigued!" Miss Banwell called out. "Lord Kelthorne, tell us of Miss Lovington at once!"

His lips seemed frozen. His lungs would not draw breath. How could he then speak and how could he speak of *her* when he had so recently been in pursuit of her? He sought for the right words. He strove to open his throat. Finally, he managed. "I believe I must say that she sings with the voice of the angels, yet not like the angels at all. I vow there is something within her that is not of this world, yet she is more of this world than you or I. Otherwise, who could explain such music as comes from her perfect throat?"

He drew in a deep ragged breath and blinked several times in an attempt to clear the vision of her from his mind. He was not aware for at least another twenty steps that everyone had fallen silent, strangely silent, badly silent.

He glanced down at Miss Currivard. Her gaze was fixed steadfastly ahead of her. He could not see her expression. "Have I misspoken?" he queried.

"I . . . that is, I have never heard such praise before. I find I am quite astonished."

"Am I overstating the case, Laurence?" he queried.

Laurence sighed. "Not by half, but I believe our dear company may have taken offence."

Good God, Laurence was right. All three ladies had sung for them only the night before and each had perfect expression, lovely voices, and interesting interpretations. None of course had compared to Judith, but what did that matter? He saw at once where he had erred.

Ordinarily he would not be such a sapskull as to have essentially lessened their efforts by praising to the skies the songs of another, but so he had and that quite unwittingly because from the first Judith had charmed him. Yet, what a hamhanded gudgeon he was, behaving more like a stripling still green behind the ears than a man of the world.

Only in stages did Kelthorne, with Laurence's aid, restore the conviviality of the party.

Arriving at the theater, however, Mr. Emborough brought a disappointment. Even in his prudence he had only been able to secure seats for the ladies. The attendance that evening had proved enormous. Word had spread throughout the county that a troupe of exceptional performers had come to Somerset and so it was that a great number of men were required by necessity to stand about the perimeter of the small theater, a real compliment to the troupe.

Kelthorne stood to the left of the stage up the aisle several rows of seats. He glanced frequently at Miss Currivard who sat not far from him between Miss Banwell and Miss Upton. More than once she turned to smile at him.

When Horace lit the limelight, the chattering audience grew hushed. Anticipation filled the air. The curtains parted and Mr. Ash, in a medieval costume, took center stage. He announced the opening performers but before he had finished speaking the names of the cast members, he was set upon in a violent manner by two of the troupe players with swords. The audience gasped as he gave every evidence of fighting for his life—a trick, of course, but quite effective.

Kelthorne smiled. What an excellent opening. The stage thumped as the actors rolled, leaped, shouted and fell with great ability. He found himself impressed that in but a handful of days the troupe had made excellent additions to the scene. A round of applause erupted as the actor, Henry Thurloxton, took his popular tumbling fall off the stage and Mr. Ash proclaimed his victory.

New costumes had appeared betwixt times as well, beautifully designed and worked. New scenery had been painted and there was even a new juggling act including a third actor by the name of Bobby, he believed. Kelthorne was as enchanted with the troupe's production as he had been the first night. There was a realism that could not help but please and often, especially during the sword fights when false blood appeared as if by magic, the ladies would squeal their fright. Indeed, he thought the troupe deserved to be on stage in London.

So it was that when Judith appeared on the stage, the audience, already charmed by the troupe, released a great sigh then fell utterly silent, just as it had on the other nights that he had attended the theater. Instantly, Kelthorne's gaze became riveted to her face. How serene she appeared for one so young, for one in command of three hundred people or so. She smiled and another sigh rippled through the audience.

She was gowned quite magnificently in flowing gold silk, more voluminous than would be seen on a ballroom floor but quite appropriate for the stage. An amber necklace encircled her swan's throat. Her chestnut hair on this evening was caught up high on her head but cascaded with curls down the center of her back. She was all that was elegant and lovely.

The notes from the pianoforte swelled into the air, she opened her mouth and such music came forth as always constricted his chest. He was caught fully and deeply by the melody wrapping its way about the chamber. Her gestures in hand, arm and the tilt of her head brought an ache to his heart. She had captured him as in a dream.

He listened enrapt, lost completely in her performance, in her mannerisms, in her voice. His mind was drawn back to the orchard nearly a sennight past now. This enchanting beauty with the song of angels on her tongue had been wrapped in his arms. He had teased her cheek and her ear. He had kissed her deeply. She had nearly lost her senses and without his support surely she would have fallen. She had spoken of chains.

He was lost now—in her song, in her beauty, in visions of having seen her swinging young Shelly about in circles until both were dizzy. He remembered his pursuit of her. He could not recall why he had ceased chasing her. His past was veiled in a thick fog. Only Judith existed. A single thought, a solitary purpose seized his mind—he must see her again—alone!

FIVE

"There is nothing for it," Kelthorne lied. "I completely forgot that I made a promise a sennight past to call upon Mr. Ash at the camp after the performance tonight. I shan't be long, perhaps an hour including the distance I must walk."

Laurence stared at him, his mouth agape. Silence returned to him from the ladies. Mr. Emborough cleared his throat and said that one's promises must always be honored. "I say," he continued, "but I should like some of that brandy we enjoyed last night."

"Aubrey, you cannot be serious," Laurence said then clamped his lips shut. His disapproval would have been obvious to a simpleton. The entire party fell silent.

It was Miss Currivard who took charge of the situation. "Then you must keep your promise," she said with a smile. "As for myself, I am with you, Mr. Emborough. I should like a little brandy as well. Will you escort me?"

"With pleasure," he said, offering his arm. The rest of the party fell in behind him.

Kelthorne watched them go. He knew he should have been overborn by a sense of remorse, instead there resided within him so great a determination to see Judith that nothing else seemed to matter. He struck off in the opposite direction without a backward glance.

He walked briskly for a quarter of a mile until he began to hear laughter and the lumbering of the troupe's wagon. He followed at a distance since several of the players were attending the vehicle and he did not wish his presence generally known. This particular visit he intended to be kept secret.

When in view of the camp, he stopped and watched the wagon as it reached the site. The unloading began, full of the high spirits usual among actors and actresses upon the completion of a performance. Once in a while, someone would burst into song or a lute could be heard being plucked, or even a drum sounded. The fire ring was set to burning and as the work diminished, the revelry around the ring increased, a concertina, a lute, the drum once more, the singing of familiar songs and ballads. Judith was among the troupe and every now and then he could hear the clear strain of her voice above the din.

Only when she finally retired, the third after Margaret and Shelly to leave the fireside, did he begin his approach. He was not certain just how he meant to invade Judith's tent but so he would. The closer he drew his blood began to burn in his veins. He was almost upon her when a whisper called to him.

"M'lord, a word," Mrs. Ash said.

Judith hummed the tune "The Joys of the Country." This was perhaps her favorite time of day, or rather night. The hour was near midnight, she had performed at her best, the earnings for the troupe were the highest they had ever been and she was preparing for bed. Most of the troupe was still by the fire, finishing what was left of the keg of beer Kelthorne had provided several days past.

She brushed her hair in long strokes but paused for a mo-

ment as she recalled taking her place on stage and seeing
that Lord Kelthorne had been in attendance. An odd inexplicable warmth flowed through her. He had been dressed
formally, in a black coat, an exquisitely tied neckcloth, black
breeches and stockings of the same color. She had nearly
forgotten the opening notes of her first song. She smiled
thinking how she had had to set her gaze anywhere but upon
him in order to regain her composure.

She sighed and brushed her hair anew. He had come to
the theater tonight. Of course he had not come purposely to
see her. Of course not. It would be absurd to think such a
thing. But he had smiled at her when she had met his gaze
while taking her bows. He had smiled and applauded quite
vigorously. She sighed. He had smiled.

Kelthorne had a wonderful smile. He should always be
smiling. He should always be looking at her and smiling.
She laughed at herself for she was being beyond ridiculous.
She must think of other things.

She glanced about her tent to see if everything was in
order. In so confined a space, she was always more peaceful
when her tent was neat and tidy. She had what each of the
players had, a bed, a wardrobe, a table, a trunk and a stool.
The niceties she had gained over a period of time added to
the comfort and beauty of her tent, her standing workbox of
course, a chair before her dressing table, and an excellent
and very safe lantern which burned oil. Covering nearly the
entire tent floor was a rug she had created by cross-stitching
canvas, which was very popular at the time. She had even
decorated the walls with several framed watercolors, painted
by her own hand and hung from loops she had stitched to the
joints of the tents. She kept her bonnets on a pegboard and
because each was fetching in its way, all of them in a row
had become as much a decoration as anything else. The single
most expensive purchase she had allowed herself was a beautiful ceramic pitcher and basin, covered in lavender flowers,
which sat on her table along with a perfume of the same
name. Lastly, a tall looking glass, used by all the ladies quite

frequently for the purpose of viewing the effects of a costume, stood beside her wardrobe.

On her feet were embroidered slippers of olive green and purple. Her nightdress she had embroidered about the bodice with a summery string of flowers as though garlanded from a fine cutting garden. Presently, she had a shawl about her shoulders, one that she had crocheted a year past and which was still in excellent condition.

How happy she was. In many places in her tent, she had secreted the money she had saved over the course of eight years. Of course, she had an account in Bath, but could only make deposits when the troupe passed through that fine city. She had pound notes and coins sewn into her mattress, the skirt about her bed, her cape, the padded inside lid of her sewing box and in every other place imaginable, the removal of which would require a very long time, indeed. In the bank she had four hundred pounds. She hoped to make another deposit very soon of no less than seventy-five pounds.

Such was her life. And tonight, when she had been able to add a full five pounds to her savings, she was exultant. She hummed a little more as she took the perfume bottle and dabbed a little of the lavender scent on her neck and her wrists. She liked sleeping with the delicate fragrance wafting to her nostrils now and again.

She was just turning back her bedcovers when she heard the flap of her tent move. There was only one person she expected to see at this hour of the night and that was Margaret. She turned around hoping to have a comfortable cose with her, then nearly swooned. There in the doorway was Kelthorne!

"I did not mean to startle you," he murmured, keeping his voice low.

His eyes appeared oddly wild. She wondered if he had been drinking and if so was she in danger from his advances?

She pulled the shawl close about her neck. "You must go," she whispered. "I can see that you are in your altitudes, but this will not do. Were I to scream, you would have to answer to John and Henry and the others. Indeed, my lord, I beg you will leave!"

He smiled. "Your friend, Mrs. Ash, knows that I am here so you are safe if that is what you fear. And I am not in the least foxed. She permitted me to come to you although she said I must be gone in five minutes. So, you see I am both here by permission and have promised to leave promptly."

"Margaret allowed you?" she queried, continuing to whisper. Well, she would certainly be quarreling with at least one person on the morrow! She stared at him incomprehensibly. "But why are you here?" she asked, wondering what he could possibly mean by coming to her in this odd fashion and so late at night with or without Margaret's permission.

"I do not know," he responded. His expression was so strange. His gaze never left her eyes.

She hardly knew what to do. She gestured to her poor stool, which would hardly be comfortable for him, and asked if he wished to sit down.

He did not even glance at the stool but rather shook his head. "I thank you, no."

"Kelthorne, I do not pretend to know you very well, but you seem overset. Perhaps you should leave now and call on me tomorrow when your mind is more settled."

He shook his head. "That will never do. I do not understand this hold you have over me. I watch you perform and it is as though you reach inside me, take hold of my heart and refuse to let go. I . . . I have changed. I wish to make a new start of it. But this, this power you exert is in no manner fair to me. I wish you would desist."

He made no sense at all for she thought it the most ridiculous thing in the world that he would blame her for his present feelings, which to her seemed odd in the extreme. In fact, so strange was his conduct that she sat down on her bed, carefully of course, and slowly slipped her hand beneath her pillow. Her dagger waited there. She had used it more than once to chase away the unwanted attentions of a man. John had taught her well the use of it, never to lift her arm, but always to keep the blade at an upward slant.

He dropped to his knees before her and placed his hands on her legs. "Let me go, Judith, I beg of you." Her hand trembled on the dagger.

"You should leave, my lord. Again, you are hardly making the smallest sense." She knew the moment was ripe, that she ought to make her sentiments more clearly known by exposing her weapon, still she restrained herself, especially since for some reason she found it quite difficult to breathe.

He searched each of her features in turn then let his gaze drift over her long, dangling locks.

He slid his hands into her hair and took hold of thick portions of it. "I knew your hair would feel like this." Leaning close, he added, "And it smells so fresh, like the earth after a day of rain."

"I washed it only this morning," she whispered, her fingers loosening from about the dagger's handle.

"You smell of flowers," he said, breathing against her neck so that chills raced up and down her side.

She was reminded of the night in the orchard and a faint groan escaped her lips. She should push him away. She should tell him to stop. She should use the dagger now!

Instead, she closed her eyes, released the weapon, and sighed with great pleasure for he was now kissing her neck, not precisely as he had on that first night, but with gentle and very moist touches of his lips in a long descending string.

"Lavender," he whispered.

"Yes," was her nearly incoherent response as she settled her arms over his back.

He leaned back and bade her look at him, but her arms remained to encircle his neck.

"Tell me what this power is that you have?" he asked.

She smiled, if sadly. "Only if you tell me what yours is over my ridiculously weak sensibilities. I had intended upon harming you." Only then did she withdraw an arm from him in order to lift her pillow and expose the small weapon.

His brows lifted but he smiled. "And you know how to use it properly?"

"I have been taught by the men of the troupe, many of which come from the worst parts of London. Yes, my lord, I know how to use a dagger."

His smile did not dim but tenderness entered his eyes. Her arm returned to lie gently across his back.

"Why do you speak as a lady of quality?" he asked. "Is this part of your acting abilities for it seems so natural to you?"

How could she tell him the truth, a truth she had spoken to no one? Once she uttered Stolford's name she knew it would be as a cry to him from the darkest places of the earth. His heart was evil and she dared not reveal to anyone who he was to her.

Therefore, she said, "If you have found me in the midst of an acting troupe, then whatever my story, it cannot be a good one. Suffice it to say, that for eight years this has been my home and these people my family."

"I suppose you are right. It hardly matters."

"The minutes are passing, my lord. You should leave now." But she did not want him to go.

He narrowed his gaze as though filled with a hundred thoughts at once. "I made a promise to Mrs. Ash that I would do so, but not just yet." Before she knew what he was about, however, he rose, pulling her up with him, and took her powerfully in his arms and kissed her.

Judith quite instantly felt just as she had in the orchard, as though each of her joints had just melted within her. Her legs could no longer support her and she was convinced she would have fallen had he not held her so tightly. Perhaps she should try to resist him, but there was something about Kelthorne that revealed the deepest longings of her heart, a yearning for the life she had forsaken so many years ago.

Therefore, she held him tightly, clinging to him as he

searched her lips and then her mouth, tasting of her and exploring her in a way she had thought never to experience. Was this love, her heart asked? Surely that was impossible for she scarcely knew him just as he knew little of her, but, oh, how sweet was the delight of embracing this man and feeling the strength of his arms about her.

In truth, no one really knew her. Though Margaret understood her best of all, even she was not privy to the deepest secrets of her heart. Could she ever reveal such depths of desire to Kelthorne?

Perhaps not in words for she hardly knew him, but she could speak her heart in how firmly she wrapped her arms about his neck, how forcefully she returned his kisses, how wet her cheeks became with unexpected tears.

He drew back. "What is this?" He still held her close, but he thumbed his own face, which had grown wet with her tears and then gently wiped her cheeks dry.

"I do not know," she said. "You spoke of needing me to let you go but tell me, my lord, what is this power you hold over me to make me feel such things as profoundly as I do? It is a very great mystery and one I would wish away for it frightens me. It is almost as though you know me to the very depths of my soul but that is impossible, or perhaps it is that your attentions cause me to want to be known."

"I do want to know you," he whispered, "desperately so." He kissed her again and again, the precious minutes waxing on and on.

The time together felt stolen. Margaret would be at her door at any moment only she did not want Kelthorne to leave. She wanted him just as she had told him in the orchard to be kept chained to her bed. What wicked thoughts and yet how sweet his lips were pressed to hers. How fierce the ache in her heart! How great her longing to have him stay with her forever.

A scratching on the canvas forced her to step out of the tight circle of his arms and to gather her shawl about her shoulders once more. "Come," she murmured.

Margaret peeked her head inside. "Ye must leave, m'lord," she said quietly. "Ye made a promise."

"Yes, of course." He held Judith's gaze for a very long moment. Finally, he drew in a deep breath, bowed quite formally to her, then turned and was gone.

Margaret remained. Judith felt tears start to her eyes before she could stop them. She began to tremble. Margaret did not hesitate but gathered her gently in her arms and held her close. Judith began to weep, incomprehensibly so. What had Kelthorne done to her that the moment he was gone she collapsed into a fit of tears?

"What is happening to me?" she whispered.

"There, there," Margaret murmured, petting her head as though she were a child.

After a long moment, she drew away and sought her kerchief. She blew her nose soundly and confronted her friend. "You should not have permitted him to come to me." More tears poured from her eyes.

Margaret's eyes were watery as well. "I did not think 'twould do ye harm."

"How can you speak so? Do you not understand that he kissed me again and that his kisses make me desire things I cannot have?"

"Why can ye not have such things?"

Judith stared at her thinking she must be daft to have asked such an absurd question. "Because he is an earl and I am a mere songstress in an acting troupe, that is why! And because he is a rogue and probably has no more real interest in me than he does for . . . for Betty or Angelique or Kitty or Lydia!"

Margaret nodded sagely. "I see," she said. "Well, then, ye had best not encourage him by throwing yer arms about his neck."

With that, Margaret shook her head at her and left her tent.

Judith stood staring at the canvas door and began to feel quite ill used. Margaret had sent Kelthorne to her. She had not asked for him to come to her tent and as for throwing her arms about his neck, just how was she not to have done so?

She dropped onto her bed ready to cry anew, but the deuced leg snapped again and the next moment she was bounced forward and did a complete somersault hitting her foot on the stool by the door.

She sat up laughing and rubbing her poor foot. She had been ridiculous tonight. If her heart was burning and even more so now because she had been kissed again, 'twas her own fault and no one else's.

With that, she rose to her feet, climbed into bed and prepared to spend the next hour or so fortifying her mind against any future assault on her sensibilities—or her lips—by the Earl of Kelthorne!

Kelthorne walked back to the castle not knowing even to the smallest degree just what he was to do with the profound desire he felt for Judith. He believed quite fully that he could seduce her if he so desired, since once she was captive in his arms, she withheld very little from him, but what of Abigail Currivard? How could he in any manner justify pursuing Judith when a lady he might possibly make his wife was presently residing beneath his roof? And what of his vow? When he had determined to reorder his life, to leave off his roguish ways, he had meant to do so. Indeed, he had. Only, he had not planned on Judith Lovington.

As he drew near the steep rise to the castle and house proper, he heard Miss Currivard's laughter coming faintly from one of the upper windows. He suspected she was in the billiard room. A moment later, he heard Laurence's voice as well and then the laughter of another female, perhaps Miss Banwell. It would seem the castle had not gone to sleep as he had hoped. In truth, once he left the camp, he had not wanted to speak with anyone upon his return. He had desired only the solitude of his bedchamber hoping for more time to reflect. Most particularly, he was trying to determine just why, when Miss Currivard was present in his house, he had since the moment she appeared on the stage tonight become obsessed with seeking Judith out.

He met his butler in the entrance hall.

"Why have you not retired?" he asked. "'Tis very late."

His butler, Coxley, smiled crookedly as was his way and shook his head. "'Tis been a long time since the castle was so merry. 'Tis no trouble, I promise ye that."

"Very well, but you must know I do not require that you wait on my guests past midnight. We all know the way to the cellars which, as you know, is all we truly want at this hour."

"Very good, very good, and just as it should be for the young folk. You will find Mr. Doulting, Miss Banwell and Miss Currivard in the billiard room."

"As I suspected. Thank you."

He made his way up the stairs to the first floor and paused outside the door to the billiard room. Laurence, clearly half-foxed, appeared to be entertaining the ladies exceedingly well for they were both laughing, almost hysterically.

"No, no!" Miss Currivard cried. "You must desist, Mr. Doulting! Oh, I cannot catch my breath! I do not know when I have had such a gay time!"

Laurence's voice rang out. "And here is the Prince Regent mounting a horse."

From the placement of the doorway, Kelthorne was able to glance inside without being seen. The ladies' backs were to him. He watched Laurence jump from his former place on the billiard table to the floor. He sported some sort of table-cloth both tied about his neck and stuffed into his breeches. A pillow underneath gave the impression of great portliness. Kelthorne rather doubted that the corpulent Prince Regent would appreciate being mimicked in such a manner as Laurence was now, attempting but failing time after time to get a leg over a footstool.

Once more the ladies began to laugh and the more Laurence made his faltering attempts, each time tumbling to the floor, the harder the ladies laughed.

"Are you in need of assistance?" Kelthorne called out at last.

The ladies immediately ceased their laughter, turning around to greet him, their eyes bright with merriment.

"You have come just at the right time," Miss Banwell cried gaily. "For Mr. Doulting has been entertaining us quite to perfection as you can see and this is his best impression yet!"

Laurence was now astride the footstool and pretending to gallop. "Hallo, Aubrey! What do you think of my mount?"

"As ridiculous as you are!"

Suddenly, Laurence stopped pretending to gallop and instead began to weave from side to side. "Why is the house moving?" he inquired.

Miss Currivard instantly left her seat and extended her hands down to him. "I told you not to drink that last tankard. Are you going to be ill?"

Laurence smiled sloppily up into her face and took her hands in his. "Never, with such beauty before me. Aubrey, is she not an angel?" Miss Currivard lifted him slowly to his feet.

"Of course she is." He moved swiftly to offer Laurence the support of his arm about his shoulder, which his friend accepted. He guided him to the sofa where he bid him lie down. "And no more ale for you, you ridiculous gudgeon."

"Miss Currivard!" Laurence cried. "The prince in a state of drunkenness." He puffed out his cheeks until his face turned red. It was a stunning likeness.

Once more the ladies burst into laughter.

"I saw him once just like that!" Miss Banwell exclaimed. "At Carlton House this very season past. Mr. Doulting, I believe you may be a genius."

Kelthorne removed the pillow and the tablecloth after which Laurence reclined his head. "You have returned just in time, Aubrey, for I am completely worn out. Now you must entertain your guests."

Kelthorne regarded the ladies wondering if he could perchance suggest that the hour was ripe for retiring, but they both met his gaze with eyes showing not the smallest hint of fatigue. "May I offer a game of pool?"

"I should like that," Miss Currivard said quickly.

Miss Banwell wrinkled her nose. "I have already lost three times. I do not intend to do so again. How glad I am there is a pianoforte in this room. I do like this chamber a great deal, Lord Kelthorne, for it offers a variety of entertainment."

"Thank you. It was the one thing I insisted upon when my sisters suggested I refurbish the house, a pianoforte in several of the chambers. I have one here, one in the drawing room, as you know, and if you have not been to the little music room off the conservatory, there is a pianoforte in there as well. "

"Well, it is an excellent notion for now I shall play for you while Mr. Doulting regains his strength and you and Abigail clatter all those balls about for the next half hour or so."

Kelthorne set up the balls and bowed to Miss Currivard who thanked him. She then proceeded to show that she was quite skilled at billiards. The conversation was lively among the four of them. Miss Banwell was quite accomplished on the instrument and could carry on a great deal of discourse all the while playing every note correctly. Laurence quickly recovered from his antics and held his part in the ongoing dialogue. As for Miss Currivard, she spoke, as she always did, with great intelligence. He only grew uncomfortable when the subject turned to the troupe's performance.

"I must say," she cried, holding her cue stick upright. "I was enchanted the entire time, from beginning to end. Really, it was remarkable that so much varied skill and talent could be found in the wilds of Somerset. I do not believe I was ever more entertained, not even at Drury Lane."

"I quite agree," Kelthorne said, realizing she had assessed the truth of the troupe's ability. "The actor, Charles Hemyock, is man of great dramatic presence and execution. He quite puts me in mind of Keane."

"I have not yet had the privilege of seeing Keane perform," Harriet called out.

Laurence twisted his head to look at her. "You have not seen real acting until you have seen Keane. Was it Byron who said when he saw Keane perform one of the bard's plays that it was like reading Shakespeare by flashes of lightning?"

"I do not think it was Byron, but I cannot think who it was."

"What an intriguing description," Miss Currivard said. "I believe I would say something similar of Miss Lovington's performance —hearing her sing was like listening to an entire Beethoven symphony in one simple song. Did you not think her extraordinary?"

Kelthorne stared at Miss Currivard remembering how he had offended all the ladies earlier by praising Judith to the skies.

Miss Currivard laughed suddenly. "But of course you do! I now confess it was unhandsome of me earlier to have thought your praise of her as coming it a bit too strong. But you were right, you know, she does sing with the voice of the angels."

"And that, Miss Currivard, is very *handsome* of you now to say as much. I will only add that I think anyone who hears her must hold just such an opinion."

"I agree. I wonder that she has not been taken up by one of the London theaters."

Kelthorne took his turn and struck the ball hard with his cue, sending it forcefully against the edge of the table and breaking apart a cluster of balls. He had wondered the same thing. "Now there is a mystery," he stated. "She ought to be in London. There can be no two opinions on that score. I wonder what has prevented her."

"I did not see her after the performance," Miss Currivard

stated. "I was surprised for all the other ladies were happy to consort with anyone who wished to speak with them. She alone was absent. I noticed it most particularly."

Kelthorne was surprised at how easily the lady on the opposite side of the table spoke of her. He wondered if she did so by design.

Laurence said, "Mr. Hemyock once spoke quite vehemently on the subject of how often the troupe pulls up its stakes on her account. She has apparently been pursued a dozen times by quite *unworthy* gentlemen, so much so that the only escape she has is for the entire troupe to steal away in the middle of the night."

"Is this so?" Kelthorne cried. "Good God!" He recalled the dagger Judith had showed him, how she had spoken of knowing just how to use it. "I confess I am all amazement."

Miss Banwell played the last note of a sonata and rose from the pianoforte. "Mr. Doulting, might I persuade you to guide me through this rather maze-like house to my room? I have grown fatigued and now desire my bed but I have a dreadful fear of spirits and old Coxley informed me Portislow Castle has at least three in residence."

Laurence sat up and yawned. "I find I am ready to retire as well. Your request comes at a most propitious moment, although I may have to lean on your arm, if but a little."

"You are welcome to it, sir!"

Arm in arm, they quit the chamber, Miss Banwell's laughter returning from down the hall. The ploy was neither unexpected nor unusual. Kelthorne thought it likely that a previous arrangement had been constructed between Miss Currivard and her good friend in order to allow for a little private conversation. He continued to play, moving around the table and passing in front of Miss Currivard. He heard her sniff, if faintly, and glanced at her wondering if she might be weeping though he could imagine no possible cause for it. There was nothing of that in her expression, however. Instead, she appeared rather stunned.

He made his shot and tried to comprehend whether she

had suddenly grown missish at being alone with him until the scent of lavender struck his nostrils, reminding him too late that he carried Judith's scent on his person. There could be no doubt that Miss Currivard had caught the fragrance as well. What was to be done?

He continued to move around the table making his shots. Silence settled in the room and it was utterly his fault. Yet there was nothing he could do to alter what had happened except to try to begin anew if he could.

"Have you been to London often?" he asked, not looking at her but lining up his next shot.

"No, not very often, three times only and just to enjoy the theaters with my father. I do not believe I could have borne London society with even the smallest degree of equanimity." She took up a seat near the table, her cue stick still in hand.

He bent over to analyze his next shot further and glanced at her. A slight frown had settled between her brows. "I do not take your meaning," he said. He adjusted his stick and slung the cue forcefully. Balls clattered again.

She was silent for a moment. "You play billiards very well. My father adores the game. He loves many things. He loves in particular the notion of his daughter getting a handle to her name."

He rose up and stared at her. "This is plain speaking."

"Yes. Sometimes it is best to state that which must be obvious regardless of propriety. The reason I could not bear the thought of residing in the metropolis for any great length of time was because Bath had already proved so full of fortune hunters that I nearly went mad. Only after six months did I begin to feel I might enjoy some normalcy in my social engagements. Therefore, I thought that were I to go to London, my experiences would be worsened tenfold."

"You were probably right." He found himself intrigued by her. "Since you have spoken so candidly, may I ask whether you wish for a handle, as it were?"

She did not answer right away, but regarded him in her

forthright manner. This he already knew about her, she knew nothing of artifice, a quality he valued very much. She would always say what she thought. She smiled suddenly, "When I was very young, yes, of course, as did every girl in my school. The only desire greater was to be a princess, but that is hardly attainable so, to some degree, being addressed as 'my lady' was the more popular game. I hope, however, that in the ensuing years I have gained some essential wisdom in that regard. The handle, I believe, would only be worth the quality of the man to whom the handle belonged."

He liked her answer very much. "And love?" he asked, curious.

"Yes, love is of the utmost importance. I will not marry where there is not love. I had rather die an ape-leader."

"Strong words, indeed!" he cried.

"Strongly held sentiment," she returned. "On this point I am firmly fixed."

He rounded the table again but missed his shot.

She rose from her seat, bent over the table and slung her cue.

"You play admirably as well."

"I flatter myself that I do!" she cried.

He chuckled. "You do not seem in the least uncomfortable with *our* situation."

"That I was invited here like a horse being displayed at Tattersall's?"

He smiled. "Precisely."

She tapped a ball gently, acquiring another point. "I thought I might suffer some distress at being here, at meeting you, but oddly I do not. Your friend in particular has quite put me at my ease and has kept me laughing so much that I have hardly had time to experience even the smallest discomfort. I understand perfectly why you keep Mr. Doulting close at hand."

"He is the best of friends in every possible sense."

She nodded. "As for *our* situation there remains only one

question to be answered—whether there can be love between us."

He watched her closely. "That is the question. I quite
agree." He moved to stand near her. She rose from her
skilled bent position and turned to face him in what was a
bold manner. He understood the invitation clearly. Never in
his life had he hesitated kissing a lady before, particularly
one who was obviously willing, her green eyes luminous in
the candlelight. There was so much to like about Miss
Currivard, not less so her willingness in this moment to be
kissed when they had only just barely met.

The scent of lavender rose to his nostrils again, however,
and he released a great breath of air. He could not kiss her,
not tonight. He did, however, catch her chin and hold it tenderly.
"I am glad you have come, Miss Currivard. Indeed, I am."

She drew in a deep breath and smiled. When he released
her, she said, "As am I." She turned back to the table, slung
her cue very hard, and missed her shot.

He followed and with two more strikes of his stick ended
the game.

The night was finished. He escorted her back to her bedchamber and learned that she had traveled extensively with
her father. The remainder of the distance to her room was
spent hearing about her experiences in India, on the hot
plains, in the cool mountains, in the humid jungles.

"You must tell Laurence of your adventures," he said.
"He always longed to travel but never had the means. He
will want to know every detail."

"Have you never left England?" she asked.

"After Waterloo, I traveled the continent, but no farther
than Italy. I did not have the bottom to cross to Greece since
there is so much civil unrest in that country. However, I
would like to do more in the future I think."

Reaching her door, she turned and offered her hand. "You
would enjoy the Far East. Well, I suppose I shall bid you
good-night, then."

He lifted her fingers to his lips. He heard her sigh quite deeply. He kissed the back of her hand and she surprised him by sweeping low and stealing a kiss from his lips. She was gone before he had realized just what it was she had done.

He stared at her door for some time. He had the profound sensation that Mary and Amy were right about Abigail Currivard that she was, indeed, perfect for him.

SIX

"I believe this to be madness," Judith said. She sat on a stool in John and Margaret's tent, staring up at the former and pleading her case.

"Ye make too much of it."

"Indeed, ye do," Margaret added. "Besides, 'twere the lady wat suggested the picnic, not Kelthorne. Have I the right of that, luv?" She looked up at her husband. Margaret was sitting on their bed, cradling and rocking Shelly in her arms. The child was fast asleep.

"'Tis true, Judith. 'Twere not his lordship. The invitation is written at the hand of Miss Abigail Currivard. Besides, I don't see why ye are overset. 'Tis only a performance."

How could she make them understand? Kelthorne would be there and as a point of civility she would be required not just to see him, but probably to speak with him as well. The last thing she wanted in the world was to do either of these things. How was she to protect herself from his advances if she was in company with him? 'Twas bad enough to see him in an audience, but a thousand times worse to actually be near him.

She had spent a greater part of the morning pondering his visit to her tent of the night before, a visit Margaret had sanctioned. She examined at length the terrible weakness she experienced whenever she was close to him, a circumstance she was convinced Margaret did not in the least understand. She wished it were otherwise, but she felt powerless in the rogue's presence. Last night, she had had ample opportunity to chase him away with her dagger, as she had done with other gentlemen. Instead she had, just as Margaret had said, thrown her arms about his neck!

"If ye be afraid that Kelthorne will make unwanted advances," Margaret said, appearing oddly sad as she spoke, "I believe there is something ye ought to know. Mrs. Marnhull, in speaking with the castle cook, was told that Miss Currivard is to be the next Countess of Kelthorne. 'Tis all but settled."

Judith stared at her. "Indeed?" she queried, stunned.

"I fear 'tis so, which makes me wish I had not allowed his lordship to come to yer tent. Fer that, I apologize. But as ye can now see, ye have nothing to fear. He will hardly chase yer skirts with his bride-to-be looking on, now will he?"

Judith blushed at her choice of words. "I suppose not."

"Besides," John added, "we are being paid handsomely, and I do not think I could prevent the engagement without a war among the players."

"How much?" she inquired.

"Two hundred pounds."

"What?" she cried, stunned all over again. "'Tis a fortune!"

"Indeed, it is."

She rose from her stool. "I did not know. Well, there can be no question now. My own concerns pale in comparison to this. I would not deny the troupe such a sum for the world."

She turned to go but John caught her hand. "Ye always were a right un, Judy. I am sorry to see ye troubled."

She patted his hand and smiled. "'Tis my own fault. I could have prevented him from kissing me. I had your dagger in hand. Oh, now do not pretend to be surprised or that you have not the faintest notion what happened last night. I know very well that Margaret tells you everything."

"'Tis not that! O' course I know he kissed ye!" he cried. "Although you are right, she does tell me, but the truth of the matter is, Judy, I cannot think wat would have happened had ye stuck a lord!"

At that, Judith began to laugh for it was funny beyond words. He was right, however. There was a great difference in doing injury to some poor farmer or son of a vicar, but another to draw blood from a Peer of the Realm.

She quit the tent still laughing but not for long. She must now prepare to endure on the morrow an entire day spent in Kelthorne's company. She must see him and try not to let her heart grow careless. She must speak with him and not desire to be fully engaged in conversation with him. She must perchance brush against him in the course of all the activities of a picnic and not desire to throw herself into his arms. How was she ever to manage?

The following morning, Kelthorne was pulling on his boots when a scratching sounded on his door. "Come," he called out.

Laurence entered the room, running a hand through his loose, curly brown hair, his face pinched in concern. "Aubrey, I have been turning our plans for this day over and over in my mind and I cannot be easy."

Kelthorne merely looked up at him from his seat on a chair by the window and continued working his foot into his snug leather boot. He had no idea just how rugged the time at Cheddar Gorge might prove, but he sported his most serviceable footwear nonetheless.

Laurence began pacing the floor but spoke in a quiet voice lest he be overheard. "I think this scheme of yours might prove to be disastrous. Indeed, I do not know what maggot got into your head that you would actually consider an outing in which both Abig—that is, Miss Currivard and Miss Lovington would be present, and that for hours at a time. How could you be so baconbrained!"

Kelthorne shook his head. "You are greatly mistaken," he began, but got no further.

"Mistaken? I think not, my good man. You simply have not considered the possibility that Miss Currivard will notice your extraordinary interest in Miss Lovington, which only a sapskull could fail to comprehend. I must tell you, you shall be in the basket, indeed!"

"You are still mistaken!"

"In what manner! Do explain that much to me! I am all agog to know!"

Kelthorne finally slipped his heel into his boot. "I am vexed every time I put on these boots from Stultz, but, by God, they fit like gloves. They are, however, even more difficult to remove."

Laurence merely crossed his arms over his chest, tapped his foot and scowled. "I still wish to know just how I am mistaken!"

"Very well, I shall tell you, but I believe you will be utterly astonished. As it happens, this picnic was not in the least my notion, not by half! And if you had heard the argument I had with my sister, who also wished to prevent the picnic, you would be even more amazed. The truth of the matter is that Miss Currivard ordered this day's amusement. There. What do you think of that?"

"What?" Laurence appeared utterly dumbfounded, his mouth remaining agape for a very long time.

"You have not misunderstood me if that is what you are thinking. Miss Currivard desired the outing. She remained adamant even though I pressed her to think the better of it. In the end, I did not feel I could refuse her. She even went so far as to express a desire to pay the troupe, from her own purse, some two hundred pounds. Of course, I could not permit her to do so and, therefore, made the arrangements myself."

"I do not understand," he said, waving his hands about wildly. "She knows of your fascination with Miss Lovington, of that I am convinced."

"As am I."

"Then why would she do something that would appear even by the most slovenly reasoning to be foolhardy at best?"

"You must ask her, I fear. I have no answer and we certainly have not discussed the details of the subject as you may well imagine."

"Good God, no, I suppose you would not have." He began to laugh and spoke in his falsetto, "I say, Lord Kelthorne, do you fancy Miss Lovington?"

Kelthorne laughed and stood up, further arranging his feet in his boots.

Another scratching on the door revealed his butler. "Yes, Coxley?"

"The carriages are ready, my lord."

"Very good, if you would please inform Lady Radsbury or Mrs. Newnott. Either will gather the ladies."

"Of course. The gentlemen are already outside. Lord Radsbury is tending to his cattle."

"Thank you."

Coxley left and there was nothing that remained but to begin a journey that promised more than a few uncomfortable moments.

As Kelthorne descended the stairs, he found Miss Currivard standing in the entrance hall pulling on her delicate lace gloves. She was the picture of picnic beauty in a flowing, summery gown of blue sprig muslin embroidered with cherries and a wide-brimmed straw bonnet which sported artificial fruit of the same variety at the base of the crown. He wondered if this was the reason she had desired a picnic. Could any lady have appeared to greater advantage?

"Faith, but what a lovely portrait you make this morning, Miss Currivard. The personification of the season, I believe."

She dipped a playful curtsy and he was struck, as he had been over the past several days, that even when she was in a flirtatious mood she still did not conduct herself with even the smallest measure of abandon. There was too much intelligence in her, he thought, to be truly audacious in anything she did, even in her flirting. He wondered quite oddly if, were he to kiss her, would she give herself so completely to him as Judith had?

He gave himself a strong mental shake. This would not do, this comparing of the two women, not at the outset of what would no doubt provide far too many opportunities to do so anyway.

Nearing the end of the journey, Judith leaned her head back and let the sun beat on her face. She felt surprisingly wonderful even though she had begun the trip full of dread. However, there was something quite healing about the fresh air and about traveling in an open wagon to a new place—she had never been to Cheddar Gorge or on a picnic—even if she would be performing throughout the day.

Her nerves had quieted after an hour of travel. She had resigned herself to the difficulty of the situation and rather than struggle against fate, chose to accept that for today she would be tried and tested and perhaps tried a little more.

Given that she would be in company with Kelthorne much of the day, she had worn her dullest gown of a very simple white muslin that had for adornment a faded pink ribbon about the high waist. Her hair was a simple braided coil atop her head, neat and tidy. The stage was the place for embellishment, but among her betters, modesty and reserve were always the proper course.

Margaret had protested loudly about her gown and her hair. So vehemently, in fact, had she remonstrated with her, that Judith had finally asked her why she had felt it was so important for her to have worn a prettier gown. Margaret had grown rather flustered and could not give her answer. Judith began to suspect that her friend was still attempting to encourage a match that was, even by her own admission, given Miss Currivard's presence at Portislow, quite hopeless. Judith had refused to change her attire.

The troupe drew onto a large grassy sward, which opened out from the mouth of the canyon. Cheddar Gorge was a place of great physical beauty and magnificence. Granite formed the impressive cliff walls, and the most delightful stream, some five miles long, trickled through the gorge itself.

The troupe began at once setting up a variety of makeshift stages and posts for the numerous acts that would be performed. Given the great beauty of her surroundings as well as her acceptance of the difficult situation, Judith entered into the festivities with a light heart and easy mind.

By the time the castle party arrived some two hours later, the members of the troupe, many of whom were in festive costumes of a medieval appearance, greeted the coaches by forming two opposing lines. Tambourines shook in the air, warm welcomes were shouted, and as the ladies and gentlemen descended their carriages, John sang for them while playing the lute. Henry plied his flute in accompaniment. The sounds were as quaint as their costumes, which lent a cheerful, romantic aspect to the arrival. Kelthorne's servants followed in an additional wagon from which an enormous hamper was removed, containing, Judith could only suppose, the day's victuals.

Judith remained as far from the party as possible, carrying Shelly about with the pretense of keeping her away from the horses and carriages, even though Margaret frowned at her and rolled her eyes. Judith laughed and said, "You know very well that children are never safe if a vehicle is moving and you know what horses are. Once they are all properly tied up, I shall relinquish her."

Margaret narrowed her eyes. "If ye did not make so much good sense, I should ring a peal over yer head, fer ye must know all the gentlemen long to see ye, though I wish a thousand times ye had not worn that ragged looking thing." Margaret held in her hand the music for the pianoforte. The instrument had been set up on a small portable stage near the stream. "And now, I must see John about just when he desires us to perform. Oh, but I have such a headache. Once I am finished with ye, John will tell ye what to do. He has the order of events."

Margaret headed in her husband's direction and Judith carried her charge closer to the stream.

"Look!" Shelly cried suddenly, pointing in the direction of the steep granite cliffs of the gorge. The castle party was gathered near the base of the cliff watching the first of many events. Some of the actors were involved in a series of intricate tumbling passes played out on a stretch of grass that had previously been examined for unsuspecting rocks.

"Horace is certainly learning well. Look at how high he can jump now."

"Not, Horace," Shelly cried. "Look!"

Judith glanced at her and saw that her gaze was fixed to the tall ridgeline of the cliffs. There were several deer, including at least two stags, grazing on fine summer grass. She was surprised that they were even in the vicinity with so much noise below. One of the deer suddenly bolted out of sight. Judith thought it would not be long before they all disappeared. "Aren't they magnificent, Shelly?"

"Aye," she responded.

Judith loved hearing her little girl's voice and squeezed her gently. She had been present at her birth and stood as godmother to her. She often wondered about the unusual upbringing the child was experiencing. She would probably never attend school and yet how much she would learn being among the troupe and how much she was loved by one and all. With the exception perhaps of Charles who was interestedly solely in what could be of benefit to him.

Mrs. Marnhull approached her. "I been told that ye're wanted, Judy. 'Tis time to sing. I'll see to Shelly. Come here, pet."

Shelly went to her easily. Mrs. Marnhull took her in her arms then slid her to the ground. She took her hand and said she could feed a carrot to one of the horses if she was very good.

Judith saw Margaret and John both wave to her. The guests, having been properly entertained by the tumblers and the lute and flute, were now taking up their seats before the small theater. She took up her place beside Margaret in the wings. With a brief introduction, John called her forth. Happily, Judith took the stage.

Kelthorne did not look at Judith directly. If anyone decided to watch him, he had no intention of revealing even to the smallest degree the nature of his sentiments. He therefore schooled his features to an expression of passivity, something he was far from feeling.

The moment his coach had drawn up to the picnic site, his gaze found her and his blood began to race. He did not know how it was that merely looking at her could cause his heart to jump about so erratically.

Since it was impossible to gaze upon her without his heart heating up to a blaze, he decided to fix his sight upon a tree limb in the distance, which though fifty yards away, was in a line of sight just above Judith's head. As she began to sing, he pondered that tree limb, the gnarled beauty of its shape, the color of the bark, the leaves shimmering and dancing in the light breeze.

When the sweet purity of her voice drew him inexorably into the song, so that the tree lost its value, he gazed upon her but strove to keep his countenance indifferent. He fixed his thoughts on her nose, a very pretty nose. Looking at a nose was a harmless business. Her eyes were very near, however, her enchanting chestnut eyes, which were dewy when she sang. If only she had not worn such a lovely gown, so elegant in its simplicity for it revealed the absolute perfection of her figure. He had held her in his arms so he knew quite well the dips and rises, swells and curves of her waist and back, even her breasts, for he had held her tightly against him. . . .

The deuce take it!

Very well, it would seem he could not even look at her
nose for his thoughts ran so swiftly astray. He tried to imagine her eating onions as Betty was wont to do and how vile
her breath would be. Not like the lavender she had worn
when he had come to her tent and found her clothed so
scantily in a soft cambric nightdress wrapped in a shawl, her
hair hanging in soft waves down her back. How her hair had
felt in his hands, how he wished he could take the braids
now that formed her coiffure and gently separate them so
that once more he might see and perhaps even feel the silky
texture. In the present daylight, the color was a pure chestnut
but in the tent it had been almost black in appearance with
reddish glints from the lantern light. Why he had knelt before her as he had, he would never quite understand, except
that he had been so lost in her presence as though she represented something to him he had yet to define. How sweetly
she had accepted his tribute and how daringly she had told
him of the dagger, which she had not used against him because, and this he understood to perfection, she trusted him.
This was what was by far the greatest advantage he possessed in his pursuit of her. He already knew precisely how
the chase would end, and how beautifully she would surren-
der to him. . . .

The devil take it!

Good God, was there nothing about her that would not
lead him into this dangerous passage?

Her shoes. She wore rather ugly shoes today, he must say.
They were black and somewhat scuffed, quite inappropriate
for a simple muslin gown. She had rather have worn no
shoes than these thick black ugly ones. They were so different from the pretty embroidered slippers she had been wearing in her tent. How small her feet had seemed peeping from
beneath her nightdress, couched in brightly patterned almost
festive colors. He wondered what her feet looked like and
how she would have responded had he removed her slippers,
very slowly, touching her ankles, maybe placing little kisses

on the top of her foot where the prettiest curve led the eye up the leg. . . .

Hell and damnation! Even her ugly shoes had diverted his thoughts into unwanted channels!

He looked away. The horses were not far. He concentrated on how many of them swished flies from their flanks. How many horses were there? He counted them. He counted the carriages and the horses, the wagons, the wheels of the coaches, wagons and carriages, then the number of whips probably used, the reins . . . finally applause sounded in his ear.

Thank God!

Laurence, sitting beside him, elbowed him hard in the ribs. "What a sapskull you are! Could you not at least have made an effort at indifference? Miss Currivard deserves far better from you and well you know it, or at least you ought to know it. She is one of the sweetest ladies I have ever known, besides being quite beautiful, and you are treating her abominably. And why were you staring at the horses?"

"Do stubble it," he whispered back, crossing his arms over his chest. "You need not remonstrate. Trust me, my conscience has barked more words than you have just now."

She left the stage and though Radsbury and Amy both cried out for an encore, and though Judith returned once to offer another deep curtsy, the stage was quickly overtaken by Mr. Hemyock who recited a long passage from *Hamlet*. Ordinarily, Kelthorne might have started yawning but Charles Hemyock did have abilities and he was soon drawn in, thankfully, to his performance. At last, Judith was forgotten.

Judith remained backstage, hidden from the castle party. She felt both relief and dismay at one and the same time. Kelthorne had taken a disgust of her and she did not like it, not by half. Perhaps Margaret was right. Perhaps she ought to have worn one of her prettier, more resplendent gowns.

He could hardly set his gaze upon her, he looked over her head at nothing rather than at her and once he saw her shoes, which she had to admit were quite atrocious, his disgust had deepened immeasurably. Finally, he had rather have looked at the cattle than at her! She wondered if she had sung poorly. But that would not fadge because the remaining guests had applauded very loudly, requiring that she return to the stage a second time to acknowledge their appreciation.

Of course, she was in truth quite relieved, extraordinarily relieved that he had lost all interest in her, that he had now begun to see her undoubtedly as a paltry songstress earning her keep in the rustic wilds of the West Country, not even fit for London, worth less than a flea really. Of course she was relieved, beyond words! And so very happy!

She sighed heavily. She would probably not even converse with him once in the course of the day. How perfectly delightful!

Once Charles's performance was complete and the applause reverberated from one granite cliff to the next, John announced that targets would be erected for the purpose of the gentlemen engaging in a shooting contest, actors and castle party alike. Judith took the moment to make her escape. She hurried in the direction of the wagon where Mrs. Marnhull had established a private area for the troupe. She found Shelly there playing with a magnifying lens. "Look, Judy! I found a dead bee!"

Judith, grateful for so innocent and simple a diversion, sank to her knees on the grass and through the glass examined the bee. "How fascinating! Why, he looks covered in fuzz."

"'Tis not a 'he,' 'tis a 'she.' I named her Molly."

A dead bee named Molly. Judith withheld her smiles and nodded seriously. "Well, Molly looks like she has been covered in yellow fuzz."

Shelly smiled broadly, then her gaze drifted up and to her left. "Hallo," she said softly. "Are ye an angel?"

Judith turned and looked up to see a lady standing over them—the one designated to become the next Countess

Kelthorne. Her hair was the color of sunshine, her eyes an unearthly green, her demeanor poised and her smile welcoming. Shelly was right, Miss Currivard looked like an angel.

"An angel?" Miss Currivard queried sweetly. "Not by half, I fear. Only tell me what you have there? Is that a magnifying glass?"

"Aye."

"And what are you looking at?"

"Molly. She's a bee but she's dead."

"Well, that is very sad. May I look as well?"

"Aye." Shelly extended the glass to her.

To Miss Currivard's great credit, she too sank to her knees, took the glass and examined the bee.

"She is the color of yer hair," Shelly said softly, as if in some awe. She reached out and touched a lock that hung forward from the cluster dangling down her back.

Judith glanced at Mrs. Marnhull, who was busily knitting a stocking, her particular contribution to their regular donations to the church. That good lady was nodding her approval of Miss Currivard.

"Molly is quite beautiful," Miss Currivard said. "Have you found a bed for her yet? Do you not think a dead bee should have a proper bed?"

Shelly's eyes brightened. "Marny, have you a bed for Molly?"

She shook her head. "Nay, m'darlin'."

"Perhaps we could make one," Miss Currivard suggested. "A few twigs, perhaps, a little grass, everything woven together with some yarn, if there were any yarn about that is." She was smiling as she glanced up at Mrs. Marnhull.

Shelly was on her feet in an instant. "Will ye give us a bit of yarn, Marny, fer a bed fer Molly?"

"Aye." Mrs. Marnhull reached into her sewing bag and snipped off a generous length of rose pink yarn and gave it to Shelly.

In turn, Shelly gave the bee and the magnifying glass to Mrs. Marnhull. "Let's go!" she cried, whirling around.

Judith rose to her feet. "Shelly, one moment."

Shelly stopped and looked up at her as though she had thrown water on her head.

Judith explained. "We have not yet made the lady's acquaintance. I think there ought to be some introductions. After all, she does not even know your name."

"I am Shelly," she stated, looking up at Miss Currivard and extending her hand to her.

"Well met, Miss Shelly," she said, taking her hand and giving it a shake. "And how do you go on?" she inquired.

"Wery well, thank ye."

Judith said. "I am Miss Lovington and I am very pleased to make your acquaintance."

"I am Miss Currivard. I dare say I should have asked for a more formal introduction." A loud burst of rifle shot ripped through the air. "But as you can see, there were none left to perform the duty since it would seem all the gentlemen must shoot and prove themselves and the rest of the ladies have gathered round to admire their effort. I have been given to understand that you are acquainted solely with Lord Kelthorne and his friend Mr. Doulting."

"Yes," Judith said, feeling uneasy. Did Miss Currivard know that Kelthorne had visited her tent only two nights before? "I have not yet had the pleasure of making the acquaintance of any of the ladies."

A soft smile touched her lips. "Mr. Doulting was right. You speak as a lady." Judith must have blushed for Miss Currivard continued on hastily, "I do beg your pardon. I did not mean to make you uncomfortable. Forgive my impertinence. Will you take a walk with me? I was hoping for a little conversation as well as a bit of distance from the guns."

"Yes, I should like that," she said, but she could not understand Miss Currivard's interest in her, not by half.

Shelly tugged on Judith's hand. "Let's go. Molly needs her bed."

"Let us, indeed!"

As they passed by the target area, watched carefully by several of Kelthorne's servants who helped in the loading of the weapons, Charles Hemyock began cursing quite loudly.

Judith explained quietly, "He is the worst shot imaginable though he prides himself on his skill with rifle or pistol."

Miss Currivard whispered. "A rather arrogant, self-satisfied sort, I dare say?"

"You have drawn his character exactly. He could not be more provoking."

"I don't like Charles," Shelly muttered. "He always pulls me braids and pinches me cheeks."

"That decides the matter for me," Miss Currivard responded. "I do not like him either."

Shelly beamed her approval. "Ye talk like Judy talks," she stated.

"I suppose I do," she said.

John's voice called out, "Fire." A volley of shots ripped through the air. The ladies jumped.

"I must say, I am grateful for the walk," Judith said. "And the more distance we place between ourselves and that noise, the happier I shall be."

"I as well," Miss Currivard said. She glanced at Judith then said, "You know, Miss Lovington, I once lived in a tent for several months but that was, goodness, five years past now. It seems but yesterday. My father is a man of trade, you see. I am excessively devoted to him and an only child. He took me, after I had begged it of him for months, on a trip to India and to the Orient. I should suppose in that, Miss Lovington, that you and I have shared a similar experience."

Another volley of shots rang up the gorge, still far too loud for comfort.

Judith was surprised to think Miss Currivard would think anything they had shared was similar in nature. "Except that I have never once left the island," she said, smiling.

"But, contrary to your upbringing, you have lived a life of some adventure, if I do not mistake the matter."

Judith glanced at her. Miss Currivard was smiling as well, but there was a serious knowing expression in her eye. "I begin to understand the comparison," Judith said.

"You have undoubtedly seen more of the world already than most young ladies are likely to in the course of a lifetime."

Judith glanced down at Shelly and patted the top of her head. "That much is quite true."

Miss Currivard started. "Were you . . . that is . . . did you attend . . . her birth?"

"I was greatly privileged to have done so."

"I think it marvelous. I know my father has every intention of seeing the family's position in society raised through my marriage, and I have strived to embrace all that is thought genteel and of good breeding. However, there are times when I am certain something grand and beautiful has been lost when one is surrounded solely by comfort, entertainment, and the supreme object of learning to set a stitch or manage a palette of watercolors properly."

"You would certainly have much to discuss with my governess. She was wont to say—" Judith said, but she broke off suddenly for she had just revealed more to Miss Currivard than she had to Margaret in all the years she had been with the troupe. She had, in essence, just revealed the truth.

"So it is true, then," Miss Currivard whispered.

Judith lifted her chin. "Is what true?" she queried. She met Miss Currivard's gaze squarely. She could see the young lady struggle in her mind as to what she ought to say next, that a thousand questions were poised on the tip of her tongue. She hoped she would not attempt it for then she would have to terminate the conversation instantly.

Miss Currivard laughed and swung an arm in a wide arc. "Is it not true that the day is beautiful almost beyond bearing. Would you not say so?"

Judith breathed a sigh of relief. At the same time, she rather thought she might have found a friend in Miss Currivard. "Yes, quite so."

More shots rang into the air, but the distance was increasing so that the sound this time did not cause Judith to flinch.

The ladies pressed on, trailing behind young Shelly as she sought out treasures from the stream, from the grassy patches, and from the base of trees. She continued shoveling her growing collection to either Judith or Miss Currivard. From behind them, the sounds of the volleys of shots grew less marked the farther the ladies traveled.

While they marched uphill, Judith responded to a question Miss Currivard had about life with the troupe, in particular about her daily regimen.

"Horace is the rock of our troupe at this time," Judith said, "though he hardly knows it. But he keeps the water flowing and, believe me, among thirteen adults and one child, a great deal of water is required. In addition, Mrs. Marnhull keeps one very large kettle full all day of steaming water. She is the soul of our group. She feeds and tends us, scolds when we are being ridiculous, and teaches any who wish to learn how to cook. I help her with the daily loaves of bread, of which many are required as you may imagine."

"You bake your own bread in such a camp?"

"The actual baking, no. But we do prepare the dough. Once the dough has fully risen in the pans, Mrs. Marnhull takes them to the local baker and for a small fee we have use of his ovens. In fact, upon arriving in a town or village, that is her first call. And if I may say so, the bread we enjoy along with goat cheese, is truly wonderful."

"I recall such experiences in India. I have come to believe that no matter how skilled a chef, there is something even more wondrous that occurs when food is cooked over an open fire in the fresh air. Do you not agree?"

"Yes, very much. During the winter, we do not camp but have to spend some of our very hard-earned shillings, upon inns and hotels. The food is rarely comparable to Mrs. Marnhull's skill. The summer spoils us in more ways than just excellent weather."

"Who makes your costumes?"

Shots once more reached up the gorge. Judith turned back to see that a great deal of smoke had accumulated near the targets but was, thankfully, drifting rapidly to the east caught on a breeze.

Resuming their conversation, Judith answered her question. "We all make full use of our needles, including the men. Margaret, John, Henry and Charles do most of the design work, creating the proper garb for the latest plays or tumbling routines or farces that have been concocted."

"Regardless of his questionable character, Mr. Hemyock is quite talented. There can be no two opinions on that score. I have truly enjoyed the juggling and the various displays of swordsmanship, but I must say that I was very pleased to hear so much music included throughout the troupe's unique presentations." She then stopped for a moment causing Judith to pause with her, and added, "I just wish you to know how much your songs have spoken to my heart. I am certain by now you must have a rational understanding of how well-received your performances are but, truly, Miss Lovington, you have a quality that I have never before heard, which must in part explain . . . that is, who could possibly not find you absolutely enchanting."

Judith felt her cheeks grow warm. She suspected Miss Currivard was referring to Lord Kelthorne. "I thank you most sincerely, but now you have made me blush."

Miss Currivard set her feet in motion once more. She began marching once more uphill. "Oh, dear," she murmured. "I keep wanting to ask you the most impertinent questions, which I know I should not. When I go beyond the pale, pray give me a setdown for I would not offend you for the world, but I am utterly intrigued by your presence in this acting troupe. There is, however, something more, something quite inexplicable about you that is even more a mystery to me."

Since she fell silent, Judith glanced at her wondering what it was she had meant to say. "Do go on," she encouraged her, "for you have quite intrigued me."

"Well, I am not certain how to say this, but I have never found it so easy, so comfortable to speak with anyone before now. I cannot explain it except that it must be something in your manner or perhaps your kind disposition."

Judith was surprised. "But I have seen you with your friends and there appears to me to exist a quite enviable camaraderie among you."

"Harriet is my good friend, but I fear our friendship is centered almost exclusively on the worst habit of gabble-mongering. But her heart is good. As for Faith, she is very sweet but scarcely has two words to say for herself and will not speak unless prodded with a stick."

"I have been fortunate in the troupe. Margaret is my dearest friend and we have a wonderful rapport. Only four years separate us. She was eighteen when I joined the troupe. So many years later, we have numerous shared experience, Shelly amongst them."

Miss Currivard turned to look at her a frown between her brows. "But that would make you, good Lord, still in the schoolroom when you came to be with the troupe."

"Yes," Judith said, "but on that subject I will not for the present say more."

The shots that reached them now were scarcely troubling.

Miss Currivard smiled. "And I thank you for saying so much as you have."

Judith did not know how it was, but she was inclined to confide in Miss Currivard. "There is one thing I am not reluctant to speak of."

"Indeed?" Miss Currivard smiled broadly.

"Well, I am not without my own plans for the future. I hope very much to one day purchase a cottage, in Devonshire, and live as respectably as a retired actress may, in some village or other."

"And you would be content after such a life as this?" She whirled about and swept a broad stroke with her arm encompassing the fair-like atmosphere at the bottom of the incline.

"More than you can imagine," Judith said. "Such a life

might be grand for a season but there is a weariness that attends the troupe, particularly in the depth of winter when traveling is labored. Tempers grow short and our funds dwindle. We must work very hard all summer to be sustaining through the dark months."

"I see. I suppose on a beautiful day such as this, I am seeing the life of your troupe as something quite idyllic but not necessarily realistic."

"On such a beautiful day as this, even I can see the troupe quite easily through your eyes."

"Do but look. There is Mr. Doulting waving to us. I see that the tables are now laden with food."

Judith called to Shelly. "We are to have our nuncheon now. Come, dearest." Shelly stepped from the stream, shook off her feet, plopped to the ground and began replacing her stockings. Once her shoes were on her feet, she began running down the hill.

Judith might have hurried after her but in the distance she could see that Margaret had caught sight of her and was even now running in her direction with her arms wide open. At the base of the hill, Kelthorne's servants were busily arranging nuncheon for the castle party and for the troupe.

Mr. Doulting approached them, his expression grim.

SEVEN

"What is it, Mr. Doulting?" Miss Currivard asked when he drew near. He turned and walked back beside her.

"That fellow, Hemyock!" he cried in some exasperation. "He will be the death of us all! I hope I do not give offense, Miss Lovington, but he is as deuced a fellow as ever was born!"

"You cannot offend me by saying such things. Poor Mr. Hemyock. I fear all his abilities are in his acting voice for in every other instance he is a perfect cretin. Only, what has he been doing?"

"I chanced to stand beside him while he was firing his rifle and I cannot tell you how many times he pointed it at me while adjusting the pan or asking the servant if he needed more powder! And worse, he did not comprehend why I kept tilting the barrel away from me or suggesting he do so. 'My hand is not on the trigger,' he would shout as though I had lost my mind!"

"It is so like him," she said, sighing. "It is almost as though there is no one else in the world beside him."

"Well, at least we are to eat."

"Are you grown a trifle peckish?" Judith asked. She could not help but smile. There was something so endearing about

Laurence Doulting. Perhaps it was his curly hair, which served to give him a youthful appearance, or perhaps the keen look of intelligence in his eyes.

"I confess that I am. Only tell me what it is you both have in your hands."

Miss Currivard explained about Shelly's bee. Mr. Doulting laughed then addressed Judith. "On another subject, however, permit me to say that your song earlier was quite magnificent. I had tears in my eyes."

"Indeed?" Judith queried.

He then whispered. "Only pray say nothing of it to Aubrey, that is, Kelthorne, or I will not hear the end of it for a twelve-month."

"Your friend seemed less pleased with my performance. He was looking at the horses."

For some reason the pair next to her began to fidget, plucking at shirtsleeves and gloves and clearing throats. She wondered suddenly if either knew of his visit to her tent two nights past. She tried to keep a blush from rising on her cheeks.

"I feel quite certain," Miss Currivard said, "that his lordship was only looking at the horses so that he would not follow Mr. Doulting's lead and become a watering pot as well."

Judith was grateful for her diplomatic response as well as for Shelly who began calling and running toward her once more. "'Tis time to eat, Judy! 'Tis time to eat."

Judith parted company with her new friend and Mr. Doulting and moved to a separate table where the troupe had already taken their seats. She was grateful to return to her more usual surroundings but was dismayed to find that the only seat remaining was at the very end, which turned out to be opposite Kelthorne. She could hardly avoid meeting his gaze now and then. Fortunately, Mr. Emborough, who proved to be garrulous, sat beside the earl and was busily taunting Kelthorne about having won the shooting contest.

Freddy addressed John quietly, "Mr. Emborough is also skilled with the sword. Mr. Doulting said as much. Maybe we could ask for a demonstration. He might show us something we could use on the stage."

Before John could answer, Charles said, "He's an amateur in every sense of the word and a buffoon."

Horace, who had risen from his seat to assist Mrs. Marnhull, stared at Charles angrily. "He helped me wi' the horses when you would not!"

"I am an *actor*," Charles stated boldly and in a voice that caused the party at the next table to turn to stare at him.

"And we ain't never permitted to forget it, are we?" Horace returned hotly.

Laughter ran around the table, but Judith had never seen Horace so enraged. Charles, however, had quite worn out his welcome. From nearly the day he joined the troupe his demands were consistently high-handed and on every occasion requested as though he held supremacy among the troupe. When Horace was not quick enough to perform a given task for him, Charles often read him the riot act.

Presently, Charles leaned back slowly, lifted his chin dramatically, raised a brow and crossed his arms over his chest. "In even one passage from Shakespeare by my reading, I am more than ye could ever be in a thousand!"

"Oh, Charles," John cried. "Do stubble it, fer God's sake, man! Ye sound like a coxcomb."

He swept a dramatic arm in Horace's direction, a young man at least sixteen years his junior, and cried, "Well, he began this nonsense."

"Then see that ye finish it."

"I should be happy to," he stated grimacing, "but I do not believe it an honorable thing to engage in fisticuffs with my inferiors."

John instantly rose from his seat and grabbed at Horace whose face was now flaming. He turned him around and walked him in the direction of the horses.

"He'll hardly grow into a man if John keeps protecting him," Charles stated.

Judith, who saw that both Henry and Freddy were ready

to tear Charles limb from limb, interjected softly. "Has anyone explored the caves yet? Miss Currivard and I passed by them but we did not venture inside. What of you, Bobby? I saw you there earlier. Did you chance to make even the smallest exploration?"

"Nay," he responded, casting a dagger-glance at Charles. "I looked in. Had I not been in costume, I should have explored as far as I could go but 'twas too damp."

Judith, seeing that Charles would speak again, once more interjected. "Mrs. Marnhull, would you pass the bread, please, and the butter? The ham looks marvelous. Angelique, you will be content today, for I know how much you like ham and that is perhaps the finest I have seen in a twelvemonth."

"'Tis a wonderful thing to have friends wat live in a castle," Angelique said.

Since Judith's request sent the food once more moving about the table, tensions dwindled in quick stages. Judith observed, and not for the first time, that it would never do to allow men to get very hungry. Tempers never raged more than with too many hours lengthening between one meal and the next.

A moment later, the dropping of a linen to the ground at the table some few yards from hers caused Judith to glance in that direction. She found that Kelthorne was looking at her in a somewhat marked manner. He smiled, nodded and in his eyes she saw his approval.

She inclined her head in response, but since her heart fairly leapt in her breast at such a smile, she set to vigorously decimating with knife and fork, the ham on her plate.

After what in the end became a pleasant dinner, Henry, Freddy and Bobby entertained the castle party with another powerful display of tumbling. All three young men were quite strong, lithe and skilled so that there were as many bursts of applause as there were sudden gasps and expressions of wonder.

Later, several of the men of the troupe exchanged their costumes for more serviceable clothes and with Mr. Doulting and Mr. Emborough, explored the caves that proved, indeed, to be quite damp. John very sweetly took Shelly within as well though they emerged but a few minutes later with Shelly in tears. "She became frightened," he explained, holding her close.

"I expect she would," Judith said. "I cannot even bring myself to go within. Shelly, you are far braver than I. Let me take her, John. I know very well you wish to return."

Since Shelly reached for her, John smiled somewhat sheepishly. "Thank ye, Judy. I do, indeed, but are ye certain? I would not wish to trouble ye."

"Pray, do not be absurd. Now go. As for you, my dear," she said drawing back and meeting Shelly's gaze, "why do we not find things to make a house for your bee in addition to the bed?"

Shelly agreed with a sniff and a quivering of her lip. Judith continued to hold her and walked back down the hill. In the distance, she could see Charles near the wagons. He was alone and she could not help but wonder what mischief he was plotting this time.

Not far distant, she saw Lord Kelthorne extend his hand to Miss Currivard as he assisted her in crossing the stream not far from Charles. Judith thought they made a rather stunning pair since they shared the same thick, wavy blond hair. The knowledge that she was regarding a future that could never be hers forced her to look away and to refuse to ponder the longings which of late had been dogging her heels.

She lowered Shelly to the ground and helped her to cross the gentle stream. They jumped from boulder to boulder and in the end both their gowns were wet to the knees. But the day was fine and they proceeded to the opposite side of the narrow gorge in search of woody treasures fit for bee-house building.

"Look!" Shelly cried, pointing up. "He's come back."

Judith lifted her gaze to the top of the cliff and there, poised at a lower edge of a narrow footpath was a young stag. She still marveled that the animals were so fearless with so many people around and wondered if they often canvassed this lower portion of the gorge for bits of food once picnickers had departed.

Suddenly, a rifle shot boomed in her direction and in a split second, the stag leaped into the air, twisting and turning then striking the granite wall once before falling to the earth but a few yards from where she stood with Shelly.

Judith was so startled that for a moment she froze and thanked God that she had Shelly still in hand. The stag, however, was still alive and quickly struggled to gain his feet, his antlers shaking about nervously. She saw that his shoulder had been grazed and was bleeding steadily, but that he could walk and worse still that his eye, wild and terrified, had become fixed on her.

"Oh, dear God," she murmured. "Shelly, get behind me. Now!"

Shelly did not hesitate but did so, clinging to her skirts and crying.

"Walk backward, darling, very slowly. There, that's a good girl. A little more. Yes, a little more."

The stag began advancing on her and in that moment, Judith realized there was absolutely nothing she could do. The animal was wounded, in no small degree of pain and frightened out of his wits.

A mere fifteen feet separated them, now ten. "Shelly, you must run to your father now. Go!" She felt Shelly leave her skirts and she could hear her small feet splash once more through the stream.

Behind her, the men had emerged from the caves and were making an enormous commotion, hoping to divert the animal but with little effect. She closed her eyes, waiting, expecting to be gored when suddenly a second rifle shot echoed up the gorge, followed by a heavy thud. The ground trembled at her feet.

She opened her eyes and, lying there with a shot through his skull, was the deer, twitching still in death.

She felt violently ill, weaved on her feet, and then nothing.

Kelthorne dropped the rifle where he stood and began to run. He had understood precisely what had needed to be done and had not hesitated. He had run to Charles, taken the weapon from him, and loaded it with speed and care. He did not give pause to feel even the smallest particle of justified rage at the fool now swaggering beside him and claiming to be an excellent shot.

Once the rifle was loaded, he lifted it to the now advancing deer, took precise aim and without considering how close the animal was to Judith squeezed the trigger, steadily and purposefully.

To his great relief, the stag had fallen at her feet.

"Is she hurt? Is she hurt?" he shouted, beginning to run toward the group now clustered about Judith. At such a distance, he could not tell what had happened since she had fallen at nearly the same moment the stag had.

Laurence was bending over her while Mr. Ash was cradling her in his arms. "No!" Laurence shouted back. "She has merely swooned. Good God, Aubrey, but that was a fine shot!"

"It was a lucky shot," he returned. A few seconds more and he could see for himself that Judith was uninjured. Her complexion, however, was a sickly white. Betty held a vial of smelling salts beneath her nose and with a weak hand she kept pushing it away.

"Ye saved her life and Shelly's as well," Mrs. Ash said to him, tears running down her cheeks. She was holding her daughter tightly in her arms.

Kelthorne saw that though Judith's eyes were open, they were dazed and unseeing. Mr. Ash began to weep and Kelthorne, without knowing precisely why, understood him. "Allow me," he said, taking Judith from his arms. "Please, tend to your daughter. She will need her father's arms about her."

Mr. Ash rose and took Shelly in his arms.

By now, the entire party was gathered about Kelthorne and Judith.

Miss Currivard said, "Bring her to my carriage. We will be able to see to her there. I am certain she will be more comfortable within."

Kelthorne glanced at her, not quite seeing her, but nodded in response. He carried Judith gently if briskly to the coach. Miss Currivard entered and after sitting down allowed Kelthorne to place her in her arms. Kelthorne stood at the doorway. "Is she all right?" he asked again. "Are you certain she is not bleeding or bruised perhaps?"

Miss Currivard shook her head. "Not a single wound, not even a bruise. Your shot was true. You performed beautifully, my lord."

Kelthorne stepped away from the coach and realized that his arms and legs were trembling. Suddenly, he knew there was business yet to take care of. He caught sight of Mr. Hemyock boasting to one of his servants of having brought the stag down first. He made a path through the crowd that had followed him to the coach and approached the actor.

Kelthorne remembered Mr. Hemyock's words earlier words to the young lad, Horace, so he said, "Unlike you, Mr. Hemyock, I do not hesitate to use fisticuffs with my inferiors." And with that, he planted Mr. Hemyock a facer that sent him flying backwards. He lay unmoving, his eyelashes fluttering.

There arose a great shout of joy and triumph at this action. Though Kelthorne regretted that he had let his temper get the better of him, there was not one present who remonstrated with him. Even his sister, Mary, who preferred everything to be proper, patted him on the shoulder. "Well done, brother! A more selfish creature I have never before seen."

"Aye!" Radsbury exclaimed beside her. "Well done, indeed!"

* * *

Judith became aware of her surroundings in small stages. She was within a coach and three ladies were speaking quietly.

"Did you see him give Mr. Hemyock a leveler?" Judith recognized the voice of Miss Banwell.

"He was magnificent!" the timid Miss Upton whispered excitedly. "Oh, Abigail, you are so fortunate to be singled out by him."

"Did he really strike Mr. Hemyock?" Miss Currivard asked.

"Indeed, he did! Do you know what else he said? He mocked Mr. Hemyock in the most beautiful manner. He repeated the very thing Mr. Hemyock had said to that young man who tends the horses only he said, 'Unlike you, I have no hesitation in using my fisticuffs with an inferior,' and then he struck him down with one blow. Oh, but he is a dashing man and to think he saved Miss Lovington's life."

Judith now realized what had happened. That Charles in his stupidity had tried to prove his mettle by firing at the stag and that Lord Kelthorne, with his already proven skill as a hunter, had saved her life as well as Shelly's. This knowledge served to shake some of the stupor from her mind and she struggled to right herself. Only then did she realize she had been reclining on Miss Currivard's lap.

"I do beg your pardon," she said, embarrassed.

"Nonsense," Miss Currivard said, smiling sympathetically. "You were exceedingly brave to protect Mrs. Ash's daughter as you did. The least I could do was offer you a little kindness."

"Have I been, that is, how long—?"

"Only a few minutes. Are you feeling better?"

"My head is swimming."

"Do you care to use my vinaigrette?" Miss Banwell asked, searching her in her beaded reticule.

"No. I thank you, no. I believe I would feel even worse."

"Harriet," Miss Currivard said. "Would you fetch Miss Lovington a little wine? Brandy, if it can be found."

Miss Banwell scampered from the coach, her voice elevated as she called to Kelthorne's servants.

"I detest being such a nuisance," Judith cried.

"You are no such thing," Miss Upton said in her soft voice.

Judith glanced from Miss Upton to Miss Currivard and thought what an excellent friendship the young ladies enjoyed, Miss Banwell included. She was envious suddenly, remembering her own cousins and being with them just like this, innocent, kindhearted, excited about all the possibilities before them. How much she had once looked forward to such a time in her life, when she would be at a country party during the summer, perhaps searching for a proper husband, hoping to tumble in love, and desiring above all that heroism and chivalry would mark the days.

How different her life had been. How utterly different, indeed!

She felt uncomfortable suddenly in the presence of the these ladies. "I think I should rejoin the troupe."

"Will you not wait for your wine?"

She had forgotten Miss Banwell's efforts. "Of course." She sat back but looked out the window. From her position, she could see the troupe taking down the portable stage and others loading the wagons with the props, costumes and tents used in the course of the day.

In a few minutes, Miss Banwell arrived with a small glass of brandy. Judith took it gratefully and began to sip, pausing as the lively young lady clambered aboard the coach, rocking it grandly. Judith laughed. "I nearly spilt it."

"How dreadful that would have been!" Miss Banwell cried. "And on your lovely muslin. I do beg pardon."

"It would not have been your fault," Judith cried. "I should have waited for you to take your seat."

"I am settled now. I hope you still wish for the brandy."

"I do, very much, indeed. Thank you for your kind attentions. My nerves, I must say, are in such a state."

Miss Banwell frowned slightly. "I find I am constantly amazed when I hear you speak." Her words were thoughtless and she blushed to the roots of her hair. "Oh, I am sorry."

Judith was embarrassed anew and sipped her brandy. The ladies had been so kind but she knew quite well just how odd her proper diction must sound in comparison to the general speech of the troupe. She felt compelled, almost driven to confide in them. "I suppose you are desirous of knowing, of understanding," she began, but she found it difficult to continue. Indeed, her eyes suddenly brimmed with tears and her throat grew painfully tight.

Miss Currivard quickly took possession of her hand. "My dear Miss Lovington, you owe us no explanation. Indeed, you do not."

"Pray, forgive me," Miss Banwell said. "I spoke heedlessly as I always do! I am so sorry."

Judith could bear no more of their kindness, for it only reminded her of how much she had lost when she had escaped a most vile stepmother and the man she in turn had all but invited to invade their home.

She finished her brandy quickly and said she must leave. She descended the coach only to find Lord Kelthorne suddenly before her, offering his hand to keep her from toppling over anew. She wanted to refuse but she was dreadfully dizzy.

"Thank you," she murmured.

He quickly wrapped his arm about hers and guided her in the direction of the troupe wagons. "Only tell me you are uninjured that I might be at ease, for I am still incapable of believing you escaped without harm."

She looked up at him. She had meant to reassure him but instead, she fell into his gaze and found no words coming to her tongue by which to speak. This was the moment she had been avoiding all day, being near him, close to him, even touching him as she was with her arm linked closely with his.

Finally, she uttered, "You saved my life. Lord Kelthorne, how shall I ever repay you? When I looked at the stag and saw the wildness in his eye, I knew. . . ." Her breath caught raggedly on a sob.

"Pray say no more," he said, crushing her arm against his. "You are well and that is all that matters."

But she was not well. Her heart ached desperately. In these past few minutes, in the carriage with the castle ladies, she had experienced the very best of the society she had forsaken and longings both powerful and deep rose to consume her. Worse still, was that she felt as she always did in Kelthorne's presence, as though she wished to stay beside him forever. She could not explain it, but certainly it was made more intense by the knowledge that he and he alone had saved her from certain death.

Once within a few feet of the last tent now being struck, she released his arm and turned to face him. "Thank you again, my lord." She offered her hand and he took it.

Lord Kelthorne looked into chestnut colored eyes and knew that his mouth had fallen most unattractively agape. "I am sorry I looked at the horses instead of you," he whispered.

At that, she smiled and even laughed. "I thought you were displeased with my performance. It was very lowering."

"How could I ever be displeased?" he said passionately. "How could anyone when you sing so enchantingly?" He fell silent. There was nothing more to say. He knew he should release her hand but he could not. He just stared into her eyes savoring this moment as though it was absolutely the last time he would ever settle his gaze upon her.

She was so very beautiful. How his heart swelled as he looked upon her. She had been quite brave in protecting Shelly and he would always hold her in great admiration for that. How many other ladies would have had the bottom to stand her ground so that the child could escape?

"Aubrey!" Laurence called to him sharply. "'Tis time to depart."

The odd spell was broken and he released her hand. He offered a brief bow, turned on his heel and rejoined his party. The time had come to leave Cheddar Gorge.

From a stool situated near the wagon at which Mrs. Marnhull was working, Judith watched the castle party coaches rattle away. The jingling of the traces, the clip-clop of the horses hooves as each equipage was set in motion, the cries of the coachmen, soon disappeared from sight and hearing.

The troupe continued packing, of course, with little conversation. An air of fatigue had settled over the members as well as a sense of concern and ill usage. A heated argument broke out suddenly between John andd Charles, not unexpectedly, of course. She was certain John had merely been waiting for the castle party to leave before he gave the much needed dressing down.

Shelly ran to Judith and crawled into her lap. "Why is papa so angry with Charles?"

"Because he should not have used a rifle to kill the stag."

Shelly buried her face in Judith's shoulder. The quarrel lasted a very long time. No one paid the least heed.

In the end, Charles sulked. Judith ignored him, taking her place on the cushioned seat in the wagon in which the ladies rode together. Shelly remained with her. She found she had grown angry that through Charles's stupidity she had nearly lost her life. She would have, too, had it not been for Lord Kelthorne.

Her thoughts became fixed for that reason on the earl and it seemed her heart began to throb almost painfully in her chest. She wished suddenly that anyone other than Kelthorne had raised his rifle and slain the buck for now, she feared, her desire for him had trebled, at the very least. A crippling frustration settled within her, of desires that could not be fulfilled, desires she had ignored for most of her time with the troupe, of memories of being with her cousins and all the silly plans they had made to cut a dash in London during their come-out season.

She wished herself a thousand miles from Somerset. Never, when the troupe had arrived at the town of Portislow, did she think she would find herself in the midst of such struggles within her own heart. It was as if a very large door, and very grand in appearance, had swung open to reveal golden light and all of her hidden desires fulfilled, only she was not allowed to cross the threshold. She was a songstress, and, at times, an actress of the troupe. Lord Kelthorne, Miss Currivard, Mr. Doulting, Miss Banwell, Miss Upton, and Mr. Emborough were as untouchable to her as the sky.

Shelly had fallen asleep. She wished her life were as uncomplicated, that she could simply close her eyes, drift into sleep and all that was troubling her would disappear like mist before strong sunshine.

Margaret asked Betty to trade places with her and once seated beside Judith, took Shelly from her. "Ye can scarcely keep yer eyes open. Lean on me shoulder, if ye like."

Judith wanted to say no, but she was greatly fatigued and leaned against her friend.

"Are ye well?" Margaret asked on a whisper.

"Aye," Judith responded. "Just a trifle sad."

"And no wonder."

"I wish I had enough set by to purchase my cottage. I believe I would do so tomorrow."

Margaret clucked her tongue. "As I have told ye an hundred times, Judy," she continued in her whispers, "a cottage 'tis not fer ye. I've seen ye with Shelly. Ye'll not be content 'til ye have a husband and were ye to make a push, even now, ye might have one afore summer ends."

Judith sighed heavily. Whispering as well, she said, "You must be as mad as Bedlam if you are thinking what I believe you must be thinking."

"Not so daft as ye might think. Just try not to discourage him should he come to call."

Judith chuckled softly. "I am a poor songstress. There is

only one manner in which such a man looks upon a female like myself."

"P'rhaps," was all she would say.

Judith fell asleep against Margaret's shoulder wondering what Kelthorne's thoughts might be and wishing, not for the first time, that he would try a little harder to not be her ideal.

EIGHT

Kelthorne traveled alone with Miss Currivard. He had not desired to do so but his sisters would brook no opposition on that score. In addition, there had arisen an understanding among the party that he was courting her quite seriously even though his heart was in no manner centered upon her. He had been unable, therefore, to avoid the intimate situation.

To her credit, she did not attempt to engage him in conversation. Rather she sat gazing out the window, her hands folded serenely upon her lap. She seemed inordinately content, something he did not understand. He found he was a trifle irritated. Did she not comprehend his attraction to Judith? Did she not understand in the least that when he was near Judith his heart pounded unreasonably? Had he, therefore, misjudged Miss Currivard's intelligence?

He groaned inwardly. Would that he had never come upon Judith trespassing in his orchard that first night. He could have fought his desire for her otherwise. The truth was that had she been a lady of quality he would be courting her now and not Miss Currivard.

But she was not a lady of quality even if her speech bespoke her birthright. For reasons he did not know, nor cared to know, she had chosen life as a professional songstress. Little better than an actress, particularly since she had been traipsing about the country in the company of several healthy young men. She could not possibly be innocent for all her protests and yet, God help him, he wanted to believe she was. Not that any of it mattered, not one whit! Regardless of the truth, even were she to attempt to reenter polite society, she would never be able to overcome the stigma of her years of living in such a manner.

He glanced sharply at Miss Currivard. "Why did you desire this picnic? I confess I did not understand it from the beginning. What did you hope to achieve?"

She smiled and shrugged. "Precisely what I did achieve."

Now she would be evasive? He was irritated once more. "And what was that?" he snapped.

She lifted her brows to him. "Have I offended you in some wretched manner, my lord, for I vow from the moment of entering the coach you have been as cross as crabs. Yes, I know you have not spoken meanly to me, but everything about you is as prickly as a hedgehog from the time we departed Cheddar Gorge!"

He drew in a deep breath feeling quite guilty. "I do beg your pardon and no, you have not offended me, not by half. It is merely that, well, I suppose I am distressed by many things not least of which that Miss Lovington could have perished today and my shot was deuced fortunate." There it was, he thought, the truth that was haunting him, just how close Judith had come to being killed by the wounded stag.

Miss Currivard leaned forward and caught his gaze, which he gave to her reluctantly. "I am not ignorant—" she began, but then checked her words, "that is, of course, you must be overset. Who would not be when another's life was dependent upon clear thinking and accurate shooting? You are to be commended a thousandfold for what you did today. At the same time, I cannot help but wonder the toll it must have taken upon you."

He nodded. "I suppose you must be right. I would wish

the moment undone. Good God, what a fool that Hemyock creature is."

"I could not agree more nor did it escape my notice that the rest of the troupe held him in much contempt for what he did. Amazingly, however, he seemed entirely oblivious to his perfidy."

"Such fellows as that," he said, shaking his head, "usually are. They often leave a trail of disaster behind them without once looking back. Even in the chance moment they do, they ascribe any such spate of misfortunes they might see to the work of the gods."

She smiled and leaned back. "Giving the subject a slight turn, however," she said, "I suppose I do owe you some explanation about the picnic for I did have a purpose as I said before, one that I achieved, which was to come to know Miss Lovington better."

"But why?" he asked, both astonished and mystified.

She regarded him carefully for a long moment and he felt certain she was trying to communicate in her silence, but he seemed to be rather doltish for no inspired meanings came to him to explain her thoughts. She finally said, "I will confess that my reasons are to a degree incomprehensible even to me, but when I heard her sing for the first time, I felt as though I already knew her. Do you not think that odd?"

"Yes," he murmured, but he believed he knew precisely what she meant. "Perhaps it is the nature of her gifts to create such sentiments in others."

"Perhaps," she said. "But at the same time, I had the strongest sense that she might be able to understand me."

He laughed in his incomprehension. "But she is little better than an actress. Do you hope to befriend her? I would think it quite ill-advised."

She tilted her head slightly. "Do you truly?" she asked.

"Well, yes. Her position in society is so far beneath yours, so far in fact that she might as well reside in another land."

"Indeed?" Though she spoke quietly and as always in a

poised manner, he felt a blade of ice cross to him and cut very quickly.

He felt rather insulted. "Yes, indeed!" he responded.

"Did it never occur to you that she and I might share something in common?"

"What would that be?" He could not imagine to what she referred.

She chuckled softly. "That neither of us belongs where we are on the Portislow estate. By birth, I do not belong in your company and she most clearly does not belong with that acting troupe. Yet there we must both perform as required of us by the circumstances of our lives. Over which I know I had not the smallest control and which I am come to believe neither did she. No lady of poor birth could sustain so perfect an accent without having been born and trained to it, which leads me to wonder again just how she came to be with the troupe."

He was stunned by her words, by her assessment of her own situation as well as Judith's. "I would never have thought of it in that manner before," he said.

"Do you think I do not feel the whispers and stares when I go amongst society, when I go *alone* in society? My father is not permitted to tread where I tread and I am at the mercy of the character of any lady that desires my presence in her home. I know that it is never by my own accomplishments that I am invited to the best houses. Sometimes I am treated properly and with great civility and other times as though I might as well be required to do the laundry as perform in the drawing room. Surely, you cannot think me ignorant of my situation in that regard?"

"Of course not," he said quietly. "Though I confess I do not think on the subject much. I hope I have not been unkind."

She smiled fully. "No, that is perhaps the most exceptional part of your present charm—you never let me feel for a moment that I am beneath your dignity."

He burst out laughing. "Well, that is because I have no dignity, or did you not know as much and are you certain you even wish to be here? My reputation is rather sad, in fact."

She continued to smile. "I think it the worst hypocrisy in the world."

"As do I," he said. "I should be treated like an outcast, not you." He breathed a sigh of relief. "I find it wonderful to be speaking in this manner. I was not certain how much you knew of me."

"I believe you have quite underestimated the *beau monde*'s love of gabblemongering."

"I always have, much to my detriment, I suppose." He fell silent for a moment then asked, "So your desire was to come to know Miss Lovington during this picnic and you say you achieved your object."

"Well, I certainly made a beginning but I must say I had a very difficult time restraining all the questions I desired to ask of her. You see I am convinced there is some great mystery surrounding her presence in the troupe. Are you aware, for instance, how much she is loved and protected by them? Betty said . . . do you know Betty?"

"Betty of the onions?"

"Oh, lord yes," she returned grimacing. "At any rate, I chanced to speak with Betty as well and she informed me of these truths and that the troupe has often withdrawn in the middle of the night to escape the attentions of some forward rogue or other and even debated doing so because of you."

"Indeed?"

"Oh, yes, so you see your reputation does precede you."

"Abominably so, I fear, and yet you are still willing to converse with me."

"So I am," she stated.

"Do you know, you put me in mind of Laurence in this moment. I believe you share a quality with him that I do value very much."

"And what would that be?"

"That neither of you fears a little plain-speaking."

"There is no point to refrain from it when one wishes to know well and to be known."

"Aye," he responded softly. He recalled that Judith had said something of a similar nature. He found that the powerful thoughts and feelings about Judith, which had possessed him, had begun to diminish. He realized that he liked Miss Currivard, even that he admired her much as he admired Laurence. There was perceptiveness in her that she also shared with his friend and it was possible that she might even match his elevated intelligence. He knew himself to be quick-witted but there was something in Laurence of brilliance. He suspected Miss Currivard might be cut from the same cloth.

She glanced out the window then frowned. "I believe I recognize those gates. That is the country house of the Marquess of Stolford where we passed the night."

Kelthorne leaned forward and caught sight of the tall iron spires just as the coach passed by. "So it is."

"You know, I dislike him very much but your sisters seem quite enamored of him."

"I believe they are but I would wish them well away from such a man."

By the time the coach drew up the steep incline to the front of the house, Kelthorne was greatly content. Judith had retreated fully from his thoughts, and Miss Currivard's candor and goodness had quite set him at ease. As he handed her down and watched her stretch her back a little, he thought this was what his marriage ought to be: open, artless, warm.

He offered his arm, his heart full of good will as he led her into the house.

"There is one thing I think you ought to know," Miss Currivard said.

"And what would that be?" he inquired as they crossed the threshold.

"That I intend to help Miss Lovington in whatever way I can." She released his arm and began drawing off her gloves. She looked up to meet his gaze, perhaps to see his reaction.

"Do you think it necessary?" He felt nervous suddenly for he strongly suspected that by helping Miss Lovington, the lady before him meant to encourage a friendship with her. He had just spent the last hour scouring thoughts of Judith from his mind but the specter which now raised its head was of Judith being underfoot. "Do you think it wise?"

"As for necessary, I actually think very little in life is truly *necessary*, but I do believe it to be wise."

He wanted to argue the point but there was something in the determined set of her chin that stopped him. Instead, he asked, "And what precisely did you have in mind?"

"I am glad you have asked," she said smiling as she removed her bonnet. "Over the last mile of the journey a notion came to me that I begin to like more and more and which I have every confidence will be greatly pleasing to all the guests in your home." He gestured for her to head in the direction of the staircase, which would take them to the drawing room above. Laurence's voice could be heard, followed by uproarious laughter.

She chuckled and looked up the stairwell. "You have a wonderful friend in Mr. Doulting. He is never at a loss as to how to best entertain anyone. I find I am always amused in his company."

"As to that, he does seem intent on making certain you are comfortable, perhaps for my sake, I suppose. He seems much taken with you and he does not generally approve of most of the ladies of our circle. He finds them full of artifice."

"Well, as you must already know, he will not find aritifice in me."

Kelthorne chuckled. "No. That he will not." As they mounted the stairs together he asked, "So what is this present scheme of yours?"

"I think that for a very fine fee, Miss Lovington should be asked to perform for a little soiree you mean to give."

His heart sank. This would not do, not by half. "Forgive

me, Miss Currivard, but I beg to differ with you on the point of wisdom."

"I have but one object," she said, though he sensed this was a whisker. "She told me she hopes one day to purchase a cottage, that she has already saved quite a bit of money to that purpose. I mean to help her in that objective. But if you disapprove, I shall understand. After all this is your home, but I warn you I will simply make arrangements elsewhere."

Kelthorne felt as though he was being tested but he was not certain in what way. He did not feel as though refusing her would in any way cause her to like him less, but if that was not the nature of the exam he was facing, then what was it? Worse, however, was the simple truth that he could not possibly confess the real reason he disliked the notion. He could hardly tell her that he feared were Judith to be in his home, he would be unable to keep from touching her. There it was, plain and simple. He did not feel he had the smallest command of himself when he was around Judith. Still, he could hardly tell Miss Currivard that.

Instead, before entering the drawing room, he said, "I would only ask that you gain the support of my sisters. Should they disapprove of your scheme, my house would become a place of great misery for everyone, not less so yourself."

She smiled, quite broadly. "You have little understanding, do you?"

"I beg your pardon?"

"My lord," she said quietly, "your sisters would grant me the moon so long as I remained beneath your roof and attempted to win your heart."

He laughed feeling wholly resigned. "You are right. Of course, you are right. My wits must have gone a-begging."

"Then it is settled and I may proceed with your blessing?"

"Yes," he responded, but his heart betrayed him by suddenly surging with delight at the very thought that Judith would soon be in his home.

A familiar clattering up the stairs prompted him to move protectively in front of Miss Currivard. "Rufus!" he called out, turning around and pointing at the dog. His faithful hound, already at the top step, stopped instantly in stride and panted.

"Come." The dog moved to his side.

Kelthorne moved away slightly and let him see Miss Currivard. "Now greet our guest properly."

Rufus, who was a highly intelligent, though incorrigible, creature, did as he was bid and held out a paw to her.

Miss Currivard laughed, leaned down and took the large, dark shaggy paw in hand. "And good day to you as well," she said.

Kelthorne watched Miss Currivard pet his head and rub his ears, just as Judith once had. He knew Miss Currivard had an excellent heart, only what the devil was he to do?

Judith bid Miss Currivard to seat herself on the stool. She was still astonished, however kind the young woman had been to her at Cheddar Gorge, that she had actually come to call, even requesting to speak privately with her.

"To what do I owe this visit?" she inquired.

After sitting down, Miss Currivard glanced around her humble abode and exclaimed, "I should have done just this when I was forced to live in a tent for all those weeks in India. How much I should have enjoyed having my things about me, a painting or two, a piece of framed embroidery, and these dried flowers hanging from your looking glass—I think it splendid!"

Judith sat down in the chair by her dressing table and smiled. How wonderful it was to be understood. "This arrangement did not occur overnight, I assure you. But once having begun, I found it afforded me a great deal of pleasure."

"Did you do the rug as well?"

"Yes, of course."

"I am utterly amazed," Miss Currivard said. Her face was aglow.

Judith waited for her to speak. She had already posed her question but did not wish to press her guest too hard. At the same time, she knew Miss Currivard's presence in her tent to have excited the greatest curiosity among the troupe.

Miss Currivard met her gaze and smiled in some understanding. "As to the reason why I have come," she began, "I wish to lay a small proposal before you. Since you were so kind as to share your hopes for the future with me, I was hoping to be of what assistance to you I can. I was wondering if you would be so good as to perform for a soiree at the castle in the next few days or so? You will be paid handsomely—a hundred pounds."

"What?" she cried.

"I thought I might give you a shock, but indeed, if you are to have your cottage before you are quite advanced in years," here she smiled more fully still, "then a little push is quite necessary. I suppose you might think of me as your patronness."

"A hundred pounds." Judith was truly astonished. "You would do this for me?"

"Yes, of course. A friend ought to be of use, I think, and I hope you will call me friend."

Nothing could have warmed her heart more than to hear Miss Currivard address her so kindly. From the time of their conversation at Cheddar Gorge, Judith had embraced the possibility of a friendship with her, however unlikely their circumstances. She had enjoyed conversing with Miss Currivard and was never made once to feel the disparity in their situations. She sensed in Miss Currivard a unique quality that, in her opinion, would make the very best of friends.

These thoughts brought her round to the more pressing difficulty—Kelthorne. The very notion that she would be obliged to spend an evening in his company sent a shiver along her spine that had nothing to do with fear. For the past two days, she had worked very hard to relinquish all thoughts of him but now, with the prospect of an entire evening in which she would be required to converse with the guests as was natural in such private settings, she became acutely aware that she would be with him far more than could ever be thought desirous.

Miss Currivard rose. "I know that the demands of this life are great so I will not keep you. Only, I do hope you will oblige me in this."

She seemed so serious that Judith could not help but wonder if there was more in Miss Currivard's plan than merely helping her to one day purchase her cottage. She could not, however, for the life of her determine just what that might be nor could she ask her directly.

"I must lay the request before Mr. and Mrs. Ash," Judith said, rising as well. "They have charge of our time and schedules."

"Yes, of course." She extended her hand and Judith shook it warmly. Releasing her hand, she added, "There is one more thing, Miss Lovington. If you would not be disinclined and should you choose to accept my proposal, then I would be greatly honored if you would permit me to accompany you on the pianoforte."

"Indeed?" Judith inquired, shocked once more.

"Do you fear I am not sufficiently accomplished? I promise you that my governess who lived in constant dread that my rank as a tradesman's daughter would sully her sterling reputation, made certain from the time I was a very little girl that I learned my scales and arpeggios properly."

"I did not mean to imply anything of the sort. I was merely stunned that, given the differences of our situation, you would be wishful of doing so. After all, we will need to practice together, and I should require several rehearsals. So are you absolutely certain this would not be repugnant to you, for I promise you, on this head, I am a severe taskmaster. Mrs. Ash and I have quarreled more than once on just this topic."

Instead of appearing doubtful, Miss Currivard merely laughed. "I see that you are something of a perfectionist, as am I. I suspected from the first that we two shared this in common. I promise you in return, therefore, that you alone shall name the date of the soiree and you shall have as many rehearsals as you deem necessary to be comfortable with my skills."

Judith felt there was nothing more to be said. She reiterated her need to discuss the proposal with John and Margaret but promised to send word to the castle by the afternoon.

"I hope you will not refuse me," Miss Currivard said. "Indeed, I am depending upon you more than you can know."

There it was again, the hint that the entirety of her motives for the soiree was yet hidden.

A few minutes later, Judith was locked in a great argument with both John and Margaret.

"But I do not think it will do at all!" Judith cried. "Without wishing to elaborate, I do not feel it wise that I engage a concert at the castle. It is not seemly."

"In wat manner not seemly!" Margaret cried. "What rubbish! Lord, Judy, I ain't never seen ye so missish."

"Aye, Judy," John agreed. "And 'tis not as though ye have not performed fer a private audience afore. Do ye not remember Shropshire?"

"And do you not remember that we were required to leave town that very night. Charles was furious!"

"I supposed that were a poor example," John said. "But Lord Kelthorne has been most kind to the entire troupe and I have seen nothing of his attentions to ye that were improper. Margaret agrees with me."

"Even though he came to my tent?"

"Even then, fer he were a gentleman just as Margaret knew he would be." He crossed his arms over his chest. "And Miss Currivard has been a perfect lady and shown great kindness to ye, singling ye out as she has. 'Twould be an insult to deny her now. Ye know as much. I know ye do."

This much was true. "But I cannot like it. I know

Kelthorne has not precisely gone beyond the pale. However, I still feel in danger."

"Aye," Margaret said softly. "But ye are speaking of yer heart."

Judith gasped. How did Margaret know? "Yes," she confessed.

John suddenly swept an arm about her shoulders. "Judy, 'twould not be bad to let yer heart be engaged a little."

Tears started to her eyes. How easy it was for him to say such a thing to her when he had been able to wed the woman he loved, but what of her? What if she tumbled in love with Kelthorne? There would be no such marriage to fulfill the dreams her heart seemed to weave the moment she was within twenty paces of him.

There seemed to be no argument, however, that she could put forth that would convince John and Margaret that she should refuse the invitation. Besides, to deny Miss Currivard was to show her unkindness when she had been so good to her at Cheddar Gorge. No, she must go.

John gave her shoulders a squeeze then released her. "Ye know wat ye must do."

"Well, if I must do this thing," she snapped, "then I insist upon sharing the hundred pounds with the troupe."

"None o' that!" John cried. "Ye know very well that earnings from any private performance is not to be shared. Those are the troupe's rules."

"It is not right," she countered.

"Nonsense. Remember Winchester, when the officers asked fer Betty and Angelique for the evening, fifty pounds a-piece."

"But that was not for . . ." She broke off blushing deeply.

John laughed at her. "And still, after all these years, yer cheeks will turn the color of a tomato."

Margaret laughed as well, but said, "Have done with it, Judy. Take the engagement. Indeed, ye have been such a blessing to the troupe, whatever Charlie says. Ye have brought audiences when no one else could. And as fer Kelthorne, if ye be worried, then hint him toward Miss Currivard."

"I suppose I could do that," she murmured, but she was not content.

An hour later, she penned her note to Miss Currivard accepting her proposal and naming the number of rehearsals she required, five for at least an hour each time and therefore setting the date of the soiree for a week's time.

So it was that on the following day, Judith found herself at Portislow Castle. Miss Currivard was giving her a tour of the principal rooms and had led her at last to the conservatory. She opened the glass door that had a view of the small vale in which the troupe was camped.

"From here," she said, stepping to the low wall, which gave warning that the hill dropped sharply away, "you can see the camp, particularly at night when the lanterns are lit and the fire ring is ablaze. It is a lovely sight."

Judith stood beside her. The day was very fine and the hillside opposite was aglow with morning light. All the hills about were heavily wooded giving the entire vicinity a lush, verdant aspect. "What a beautiful sight," she cried.

"Aye, so it is."

"Where does this path lead?"

"To the left is a long slope by which one can reach the stables at the bottom of the hill and to the right the path connects with another that meanders to the top of the hill." She turned to her suddenly. "I ought to give you fair warning that you are to stay to dine with us."

Judith felt her heart constrict in her chest. "Oh, but that is impossible. You must see it is! Indeed, I cannot. . . ."

Miss Currivard cut her off swiftly with a wonderful trill of laughter. "My dear Miss Lovington, I will brook no opposition. Your presence is required."

"By whom?" she asked, feeling suddenly frightened. She understood Kelthorne's sisters to be quite fearsome.

"By me, of course."

Judith stepped away from Miss Currivard. "I beg you will excuse me," she said earnestly. "No good can come of this."

Miss Currivard held her gaze firmly but her expression softened in quick stages. "I believe I understand your reticence and if my intentions were of a simple nature, I would allow you to be excused but, for reasons I cannot explain, you would be doing me a very great favor."

Judith might have protested but there was such sincerity in her looks that she found she could do little more than smile, if feebly, and acquiesce.

"Shall we?" Miss Currivard gestured to the small music room that adjoined the conservatory.

"Yes, of course."

Whatever her fears about the awkwardness of the social situation, the rehearsal pleased Judith enormously. Margaret had a great deal of ability, there could be no two opinions on that score, but Miss Currivard had something of brilliance, even perfection, in her playing. After a very short time, Judith felt as though she had been performing with Miss Currivard forever.

When some time had passed and Miss Currivard was stretching her arms overhead, Judith glanced at the clock and cried out, "Good heavens! We have been here for two hours! I would not have believed it possible. I feel as though only a few minutes have passed. Indeed, I must confess I have never enjoyed myself more."

"Nor I," her patronness said, rising from the stool. "Do you know how many times little shivers traveled all over my neck and arms in listening to you sing? You have an extraordinary voice."

Judith was embarrassed by such a profound compliment but thanked her nonetheless.

Mr. Doulting appeared at the door of the conservatory. "We have just been informed that nuncheon is served. The rest of the party has gone from the front of the house, but Aubrey and I have come to collect you."

Judith barely had time to compose her nerves before

Kelthorne arrived from the hallway on the opposite side of the conservatory. How was it she had forgotten just how tall he was, how noble his features and how bright and warm an expression was perpetually in his eye?

"Well met, Miss Lovington," he said, bowing slightly to her. "I trust you are recovered from your ordeal at Cheddar Gorge."

"Yes, very much so, thank you." Though his concern was genuine, his words took her instantly back to that moment of seeing the stag fall almost at her feet and of later learning that it was he who had fired the shot that saved her life. "I owe you so very much," she said, half laughing, as though relieved all over again.

He shook his head as well, as though he too had just recalled the entire ordeal.

Mr. Doulting said, "I trust Mr. Hemyock is being forbidden the use of the troupe's firearms."

Judith turned to him and laughed. "He has suffered wretchedly since that time, most fortuitously. His arrogance continued unabated until it was finally borne in upon his stubborn mind that not one person believed him guiltless. Indeed, John—that is, Mr. Ash—nearly came to fisticuffs with him over the matter. But Mr. Hemyock is a brilliant player, as I am sure you must agree. He just lacks sense."

Mr. Doulting offered his arm. "You are being too kind to say he lacks sense. I am come to believe he lacks a brain."

Judith laughed, as did Miss Currivard.

"And now, Aubrey, lead the way with our lovely Miss Currivard."

Judith glanced up at Mr. Doulting, who gave her a wink and allowed his more exalted friend to take the lead.

Mr. Doulting's company as they made their way to the dining room on the opposite side of the house was as engaging as it was amusing.

"What are your interests, Mr. Doulting, other than an enjoyment of ale and the like?"

He shook his head and grimaced playfully. "This is a very

bad beginning if this is your only opinion of me. And I have been trying so hard to curtail my, er, *interest*. I am desolate at having been discovered."

Judith would have answered him in kind, but she saw that his gaze was fixed to Miss Currivard, who upon reaching the end of the hallway had turned to speak with Lord Kelthorne. Instead, she ventured, "She is quite beautiful."

Mr. Doulting sighed heavily. "Fearfully so," he said. He then eyed her uneasily and added hastily, "Of course, everyone thinks so."

"Of course," but she smiled regardless.

"I believe I must confess to you that when Aubrey and I reached the hallway beyond the conservatory, we heard you singing. We could not help but wait and listen for some few minutes, 'twas so beautiful. Do you despise us for spying on you?"

"Had you been discovered," she said, "I should have supposed you were being considerate in not interrupting our rehearsal."

"Why, yes, now that I think on the matter, I believe that is precisely what we were doing."

Judith chuckled. She liked Mr. Doulting very much. He was forthright in everything, a good, just, tolerant man and obviously an excellent friend to Lord Kelthorne. She wondered if the earl realized, however, that Mr. Doulting was in love with Miss Currivard. She had noticed his interest before. She had noticed how he strove to entertain her when Lord Kelthorne was absent from her side. She also noticed that not once did he cross the bounds of propriety or even of friendship for she sincerely doubted that Miss Currivard had even the smallest notion of his *tendre* for her.

NINE

Judith was quite surprised by how easily she adapted to genteel society. Miss Currivard had insisted she dine each day with the castle party, following their rehearsal, and so she had. Because she had been raised in just such an environment, in a home that was lovely with tradition, beauty and elegance, her manners more than once caused Lady Radsbury to start and, on the third day of rehearsals, to say, "Good God, Miss Lovington! I vow I have told you things I have not even told my sister and you, an actress!" She then regretted her words. "I beg your pardon. I was not thinking. You see how confused I am about who you really are. It is no wonder that my brother . . . that is . . . I beg you will forget everything I have just said to you."

She rose from her seat quickly, the yarn she had been gathering into a ball from the same strands spread between Judith's arms, dropped to the floor. She even quit the drawing room, leaving Judith to stare at the empty seat a blush descending hotly on her cheeks. She felt tears spring to her eyes and might have given way to such powerful feelings had Kelthorne not come to her in that moment and picked up the yarn. As one who had assisted his sisters in such a task, the earl sat down and began winding the yarn.

"I see Mary has taken a pelter but I would not refine too much upon it, Miss Lovington. She is often out of frame."

Judith was not certain what to say. She was still so astonished by Lady Radsbury's conduct and at the same time shocked by her own feelings that her mind would not settle. She moved in rhythm with each winding of the yarn, her own arms rising and dipping to better facilitate the task.

"Indeed, Judith," he said very quietly. "Please do not be distressed."

She looked up at him as he continued winding the ball. "I am trying valiantly not to be," she said at last, taking a deep breath. "And I promise you, your sister was not angry or offended. Merely—" Judith looked away from him unable to complete her thought.

"What, then?" he asked, again very quietly.

Judith glanced about the chamber. Mr. Doulting was seated at the pianoforte entertaining Miss Currivard who in turn was laughing and holding her side. Miss Banwell and Miss Upton were pouring over the latest issue of *La Belle Assemblee* as though nothing in the entire world could be of greater importance. And the rest of the party was gathered about the whist table from which place a sudden groan erupted from two of the players and cheers from the others.

Judith gathered her thoughts. "Merely, your sister became quite flustered when she remembered that I belong to the troupe camped in your vale."

"Ah," he said, smiling and nodding. "As to that, I believe we have all had such an experience over the past several days. After all, there is nothing in your manners or speech that would set you in the smallest way apart from the guests in my home."

She smiled, liking the intimate conversation very much. Without giving it too much thought, she said, "My governess would have been so pleased, you cannot imagine how much your words would have delighted her."

"Your governess?" he queried, lifting a brow.

She knew what he was thinking, that she had just revealed something of her past to him and that for several days she had been able to parry his inquiries quite masterfully. In this moment, and perhaps because of his kindness, she was not so reluctant to keep such information from him. "Yes, my governess. She was an excellent woman, highly intelligent, and a good friend to me in a time of great need. Yes, she would be happy to hear you say that I had not disgraced her excellent name."

"Do you never write to her nor hear from her?"

"She left England some time past and moved to the Colonies."

"Would that be eight years past?"

Judith nodded.

"I see."

"And do you miss your home?"

She could hardly speak for fear her feelings would best her. Finally, she said, "You can have no notion how very much."

"Did you live in a castle?" He was smiling, but she saw great sympathy in his eyes.

"No, but my father's home was quite lovely. A small manor of ancient origin and design and in a prosperous area of Sussex."

"I wonder that you were ever able to leave it," he said quietly, regarding her closely.

She held most of the memories at bay, save a very sweet one of seeing her father sitting in his Bath chair beneath an apricot tree. A thick blanket covered his legs and though the day was lovely, like these dreamlike summer days she had been enjoying of late, he'd had need of a layer of warmth. Though he'd been ill, he was smiling that day, watching her try to fly a kite on a perfectly windless day. She had run up and down and up and down a hundred times, a thousand times. He had laughed at her so. Maybe that was why she continued to try to fly her kite when even the leaves on the apricot tree were silent. How she had loved his smiles.

She knew she had told Kelthorne more than in any previous conversation and ordered herself to be more guarded. She therefore ignored his searching comment and instead, said, "I think you would have liked my father. He was such a good man and not in the usual style. He often said he would forgive a man anything were he just to live without hypocrisy before the world."

Lord Kelthorne paused in the yarn wrapping. "That is very broad thinking, indeed."

She smiled. "I said you would have liked him."

He smiled as well. "I suppose I would."

A burst of laughter erupted from near the pianoforte. Judith's gaze was drawn to Mr. Doulting and Miss Currivard. Once more, she glanced at Miss Banwell and Miss Upton. They were smiling and laughing together as well.

"You have been doing that all day," Kelthorne said quietly, once more wrapping the yarn about the growing ball.

Judith brought her attention sharply back to the earl. "What do you mean?"

"I have observed you several times watching the others with an expression very near to longing in your eyes."

Judith sighed. "How could I not when Miss Banwell and Miss Upton put me so forcibly in mind of my cousins? They used to reside in Kent, but since they were older than I and very beautiful, besides being in possession of excellent dowries, I would expect they are married by now and living in other places."

She watched a frown grow between his brows. She felt uneasy. She should not have alluded to her past for it was most dangerous. She had even given clues to her identity that ought not to be given.

He looked at her, his penetrating blue eyes piercing her heart yet again. He opened his mouth but she spoke hastily, preventing his speech. "Pray do not ask," she whispered, "for I cannot give you answer."

"Why?" he asked bluntly.

She felt a blush creep up her cheeks. Her heart beat strongly in her chest. "Because I cannot."

"How is it you left your home and your good father to take up with an acting troupe? How could he have let you go?"

How could she tell him he was dying when she left or anything else about that wretched day eight years past. "Some decisions, even despised, are absolutely necessary."

He ground his teeth. "Are you to remain a mystery forever? Why will you not trust me with the truth?"

"Why will you not trust me that I simply cannot?"

He shook his head but she supposed the logic of her response made some sense to him for a small smile, reaching to his eyes, appeared on his lips.

Once more her heart gave pause. She met his gaze fully and tried to breathe but, as often happened, she found it impossible. Of course he was handsome and that might normally have accounted for the breathlessness that overtook her. However, in this moment, she rather thought the present enchantment that descended on her had more to do with his interest in precisely who she was. She found she desired nothing more than to tell him everything, to tell him of Lord Stolford's heinous conduct and of her stepmother's wickedness, yet she could not. She still feared that were Stolford to learn of her whereabouts he would once more pursue her, particularly since she had been given to understand that his county seat was in Somerset as well. The thought that he might not be far from Portislow caused her to shudder inwardly.

She was relieved of having to continue the conversation with Lady Radsbury's announcement that the coach was ready to take her back to camp. If the hour was earlier than anticipated and even if Miss Currivard appeared quite surprised that she was being sent away, Judith for her part found herself grateful. There was too much temptation for her at Castle Portislow, and that of a varied sort, to allow her to remain with a proper degree of equanimity. She feared revealing too much to Kelthorne and she was growing far too comfortable in her discourse with Miss Currivard. In her opinion, Lady Radsbury had shown great good sense in sending her away so she could not repine.

Perhaps because of Lady Radsbury's concerns, the two remaining rehearsals were kept both secluded and brief although Judith was still continually overwhelmed by how easily and rapidly she fell into conversation with Miss Currivard. She shared with the tradesman's daughter so similar an opinion on so many subjects, that by the last day of rehearsal it seemed to her that she might as easily have been friends with Miss Currivard for years rather than a scant sennight. If more often than not she lay awake at night in her tent, yearning for that which she knew could never be, in what was proving to be a beautiful stolen season, she felt such longings to be a small price to pay for the pleasures of Miss Currivard's understanding, friendship and daily tea with her in the small music room at the castle.

"You seem to like Mr. Doulting exceedingly," Judith observed.

Miss Currivard immediately chuckled. "He amuses me vastly. I am never in his company but a few minutes before my cheeks ache with so much laughter."

"And what of his prospects?" she asked, sipping her tea, her feet settled comfortably on an embroidered footstool. Miss Currivard reclined gracefully on a chaise lounge.

She threw her arm over her head and sighed. "He has none to speak of. He has resided these many years and more in the various homes of his friends, whether in the city or the country, as many younger sons of the nobility and gentry do. He has confided in me that neither the law nor the army would do for him and since he was wholly unfit for the church, the only occupation of some merit to which he seems greatly devoted, is to 'scribble his poems,' as he once said to me."

"Have you read his poems?"

"A few." She sat straighter on the lounge. "I believe they have merit but, not being of a scholarly turn, I daresay I am not fit to judge them properly."

"He has hopes then of seeing his work in print?"

"He does not say as much but I believe he does."

"Perhaps he needs a push."

"Aye," she responded, her expression growing thoughtful as she too picked up her teacup and began to sip. After a moment, she said, "I have been encouraging Harriet in his direction. She is well-dowered and they seem quite nicely suited to one another in temperament although Harriet is not nearly as intelligent as he, but she would make him an excellent wife. I fear, however, that she disappointed him last night by saying of the one poem he was willing to read to her that it spoke of trees far too often." Miss Currivard laughed. "He responded dryly, 'But Miss Banwell, do but think. Should my efforts see the covers of a book, it would be very fitting since there would be so many *leaves* within.' "

"Oh, dear," Judith murmured also laughing. "And what did poor Miss Banwell say?"

Miss Currivard smiled broadly. "Only that she supposed he was right if his book was used for pressing such objects as was found in a forest."

Judith groaned. "Quite hopeless. Poor Miss Banwell. Yet you believe they would suit?"

"Yes, I think so," she responded, but not convincingly. "There is no dearer soul on earth than Harriet. Yes, she would make him a most admirable wife and her rather fine dowry would secure their future."

"You seem to have thought it through rather carefully."

Miss Currivard shook her head. "I am being ridiculous, I suppose, but I should like to see Mr. Doulting well-settled."

"You are rather fond of him."

"I am," she stated as one who had just discovered a significant truth.

Judith said nothing more and the subject soon slipped from Mr. Doulting and his poetry to the forthcoming recital. "Are you very nervous?" Miss Currivard asked.

"Not a bit. After a thousand performances in every imaginable location, I confess I find nothing but pleasure in the whole process. Besides, you play beautifully, even better than dear Margaret, and I have never known such a companionable experience between song and instrument."

"Nor I," Miss Currivard stated firmly. "Which quite settles my mind that this shall not be the last. I am rather determined on it."

Judith sighed. "If only that were possible, but the troupe will leave in a fortnight or so with the traveling fair that is due to arrive any day now."

Miss Currivard shrugged. "We shall see. What a surprising visit this has become. I had not expected to enjoy myself so completely. The experience at Cheddar Gorge was absolutely delightful, though frightening toward the end, and playing these ballads for you has been the best musical exchange of my life. With a fair on the horizon—I vow I could not be happier. Do you suppose there will be gypsies and all manner of fortunes told at such an event?"

"Undoubtedly."

The following evening, Judith dressed carefully for her performance at the castle. Margaret had dressed her hair, catching it high upon her head and creating a crown of ringlets into which she tucked sprigs of lavender. She wore a simple gold necklace with an amber cross, one that her father had given her just before she had left home. She donned the purple gown of figured silk, which she had just completed that day, straightening the point lace that edged the scoop line of the bodice. Pulling on her long silk gloves, she turned to regard herself in the mirror.

"My hair has never looked more beautiful," she said, turning toward her friend.

"Ye are that pretty," Margaret returned clapping her hands. "That ye are! I expect all the gentl'men to tumble in love with ye afore the night is over."

"As though I give a fig for such a thing. My only desire is not to disgrace either myself or the troupe by missing my notes or forgetting my words."

"Ye have never done so afore. Ye will not do so now."

Margaret was beaming. Judith, feeling oddly unsettled by

the forthcoming event, hugged her, strange tears coming to her eyes. She did not understand why she was as nervous as she was.

"There, there," Margaret murmured. "'Twill be all right, Judy. Indeed, 'twill."

Judith pulled back and dabbed at her eyes gently with her gloved fingertips. "I feel as though everything is changing," she whispered. "I do not want things to change. I do not think I can bear it!"

Margaret took hold of her shoulders and gave her a squeeze. "All will be well," she said.

John appeared in the tent doorway, his eyes wide. "How pretty ye are, Judy, and very fittin' this evening, especially since Kelthorne is come fer ye."

"Kelthorne?" she asked, dumbfounded.

"Aye. In his coach."

"I had best go then." She picked up her white silk shawl, embroidered with yellow buttercups, and arranged it over her elbows with a long loop behind, as was the prevailing fashion. John offered his arm and, given how her knees had begun to shake, she gladly took it.

Once Judith neared the coach, Kelthorne descended, his expression troubled. She wondered what was wrong.

She climbed aboard and after taking her seat and arranging her skirts, he sat down opposite her at the same time commanding the coachman to give his horses the office to start. He was still frowning.

"What is it?" she asked. "Is something amiss?"

Lord Kelthorne regarded the beauty opposite him. The fading light of evening did little to diminish the elegant line of her brow, her neck, the easy curve of her arms as she held her hands clasped loosely on her lap. He could hardly tell her the true scope of his thoughts, that she had become a perpetual image in his mind, and that whenever he was in her company, he grew increasingly reluctant to part from her.

He had also lost the ability to discern what was appropriate conduct toward her. He feared that he might have given rise to expectations he could not possibly fulfill.

"There is something I must say, lest you misinterpret any of my attentions to you." To his surprise there was a glimmer of a smile in her eyes.

"If you think for a moment," she said, not waiting for him to explain, "that I am in hourly anticipation of a proposal, I beg you will not distress yourself. I have nothing but appreciation for our conversations and since I am at the same time fully aware that your interest is directed toward Miss Currivard, and that with the blessing of your family, please understand that I hold no illusions . . . on any score."

He was relieved and yet he was not. Even if there were to be a measure of understanding between them, such a circumstance would not end the powerful feelings that possessed him whenever he was with her. "Then we are of a mind."

"Yes."

"I only desired to bring the subject forward because of, well, because of the yarn. Both my sisters gave me such a dressing down—you can have no notion! I should never have come to you in the drawing room that day."

At that, she leaned forward. "I cannot agree at all," she cried. "What you did was quite honorable, even chivalrous. Your sister left me so abruptly that I have little doubt most every one in the drawing room thought I had given offense."

"She later told me she feared both she and I were giving you reason to hope."

"I beg you not to distress yourself. I understand quite to perfection how my presence in an acting troupe does not make me fit for a proper drawing room. I have long been resigned to that fact."

Again, he was surprised for there was not the smallest hint of bitterness about her. Without thinking, he possessed himself of her hands. "But you should not be with this troupe!" he cried.

She was shocked. He could see as much in her eyes and

in the way she quickly withdrew her hands from his. "And yet I am. But if I am to continue to be comfortable at Portislow, I beg you will not importune me again."

He looked out the window, his frustration rising. What manner of foolishness had ever caused her to leave her home in the first place?

"I did not mean to *importune* you. I meant nothing of a romantic nature. One does not, you know, when one intends to scold."

"To scold?" she inquired, a slight frown marring her perfect brow.

"Yes, about your absurd decision to become an actress, when it is clear in every word you speak, every graceful gesture of your arms, every turn of your countenance, that you are a lady of quality. Someone should have given you a severe dressing down before you embarked on this imprudent course. You could not have been so wholly without protection. Why did you not go to your family in Kent? You spoke of having cousins there. Why did you not go to your aunt or uncle?"

Her expression dimmed and for a dark moment she seemed inexorably sad. "I was fourteen," she said. "I did what was necessary given the truly wretched circumstances at the time. Even my most excellent governess did not see what else I could do if I was to preserve . . ." She broke off, apparently unwilling to complete her thought, then continued, "But if it is of use to you, my first effort was to seek refuge with my uncle but it was too late for that."

"Did you bear a child?" he asked, for he could think of no other meaning behind her words.

"What?" she cried obviously shocked.

He shrugged. "You would not have been the first lady of genteel birth to have done so."

"You would think such a thing of me," she responded, horror in every line of her face. "I was but fourteen!" Tears brimmed in her eyes soon afterward and he knew then how badly he had erred.

Conversation ceased at that point. She did not open her mouth again except to thank him for fetching her when at last they arrived at his front door. Nor did she speak as he escorted her into the house. She addressed his butler, asking where she should go until summoned for the performance.

"Miss Currivard awaits you in the small music room."

"Thank you," she said. She turned away without so much as a nod in his direction.

Once in the music room with Miss Currivard, Judith was far too overset to begin.

"Whatever is the matter?" she asked, rising from the pianoforte and crossing to her. She took her hands immediately.

"I should not have allowed him to send me into the boughs," Judith said, shaking her head.

"Was it something Lord Kelthorne said to you?"

Judith nodded. She could hardly speak, but she feared if she did not address what was troubling her, she would be unable to sing. "He . . . he asked me why I left home. Of course I could not tell him. I can tell no one the truth. But he asked me if I had had a child."

At that, Miss Currivard gasped, then laughed aloud. "Tell me he did not! What a gudgeon! A complete gudgeon! Has he no perception? Does he not know what I know and what your dear Mrs. Ash has promised me is utterly true, that you are an innocent caught in a difficult situation?"

"I suppose he does not," Judith responded. Her friend's entire speech had surprised her and she did not know which part of it to address first. She began, however, with what disturbed her most, "Then you do not blame him for thinking such a thing of me? Am I wrong to be offended?"

"I think he is trying very hard to find fault with you."

"But why?" she cried.

"Now who is being a simpleton," Miss Currivard said, but she suddenly appeared very sad. "But if you must have an answer, 'tis because you are so pretty and your voice speaks to him, to all of us, of the angels."

Judith saw the rather haunted expression in her eye and

began to understand even though Miss Currivard was merely hinting at the truth. "I am sorry," she murmured. "I knew this was a terrible mistake. I should not be in this house. I should not be here at all. You know I should not. I cannot think what made you bring me here."

"Because you belong here, perhaps more than I do."

"But can you not understand how I am being tortured? Every hour I spend at Portislow makes me long for what cannot be."

Miss Currivard did not speak for a long moment. "Well, I think I can comprehend what you are trying to say, but I am convinced you are mistaken."

Judith realized there was no possibility of convincing her otherwise. She drew in a deep breath and released a sigh. "I suppose it would be useless to argue, but I must disagree."

"There must always be disagreement in any good friendship," she stated smiling. She took up her seat at the pianoforte and added, "Time will answer everyone's questions and concerns, of that I am convinced. And now, shall we warm up *your* voice and *my* fingers?"

An hour later, after having her nerves calmed through the rehearsal of the music, Judith strode confidently into Lord Kelthorne's expansive drawing room in which were seated no less than fifty of the surrounding area's gentry and nobility. She took up her place beside the fine Broadwood instrument. Kelthorne stood in the back of the chamber, but she did not look at him. Miss Currivard was right—any questions or concerns would surely one day be answered to everyone's satisfaction.

Nodding to Miss Currivard, who was seated at the fine pianoforte, she began her performance with the ballad, "Fly Not Yet." Within a few seconds of beginning, she grew lost in the habitual magic of extending herself in song to an audience. There was a play of reaction that fed her soul and swelled her voice so that by the time the last notes of the song had vanished, a warm flood of applause flowed over her. She did not forget to honor her accompanist and was delighted that the audience recognized and subsequently applauded Miss Currivard's excellent performance with equal vigor.

So the concert continued warm and wonderful, at moments sublime. Each song brought a new form of expression and meaning and another chance to delve quietly into the lives and experiences of those gathered in Kelthorne's drawing room.

When at last a second encore had been performed and exclaimed over, Judith finally quit the chamber with Miss Currivard who hugged her arm tightly. Returning to the privacy of the small music room, Miss Currivard squealed her absolute adoration of the experience. "Never in my entire existence have I enjoyed my music more than during the course of this evening. It is no wonder that you travel with the troupe as you do, that you have not settled somewhere as a mere governess or companion as might be expected in one of your circumstances. How can you even think of taking a cottage in Devonshire? How could you ever relinquish so exquisite an experience as this?"

Judith was shocked by everything she had just heard. "I am deeply gratified to know that you took pleasure in our efforts just now but truly you must believe me when I say that I would trade it all were I able to do so. Only the worst of events could have forced me to take this path. You must understand that."

Miss Currivard recovered her usual restraint and good breeding. "I suppose I have spoken foolishly," she said. "I must confess the entire experience has overwhelmed me. I only hope that we are able to perform together again."

"It was wonderful," Judith said. Hearing voices in the distance, she added quickly, "And now, I intend to walk back to camp. No, I beg you will allow me to do so. Try to understand. I do appreciate all that you are doing for me, but 'tis too much."

With that, she picked up her shawl and threw it quickly about her shoulders. "I shall leave by the conservatory so that I will not be seen. Thank you again. You have permitted me to hope that my cottage is not far distant."

Even though it was clear that Miss Currivard would have remonstrated with her, Judith hurried away. A moment later, she was walking briskly down the steep path at the side of the castle.

Kelthorne entered the music room to find Miss Currivard alone and seated at the foot of the chaise lounge. "She is gone," she said.

He glanced at the door of the conservatory and saw that it was slightly ajar. "I see. She did not wish to meet our guests?"

"No, she was a little overset, I think. I wish she had stayed."

"Perhaps it is just as well."

Miss Currivard rose and when he approached her, she took his hands. "Were you not utterly enchanted this evening?" she asked, her expression enrapt.

"Y-yes, I suppose I was," he responded.

"I have never felt such exhilaration before," she cried.

He smiled and felt a little relieved since his thoughts had all been for Judith. "You played beautifully," he said, thinking how grand and generous he could be.

Sudden tears filled her eyes. He thought he understood her, that she was overwhelmed by accompanying Judith and by his compliments. "You must go to her," she cried quite suddenly.

"Go to whom?" he asked.

"To Miss Lovington."

"Wh-why would you say such a thing?" he asked startled. "Why would I wish to do so?"

She smiled but in her eyes was a surprising sadness. "I was not thinking of you," she said. "I merely do not like to think of her walking home alone. No lady is ever truly safe even in so gentle and sweet a place as Portislow. Pray, go to her, my lord." When he hesitated, she pressed his hands, and continued, "Indeed, I will not be easy until I know that she is returned safely to camp."

He was about to protest, but she added, "I beg you will do so, for my sake. I will not rest until I know she is safe."

"Very well," he murmured. He knew she was speaking sensibly. "A young lady ought not to be on foot, at night and unprotected—especially Miss Lovington. I have always thought her a rather capable female, perhaps even able to protect herself for I know that Mr. Ash has taught her how to do so. However, I should go. I believe you are right. Yes, of course you are right. I shall do so at once."

He released her hands and offered a bow, then returned to the adjoining conservatory.

If the moment he passed through the doorway into the cool night air his heart began to beat a little more strongly in his chest, he ignored such a ridiculous thumping. He would do as Miss Currivard—the woman he knew he should make his wife—had bid him. He would escort Judith back to her tent, he would leave her and that would be the end of the matter.

Once he reached a breach in the path that afforded a view of the narrow valley below, he caught sight of Judith in the lane. He knew she could not have left but a few minutes before, yet he was surprised by how far she had gone.

He began to walk faster.

TEN

"Miss Lovington!" he called out.

Judith had just reached the edge of the apple orchard, through which she meant to take a shorter path to camp when Kelthorne called to her from behind.

She was greatly surprised and not a little dismayed. She did not understand why he had followed her. Indeed, she wished he would go away. She waited for him but as soon as he reached her, she lifted her chin. "I cannot imagine why you have come to me," she cried. "Indeed, I wish you would go away." She was still stinging after his impertinent and wholly inappropriate question.

"I have been asked by Miss Currivard to escort you to your camp. She has insisted quite adamantly so I beg you will indulge her directive and not bite my head off. 'Twas not my notion."

"Very well, but I mean to traverse your orchard unless, of course, you have an objection for someone of my low character to do so."

He lifted his chin as well. "I have no objection."

She seethed. "Very well, then." She had no intention of speaking with him. He might accompany her but that hardly demanded conversation.

After a third of the rows had been accomplished, he said, "I suppose I must beg your forgiveness." He did not sound in the least penitent.

"I would not desire you to *strain* yourself, my lord."

"I think my supposition was reasonable," he said in his defense, but his tone was much softened. "Given the strength of your reaction, however, I must deduce that I was incorrect."

She did not want to give him answer. She did not see why she must justify to him anything she did. Yet, there was something in his voice that compelled her to at least say, "You were."

He stopped her suddenly. "Will you not then tell me how it is you came to be with the troupe, for I can think of no other reason for you to have done so than that you had disgraced yourself. And yet, knowing you as I do, I cannot imagine how that might have been."

She looked up into his face. Moonlight through the leaves of the apple tree once more dappled his face. She could see that he was wholly sincere, even concerned. "My lord," she murmured, laughing in frustration, "I cannot tell you. To do so would be to reveal things that would place me in harm's way. You must trust me in this."

He began walking again but slapped the lower branch of the next tree. An apple thudded to the grassy turf below. "Very well," he stated. "I suppose I must allow it."

"'Tis not about your allowing it," she said feeling rather cheerful. "The truth is that you can have no choice in the matter and I believe that is the thistle in this field."

He growled his frustration.

She chuckled. Perhaps she had come to understand him a little after all. "So tell me, how did you enjoy our performance this evening?" Perhaps a change of subject would set their uneven friendship to rights.

He chuckled and shook his head. "My God, where do I begin in answering this question? I was enchanted, charmed, cast completely beneath your spell as was everyone in the room, I have little doubt."

She felt her cheeks grow warm. She had not meant to solicit so many compliments. "Thank you. I am gratified but I must confess that though Margaret plays quite well for one who was never before schooled in the art, Miss Currivard's abilities made the experience rather sublime for me."

"She is an angel."

"She is a good friend." Judith remembered her kind words in the music room.

"She seems to take a great deal of interest in you."

"Yes," she said, remembering their cryptic conversation. "Though I must say I am not certain why that is, save that we seem to have a very natural and warm rapport between us."

"Indeed?" he said, meeting her gaze.

"Aye," she responded. "Were my circumstances different, I think we would become the best of friends. There is a great sensitivity and understanding of the world in Miss Currivard that one does not often find. I admire her a great deal."

He frowned a little. "I believe you are right."

For Judith, this agreement softened her feelings toward him. "I wish you to know that I do think of you as a friend as well and I do not mean to offer offense by not being more forthcoming about my past."

"In turn, I have pressed you beyond what is acceptable. Although I must say, I would hope that one day you would be able to trust me to such an extent that you would feel safe in confiding in me, but perhaps that is far too much to expect."

Judith sighed, for this speech reminded her that the troupe would not stay forever in Portislow. Such knowledge, however, made her feel less threatened in his presence. She liked him very much. Indeed, there were moments when her longing for his company was so strong that she wondered if perhaps Cupid had touched her with one of his gold-tipped arrows. Were she to remain in Portislow, therefore, she did not think she would have dared say, as she did now, "I have been very happy here. There have been occasions when I have wished I might remain in Somerset forever. There is much to the county and to this vicinity that quite enchants me. Were you often at the castle before you inherited?"

"No," he stated with a laugh. "And had you known my uncle you would understand quite to perfection why it was that I was not."

She chuckled. "Not everyone is made for society. I dare say your uncle was just such a sort."

"To say the very least, I assure you."

"You seem on excellent terms with your sisters."

Again, he chuckled. "If you mean they feel obligated to offer their opinions on every possible subject pertaining to my private affairs then yes we are, indeed, on excellent terms."

She smiled and found that she did not wish to hurry to camp so quickly as before. She slowed her steps and he kept pace. "I envy you your sisters. I had no siblings. My mother died when I was very young, two or three, I believe."

"And did your father remarry?"

"Yes, but there was no issue. He fell very ill after a time." The words spoken into the night air brought so much sadness flooding her heart that she had to give herself a strong shake. "There are no Lovingtons other than I."

He glanced at her. "And is Lovington your real name?"

"No, of course not. 'Tis a ridiculous name, but fit for a songstress I think."

"Indeed? And what is—"

"I shan't tell you!" she cried, but she was smiling. From the first, this was what she had enjoyed in being with him. When they were not brangling, there was a natural, teasing quality to their discourse that pleased her immensely.

He pressed his hand to his heart. "I feel quite overwhelmed that you have confided at least this much in me, that you are not Judith Lovington. That must account for something."

"Yes, it accounts for my stupidity."

He laughed quite heartily. "How you delight me," he cried.

She glanced at him, another warmth climbing her cheeks. Could he have said anything in this moment that would have pleased her more? She thought not.

The subject quickly fell to questions he posed her about each member of the troupe. More than once she stopped their progress entirely in order to turn toward him and tell him some anecdote or other about the troupe's numerous experiences throughout the kingdom. Finally, he led her to an old log upon which he overlaid his coat that her skirts might not become soiled. She sat beside him listening to undoubtedly somewhat abbreviated tales of his many adventures.

She observed, "Do you not believe that having lived in a manner that was not in the least traditional—as I have and even as Miss Currivard has—that one gains a perspective of life that one would not have otherwise? I have thought so often, for instance, that in any class of people, there are those who live and walk with integrity and those who would find it impossible to offer a definition of the word in their speech, manners and especially their conduct. Many, for instance, who go by the name of gentleman are nothing of the sort. And I should in turn happily apply the term to any number of men I have known in our travels even though they might speak with so thick an accent as to be unintelligible."

Kelthorne looked into her eyes, glittering as they had that first night, beneath the scattered moonbeams piercing the orchard. "I believe I must agree quite wholeheartedly with you," he said, surprised a little that his voice had fallen to little more than a murmur. A breeze swept a dangling curl over her cheek and instinctively he brushed it back toward her ear, his fingers touching her skin. He heard her sigh softly.

He met her gaze fully once more. He had never, throughout their slow walk through the orchard, considered kissing her, but the thought entered his head now with such force that before he could consider what he was about, he slid his hand behind her neck, leaned forward and placed his lips gently on hers.

She did not withdraw, a circumstance that gave him courage. The hand that supported her neck now slipped behind her back and drew her close. He felt her hand settle upon his arm, even fingering the soft fabric of his shirt and he deepened the kiss. How readily she parted her lips and received him. How greedily he responded, kissing her as though 'twould be the last time he would ever kiss again.

Suddenly, she pushed him back. "You should not," she said softly.

"Of course not," he whispered. "But I cannot seem to resist you in this moment." He drew her to her feet and kissed her again.

Judith was bewitched. She could account for her conduct in no other way. She was allowing Kelthorne to kiss her, the man who would soon be betrothed to a lady who had befriended her, who had shown her great kindness, who was making her dreams of owning a cottage one day come sooner than she had ever thought possible. But, oh, the magic of his caress! She did not understand why he could command her so easily except that they had been talking for an hour or two in the most delightful, the most intimate manner, sharing thoughts and ideas. How she treasured each second that he possessed her in this sweet, wondrous way, for she would soon leave Somerset.

She clung to him, to an impossible dream that she refused even now to acknowledge fully, a desire that she could have what she had grown up to believe she would one day have— a husband, children, a home shared with the man she loved. As he plied her lips so tenderly, she wondered if she loved him, if that perhaps might explain how easily she could lean into him in this scandalous manner. Did she love him?

She drew back again and searched his eyes. He held her hand close to his cheek and kissed her fingers. The hour was late. Margaret must be waiting for her. She must go.

"I must return to camp. Margaret always waits for me."

"Of course." He retrieved his coat and put it back on.

Perhaps a quarter mile yet remained, but never had so short a space required so much time to traverse. That Kelthorne stopped to kiss her again and again made the approaching destination a hated thing. Judith felt agitated, even when she kissed him, as though each kiss would be the last and that as soon as the sun rose on the morrow, some great breach would occur to separate their worlds even more.

In this moment, she resented Lord Stolford more than she ever had before. It was his doing that now prevented her from being worthy of Kelthorne and yet it was his doing that had brought her to Portislow this summer. How great an irony!

"I shall remember this night as long as I live," she whispered. She stood with him now at the edge of the orchard. They were but a few hundred yards from the camp. She searched his eyes, barely visible in the pale moonlight. She could not imagine his thoughts.

Kelthorne wanted more of Judith, particularly since with each day that passed, the hour drew near when not only would the troupe leave with her forever, but he would be forced to oblige his family and take a wife. He felt angry suddenly, angry that she had made him feel things he did not wish to feel, that perhaps love was possible after all. Yet the woman he desired was not fit to be the Countess of Kelthorne.

He kissed her roughly, his hand traveling along her cheek, her throat and sliding firmly over her breast. He might as well take now what he could not have in marriage.

As soon as these thoughts entered his head and as soon as his hand gave a delighted squeeze, she drew back abruptly, pushing his hand away. She did not speak but reproached him with her gaze.

He was angry. "You permitted me to kiss you well enough," he whispered, trying to draw near again, but she backed away.

"I beg you will not," she returned sharply.

"Why do you demur now?" he spat. He tried to take her in his arms once more, but she crushed the heel of her shoe against the soft top of his foot and he reeled back in pain.

"Good night, my lord," she stated firmly. He saw the tears sparkling on her lashes.

She turned to go but even in his pain he lunged and caught her elbow. "How dare you pretend to be what you cannot possibly be!" he cried, not knowing why he was speaking so cruelly to her.

"And you, on the brink of offering for a wonderful young lady! Are you no less a hypocrite, if I am so? What manner of libertine are you? I begin to think you as bad as Stolford!"

He glared at her for a long moment. "Were you a man, I should call you out for that remark."

This time, when she turned and began the last part of the journey back to camp, he let her go. He watched her until she was safely past the first line of tents. Only then did he make his way back to the castle.

"You are quite mistaken," Judith cried. "I am not overset in the least!" She pushed past Margaret who was standing in the middle of her tent and stubbed her toe on her dressing table. "Ow!"

Margaret held her hands wide. "Ye have been in high dudgeon all morning. Ye have and that!"

"I do not know of what you are speaking!" Judith cried. "Now, if you please, I am gathering clothes to take to the church."

"I have two shirts finished as well," Margaret said. "And Mrs. Marnhull has several stockings she knitted."

"Why do you stare at me in that manner?" Judith inquired hotly. "I promise you I am perfectly well!"

Margaret's shoulders slumped. "As though I have not known ye these eight years."

Judith tossed her head. "Well, today ye are mistaken!"

"Now I know ye are troubled fer ye never say 'ye'!"

Judith sat down carefully on her bed and covered her face with her hands. "I—I should not be so upset! I am being ridiculous! I have always understood the opinion in which I would be held by any of the gentlemen I would meet or even engage in rational conversation. I am not so naïve and yet . . ." She began to weep. She had not meant to weep. She despised herself for becoming a watering pot, yet it would seem the tears must come.

Margaret knelt before her and petted her head for her hair was still undone and her long chestnut curls hung down her back. "What terrible thing did 'is lordship do?"

Judith sniffed soundly and withdrawing a kerchief from the pocket of her gown blew her nose. "How do you know it was his lordship?" she asked, as though pretence had any meaning at all.

"And who else 'twould it be, Judy?"

Judith swiped angrily at two more tears daring to roll down her cheeks. "I . . . I have grown so attached to his company. And last night, we talked and talked for hours. Well, you know how late it was, nearly two o'clock."

"And I saw that ye were overset."

"I was. I am. At any rate, I could not credit so much time had passed but we dawdled so in the orchard. Only with the greatest effort did I keep myself from revealing all of my past to him but even so he knows now nearly as much as you do. Then . . . then he kissed me."

Margaret sighed. "And to kiss such a man."

"Yes, I know. And it is far better than one can even imagine for he is the most tender of men. Is that not surprising when he is such an athletic sort?"

"Aye, very surprising. But a kiss does not sound so very bad."

"'Twas more than one kiss. Perhaps two score."

"Oh," Margaret murmured. "I see. Is that why ye are so

distressed? That ye kissed him in what he might have thought were an unseemly manner?"

"An *unseemly manner*? You are beginning to sound like a lady of quality."

"Split me corset, I am and that!" she cried, smiling broadly.

Judith laughed and blew her nose once more. Her amusement faded abruptly. "He became quite rude in the end and I do not precisely comprehend why."

"What did he say?"

"I fear it was not just what he said, but rather that he became agitated and I fear he touched me as he should not have and then he said, 'How dare you pretend to be what you cannot possibly be?' I was mortified and so angry. I cannot tell you how angry I was. I thought my head would come off!"

Margaret leaned back on her heels appearing pensive. "I think he might have grown afraid of ye in that moment."

"Afraid of me? What do you mean?"

"Afraid of his feelings fer ye. Like he realized he was in love with ye but could do naught about it."

Judith shook her head. Was it possible? "It seems so unlikely. I truly felt he was judging me again by my situation."

"Think, Judy," she said, clasping her hand firmly. "From what ye've said, there be a great bond between the pair of ye. To talk fer hours, 'tis not so common as ye might think."

"I think he wished for me to become his mistress," she said mournfully.

"That would make things simple fer him but 'twould not make him happy. There is only one thing 'twould make him happy and ye know wat that be."

"I do not," she said, sitting up very straight. "How can I possibly know what would make him happy?"

"Because, my girl, ye've been kissing him all night. Yer in love with him and he is in love, too. I've little doubt."

Judith covered her face again. She could not listen to her

for to believe such things was to allow thoughts in her head that ought not to be there.

She rose suddenly to her feet. "I must go. No, no, I beg you, Margaret, let us discuss this no more. I do not think I can bear it a moment longer. Let me walk to the church. Perhaps my head will clear with a little exertion."

Margaret stayed her, however. "At least let me fix yer hair."

Judith touched her hair and laughed. "I forgot that I had not yet dressed it. Oh, dear!"

An hour later, Judith found herself nearing the church, the basket of clothes in her arms growing, as it always did, surprisingly heavy after a mile or two on foot. A walk had been quite beneficial and she was calmer than she had previously been. She had reconciled in her mind that she thought it likely Kelthorne had become uneasy in the depth of his regard for her and had provoked her in order to end so sweet and magical and, indeed, quite hopeless an evening. She had, therefore, resigned herself anew to keeping her distance from him especially in the light of her growing friendship with Miss Currivard.

In this particular aspect of her conduct of the night before, she could not be content. Miss Currivard was her support, her friend, and her patroness. She had in that sense used her quite ill and meant not to do so again.

Fortunate for her that she had made such a resolution for when she entered the ancient Norman church, she met Miss Currivard who bore in her arms a large bouquet of roses and ferns.

"Well met, Miss Lovington," she cried. "I have come with Kelthorne's sisters to decorate the church."

"How beautiful," Judith murmured, the fragrance of the red roses filling the air all about her. She glanced in the direction of the nave and saw that Lady Radsbury and Mrs. Newnott were conversing with a rather tall, thin gentleman who seemed vaguely familiar to Judith. The dark interior of the stone church did not easily allow for recognition. "I have come on a mission of my own. Some of the ladies of the troupe sew for the poor and I have come to bring our little offering."

Miss Currivard settled her roses on a table nearby and recommended Judith do the same. She was grateful to set the basket down. Miss Currivard then picked up a boy's shirt. "Is this your work?" she exclaimed.

"Yes, that one happens to be."

"It is very fine. And how wonderful to see little dogs embroidered down the front. Charming! Truly charming!"

"I always feel so guilty though in taking the time to do the embroidery work when there is so much need for clothes generally. I suppose with the same effort I could have sewn another garment entirely."

Miss Currivard shook her head. "You are too severe upon yourself. You worry excessively. My thoughts are very different. Were I a little boy, in such desperate circumstances, I should be comforted by all these little brown pups in a way that I could never be by a mere plain shirt. Yes, Miss Lovington, too severe by half!"

Judith laughed and thanked her for her compliments and her kindness.

Miss Currivard glanced up the aisle in the direction of Kelthorne's sisters. She appeared to hesitate and a slight frown creased her brow. "I believe I must make the introduction," she said, her voice low. "Propriety demands it but I truly wish it were otherwise. Pray, forgive me."

"Now who is being severe," Judith returned laughing. She could not imagine any friends of the castle party being in the least objectionable.

As Judith turned to walk up the aisle with Miss Currivard, she wondered whom the gentleman might be. In quick stages, since her eyes had by now become better accustomed to the dim interior of the church, she realized who he was. Dizziness assailed her causing her to grasp Miss Currivard's arm more tightly than she ought.

Stolford.

"Is something amiss?" Miss Currivard inquired quietly as they moved together.

"No," Judith whispered, struggling to regain her composure as quickly as possible. She took long, deep breaths and avoided Miss Currivard's curious glances.

Once Judith had greeted Kelthorne's sisters, Miss Currivard made the introductions. "My lord, may I present our famous local songstress, Miss Lovington."

"Miss Lovington, the Marquess of Stolford."

She dipped a proper curtsy and bowed her head. She rose slowly.

He bowed as well. "I have heard much of you, Miss Lovington. Lady Radsbury praised you so highly in her last letter that I found I—" he broke off and stared at her. "You are very familiar to me, but I cannot quite—"

Recognition dawned, of that she was certain. Judith struggled to keep her composure. Fear had taken strong hold of her.

A familiar smile shaped his lips, one that set her knees to trembling. His eyes grew clouded. She wondered if he meant to betray her identity even in this moment.

"But I am being uncivil," he said. "Forgive me for staring at you but I thought for a moment I had met you in London this season past but now I am certain I am utterly mistaken. I hope to hear you sing very soon."

"The troupe with which I am presently engaged will be performing this Saturday when I am given to understand the fair will have arrived in Portislow." She then dipped another curtsy. "I beg you will excuse me, Miss Currivard, Lady Radsbury, Mrs. Newnott, but I am frightfully late for a rehearsal and I must speak with the good vicar before I depart." She turned and moved back down the aisle, picking up her basket on the way.

Once outside, she moved more swiftly, not stopping until she had reached the shrubbery nearest the entrance to the vicarage where she paused. Tears filled her eyes. She trembled from head to foot. She leaned forward slightly and felt for the dagger she kept concealed beneath her skirts in a sheath strapped carefully to her leg. What comfort to feel it against her hand. Only then did her heart begin to grow quiet and the trembling grow less marked.

Slowly, she made her way to the door and left the clothes with the serving maid.

Her worst fears had been realized—Stolford, even though by accident, had found her at last.

"Where were you?" Laurence asked.

Kelthorne looked up from the stirrup he was adjusting on his favorite gelding only to find Laurence glaring at him. "I have been out riding. Why do you ask? More to the point, why are you in the boughs?"

Laurence ground his teeth. "You will not be flippant with me. Not me. Not this time, Aubrey. I won't have it! I will have an answer!"

Kelthorne turned his horse over to his groom, whose eyes had grown rather wide with surprise. He said nothing until the servant had led the gelding away. "For God's sake," he murmured, tossing his head in the direction of the groom. "What the devil was that? You know better than to come the crab before the servants." He began easing off his riding gloves as he spoke. He could not help but be astonished by his usually sanguine friend.

"You know I have reason enough," he growled.

Kelthorne frowned at him. "I cannot say that I do since I do not know what it is I have done to so offend you." With one glove off, he let the other remain that he might concentrate fully upon Laurence.

"You must have feathers in your head if you have not the smallest understanding of . . . that is . . . Aubrey, have you not noticed how she looks at you?"

"Of whom are you speaking? Judith?" His head had been

full of her all morning; of the latest kisses he had taken from her, of her refusal to share her charms with him and of his truly wretched words to her.

"Judith?" Laurence cried, a web of small veins standing out on his now crimson forehead. "You think I am referring to Miss Lovington?"

Kelthorne stared at his friend. "I now apprehend that you are speaking of Miss Currivard, but I do not understand. Of what are you speaking?"

Laurence glanced apace about the stables and since more than one groom was present, he jerked his head to the doorway and stomped in that direction. Kelthorne began working his second glove off as he followed after him. He tried to determine in just what manner he might have erred with Miss Currivard but he was damned if he could think of anything inappropriate he had said or done to her.

Catching up with his friend, he said, "Speak plainly, for I fear I am at a complete loss."

"So it would seem," he responded coldly. "I will tell you, then. I sat with Miss Currivard until two o'clock in the morning—this morning! She was awaiting your return. Apparently, she needed to know that Miss Lovington was returned safely to her tent. So, was she, Aubrey? Was she returned safely? Did no particular harm befall her? No horrible accident requiring the fetching of a surgeon, let us say, from Wells or perhaps even Bath, that might per chance account for the tardiness of your return to Portislow!"

Kelthorne's heart sank. "It never occurred to me that she would be waiting for me."

"Are you completely shatterbrained?" he asked hotly. "Have you no sense, no powers of observation at all? Miss Currivard is in love with you, man! Even a simpleton could see as much and you have, well, you have insulted her profoundly."

"I did not want to escort Jud—that is, Miss Lovington back to her camp. 'Twas Miss Currivard who forced the matter. I did not think it at all necessary or even wise. She all but forced us together. Besides, I am not in the least persuaded she is in love with me."

Laurence squeezed his eyes shut, clenched his fists and growled a little more. "You will now make excuses for your conduct? Or did you think her such a ninnyhammer that she would believe your absence only meant that you were looking at the night sky for four hours?"

"I confess I did not think of her at all," he replied.

"Then what happened? Did you have your way with Miss Lovington?"

"Good God, no," he cried. He felt uneasy now. His conscience prickled him sorely, but he resented having his misdeeds thrust in his face. "Though I do not see why I must justify anything I have done—especially not to you. This is not like you, Laurence. Since when were you ever concerned about the appetites of one of the acting corps? Or even of mine?" He laughed, hoping to lighten the situation but there was no answering smile on Laurence's face.

"I will tell you," Laurence said, "because you have never been on the brink of offering for a lady before. Everything has changed yet you seem unable to comprehend as much. You cannot dally with Miss Lovington and think for a moment a young woman of Miss Currivard's stamp will be accepting of your exploits even before the marriage documents are drawn."

He was right. Kelthorne knew he was right. He had been foolish beyond permission last night in many respects just as he had been that first night upon chasing Judith down on horseback.

"I am a very poor suitor," Kelthorne stated. "Good God! I have been rather wretched, it would seem. But . . ." He could not complete his thought, for his mind had grown suddenly full of Judith and how he had felt the night before in her company, how much he had delighted in being with her and never would he have thought so many hours had passed while strolling in his orchard with her. "It was as though time had changed in a way that made no sense. I vow I did not believe I had been gone so long. I was never more shocked upon finding that when I reached my bedchamber, the clock in the entrance hall was chiming half past two."

"Are you in love with her?" Laurence asked nonsensically.

"The devil take it!" he cried. "Now who is shatterbrained? Judith Lovington is an actress. I admit to a mild *tendre* for her but nothing more. In love with her! What a stupid thought! A very . . . very . . . well, it is quite absurd!"

"A mild *tendre* that somehow has the power to bend time?"

"Now you are being dramatic."

"Am I? Well, it does not matter. Merely, I beg you will be more considerate of the feelings of the lady you mean to make your wife."

"I shall," he responded sincerely. "Of course, I shall. I must do better and I will. I promise you I will."

When Kelthorne reached the drawing room, he found Miss Currivard and her friends within, all standing at the window looking out over the valley below.

"Come!" Miss Banwell cried. "There is such a sight!"

"Indeed!" Miss Currivard echoed. "You must come at once!" Rufus, who had been sitting by her side, trotted up to him.

Kelthorne petted his head and glanced at Miss Currivard. He had used her very badly, indeed, but he would do better. Chastened by his friend's admonishments, he went immediately to Miss Currivard and smiled warmly upon her. "What is it?" he asked.

"Do but look! They are setting up even more tents. I vow before long it will appear as though an entire regiment is camped in your vale."

Kelthorne looked out at what was becoming a sea of tents.

"The fair!" Miss Upton cried. "The fair is come!"

ELEVEN

On the following day, Kelthorne glanced to his left and then his right then back again. The fair had come to town and there were at least two score of stalls to see. Hundreds of people were milling about, children squealing, dogs barking, sheep and cattle joining in the noisy fray and hawkers of every sort exclaiming the benefits of their wares.

"So what is it?" Miss Currivard asked loudly in order to be heard.

"I beg your pardon," he returned.

"Were you not listening to me?" she asked. "Do you see that, Mr. Doulting? Lord Kelthorne was not attending me. What do you think of that?"

Kelthorne already knew Laurence's opinion and was not surprised when he cast him a rather scathing glance over Miss Currivard's head. "I do beg your pardon," Kelthorne began, "but fear I am grown distracted by all these stalls. Look at this one. There must be a hundred different kinds of whistles and all carved by this man."

"Ye be right, sir," the whistle craftsman said. "I'll be happy to demonstrate them all, if ye like."

"Why do we not purchase one for that little girl, the one in the troupe?" Miss Currivard suggested.

Kelthorne glanced at her and the strangest burst of excitement rushed through his veins. "I think it an excellent notion." He could give the whistle to Judith for her to give later to young Shelly. Perhaps he could speak with Judith and beg her forgiveness for his conduct in the orchard. Perhaps he could walk with her again, a midnight stroll beneath another spate of moonlight and he would brush another curl from her cheek. He gave himself a shake and turned to Miss Currivard fully. "You are very good," he stated. At the very least, a compliment was in order.

"Am I?" Miss Currivard inquired. "How kind of you to notice." She laughed brightly then bid the craftsman to wrap up the whistle. "For it is to be a present for a young friend of ours."

"Wery good, ma'am."

Kelthorne met Laurence's disapproving gaze. He had erred somehow, both his friend's scathing expression and Miss Currivard's odd laughter told him he had given offense, but unless Miss Currivard could actually read his thoughts, he did not know in what manner he had been unkind, if indeed, he had been!

He strove to become more attentive to Miss Currivard, which served, oddly enough, to set a rather grim expression on Laurence's face. He began to wonder what was wrong with his friend. He was never satisfied these days and he was frequently as cross as crabs.

Two full days had passed since he had last seen and kissed Judith. During that time, he had attempted to right his conduct toward Miss Currivard yet strangely enough she had grown somewhat guarded, though he believed except for having arrived home so late the night he escorted Judith back to camp, he had not otherwise given her reason to doubt the sincerity of his intentions toward her.

If he was distracted today, however, with all the sights and sounds of the fair to confuse him, how could she possibly find fault with that?

He was about to offer his arm when he heard Judith's voice as clearly as if she were but a few yards away.

"Did you hear that?" he inquired sharply, turning toward Laurence.

"Hear what? That man selling his sheep is squawking so loudly that I can scarcely hear anything else!"

"There it is again!" he cried. "I believe it is Jud—that is, Miss Lovington. I beg you will excuse me."

He moved in the direction they had just come. To the right there was a breach in the stalls forming a long alleyway. He went down the breach and heard her again.

"I beg you will not, my lord!" she cried. "Else I shall not be able to account for what I must do next."

He turned the corner and felt a bolt of rage pass through him. Stolford had pressed Judith up against a wagon. He was laughing and kissing her neck because she was bent sideway.

"To think of finding you here," he said, laughing a little more.

Kelthorne moved quickly in their direction. He watched Judith lift her skirt on her right side and saw what looked like a leather sheath strapped to her leg. Good God, her dagger!

"Stolford!" he called out sharply. "A little early for such mischief, is it not?"

The marquess let her go and at the same moment, Judith, whose cheeks were flaming, lowered her skirts. He had expected to find her in near hysterics. Instead, the look in her eye was nothing short of murderous. In that instant, he glimpsed the last eight years of her life.

The marquess recovered swiftly. "Ah, Kelthorne. 'Tis only you. By God, are not the ladies of this troupe some of the prettiest we have ever seen? This wench, I believe to be the loveliest of them all." He took Judith's arm, but like a cat twisting in mid-air, she jerked from his hold and before Kelthorne could caution her, she struck Stolford hard across the face.

Before Stolford could respond, Kelthorne was beside her instantly, an arm stretched between them. "Enough, Stolford. The lady has made herself understood. I beg you will leave her in peace and depart."

He watched as a shuddering passed through the marquess. The years had served only to toughen him. He was quite lean, even athletic and more than once he had witnessed Stolford taking a boxing lesson from Jackson in London. He was capable of inflicting brutal damage.

Stolford's brown eyes flashed a fiery glare as he met Judith's equally angry countenance. She lifted her chin. "Do not think for a moment," she said, "that I am still a child of fourteen. I have learned a great deal in eight years and I give you fair warning that if you come near me again, I shall not answer for the consequences."

Kelthorne was stunned. At last, he understood all of it.

Lord Stolford relaxed his countenance and began to laugh. "Well, I did not expect to have so much fun at a fair. Good day to you, Miss, er, *Lovington*. I trust when we meet again, you will have forgiven my, shall we say, improper comprehension of your wishes." He even bowed.

When he was gone, Kelthorne finally lowered his arm and looked at Judith. Once more, he expected hysterics instead there was an expression of dismay. She pressed her hand to her forehead. He did not know what she was thinking. Finally she said, "I must go. At once. Margaret is waiting for me."

She moved away, but he caught her arm. She withdrew from his hold sharply and turned to stare at his hand. "I beg you will not!" she cried. She appeared horrified.

"I am sorry," he said softly. "Judith, indeed, are you certain you are all right?"

"I am perfectly well," she responded in a flat voice, but her hands were frozen in mid-air. "I must go."

"Not until I am persuaded you are uninjured."

She stared at him for a long moment. Something in her eyes began to clear. Her breathing became steadier. "Lord Kelthorne," she stated as though seeing him for the first time. She lowered her hands and arms.

"Yes, that is much better," he said, drawing close.

"He surprised me," she explained. "I was just passing

there." She turned and pointed between a pair of tents. "The next thing I knew, he had pulled me over to this wagon. How I despise him!"

"Would you have done it?" he asked, searching her eyes.

She shook her head and frowned. "Done what? I do not take you meaning."

"The dagger. The one you keep strapped to your leg. Would you have done him an injury?"

"Of course," she stated in such simplicity that a chill went through him.

"But do you not realize what the consequences would have been?"

She chuckled but her amusement was dark. "And what would the consequences have been had I not used my dagger? Will you answer me that? Will you tell me that such a fate would be preferable?"

"To death, yes," he cried emphatically.

"I had rather be dead," she returned.

He stared down at her trying to comprehend how she could possibly believe such a thing.

"Pray do not remonstrate with me," she added, her eyes growing wild once more. "For I fear I could not bear it."

Compassion flowed through him and without pondering the right or wrong of it he took her gently in his arms, holding her close. "All will be well," he murmured. "All will be well."

He felt her begin to shake. She gasped in deep breaths in an effort to keep from sobbing.

After a time, he asked quietly, "Do I understand now that Stolford is the reason you left your father?"

"Yes. Papa was very ill and my stepmother had made an arrangement with Stolford. She had all but sold me to him. My governess helped me escape while she fled to the Colonies for fear of his retribution. I tried to go to my uncle's but by the time I reached his house, Stolford's carriage was in the drive. Though I remained, waiting and watching for an opportunity, his servants seemed to be everywhere, anticipating my arrival no doubt. I slept in one of the out-buildings but grew so hungry and still Stolford remained. Finally, in my young mind, I concluded 'twas hopeless. I traversed the countryside in a northerly direction, stealing food from gardens and orchards. I wandered for days until I found the troupe. Margaret took me in."

"Good God," he whispered, holding her tightly. "How you have suffered! My dear, Judith, I am so very sorry." He patted her gently on the back but fell silent as he pondered these revelations. He had heard horrible things of Stolford over the years and here was just one example of his wholly debauched character. Fortunately, the marquess had failed in his attempts to do injury to Judith. He could only imagine the horror she was feeling at having been found after eight long years.

He felt her body relax in stages and at last the trembling ceased. "Thank you," she said, drawing away from him. She drew a kerchief from the pocket of her gown and wiped at her cheeks.

He looked down at her, wishing only one thing, that she were still locked in his arms. He wanted to hold her forever, to comfort her, to make a thousand promises that the world would now be right for her. He realized that somewhere in the middle of it all, a great sensation of love had formed in his chest. Good God, was it possible he did love her as Laurence had suggested?

At last, she drew in a deep breath. "But there is something you must promise me," she said, looking at him intently.

"Anything, you have my word."

"You must not tell anyone what I have just revealed to you."

"But Stolford should be exposed," he cried. "You should be allowed to resume your life. 'Tis not right!"

"Perhaps there will be a proper moment, but not now. You must let me see this to its conclusion in my own way."

"But why?"

"Because I fear, as I have from the first, that he would do harm to my uncle and my cousins were I to make public his conduct toward me."

Kelthorne knew quite well that the Marquess of Stolford wielded considerable power. He was a man of great wealth and extensive political connections. In this, Judith was right—perhaps more than even she knew. He thought of his sisters and their belief that Stolford had reformed his character. If the marquess took offense against them, what manner of retribution would he exact? He had but one choice in this situation, to acquiesce.

"I will only say this," he began, "that if an appropriate moment arises, I will see the deed done, but not so long as you are in the vicinity. Do not be concerned. I will not bring your name forward on any account."

"Thank you," she said. She looked up the alleyway. "There are Miss Currivard and Mr. Doulting." She blew her nose.

"They were with me when I heard you." He turned and waved.

"You heard me?" she inquired, staring up at him as one shocked. "But how is that possible with so much noise? I vow I can hear nothing of the moment but that wretched man hawking his sheep."

Kelthorne smiled. "I cannot account for it, but I did hear you. We must have been," he glanced around at the adjoining tents and gestured at several to the left of Miss Currivard and Laurence, "there, beyond which is the stall with all the whistles for sale."

"I still cannot believe you heard me."

Judith knew the time had come to leave him, but she found she did not want to. Of course, she was still overset about his previous conduct, but his presence today in helping to disrupt Stolford's wretched advances as well as his tenderness in comforting her allayed much of her former distress.

Miss Currivard waved to her. "Will you join us, Miss Lovington?" she called out.

Judith felt certain she should not.

"Yes, will you please," Kelthorne said. "I should like Stolford to see you with us, that he might know his advances are not only unwelcome by you but by me and by Doulting as well."

He offered his arm. Again, she felt the strongest need to leave him on the instant, but she could not. She took his arm. "Thank you. I am most grateful."

"You are quite welcome."

Leading her to Miss Currivard, he felt obliged to say in a low voice, "I found Stolford here."

Laurence started and Miss Currivard frowned heavily as she searched Judith's face. "I have always heard he was the worst of libertines," she said. "Did he, that is, did he do you an injury?"

"No," she answered, but the tears started to her eyes again.

"He tried, though," Kelthorne explained. "I thought it might be wise if Miss Lovington walked with us for an hour or so in order that *his lordship* might begin to comprehend that she is not without friends."

Miss Currivard straightened her shoulders. "Indeed, she is not!" she cried, taking up Judith's other arm. "Come! You will pass the day with us and, hopefully, our paths will cross that beast's a score of times and we may all smirk at him."

"Well done," Mr. Doulting said.

Judith glanced at him and noted the warm expression in his eye as he smiled upon Miss Currivard. *How much he loves her*, she thought. She could not keep from looking up at Kelthorne to see if he, too had noticed the state of his friend's heart, but his gaze was fixed on the numerous people passing by.

"Well, I know the first thing we must do!" Miss Currivard cried. "We must have our fortunes told, all of us! Have you yet seen the Gypsy?"

"No, I have not," Judith returned, finding it difficult to enter into the spirit of the adventure.

"She is not far. In the next line of stalls, I believe. She is quite swarthy in appearance, so much so that I vow she must be a man in disguise. She has long whiskers to either side of her upper lip. She wears more gold, however, than I possess. Let us cross."

Mr. Doulting spoke quietly. "And there is Stolford. Come, let us make a jolly parade of it!"

"An excellent notion," Miss Currivard said. "Leave this to me. Come, Miss Lovington, walk beside me."

Judith released Kelthorne's arm and felt Miss Currivard wrap hers more firmly about her own. She then lifted her chin haughtily and led her not away from the marquess but in his direction, the gentlemen following.

"Why if it is not the Marquess of Stolford," Mr. Doulting cried out, a hard edge to his voice. "How do you go on? Have you met our friend, Miss Lovington?"

Stolford took in the entire party and lifted a rather indifferent brow. "Yes, of course, at the church but a few days past. How do you do, Miss Lovington? Are you enjoying the fair?"

Judith met his gaze squarely. She resolved never to forget this moment. She must never forget how devoid of character, principle and even the smallest proper sentiment he was, never to underestimate the depravity of a depraved man. "Prodigiously," she responded coldly. "We are to have our fortunes read, but mine I already know."

He bowed to her. "How very singular, to be sure."

"No, my lord. 'Tis purposed."

He bowed again. "I beg you will excuse me." He turned and moved away, waving to Lord Radsbury.

Once he was gone, Miss Currivard addressed Lord Kelthorne. "I cannot credit that your sisters would wish him at Portislow. Do they not know what he is? I was not in the least comfortable passing the night at his house. He leered at me so. I was only too grateful to be going on the following morning, I assure you."

The next hour or so proved extremely pleasant for Judith.

Mr. Doulting never permitted the conversation to falter, not even for a second. At the same time, since many of his remarks seemed to be directed toward Miss Currivard, who in turn laughed heartily at his many jokes, Judith found herself more often than not engaged in a lively discourse with Kelthorne.

She was not quite certain how to account for the ease of their exchange except that given the great number of people at the fair and the frequent interruptions by Doulting with some amusing observation or other, she began to feel safe once more. After all, what harm could there be in strolling from stall to stall, conversing on every subject imaginable and, in the end, parting from him near the camp with a shake of the hand and a final offering of thanks for his intervention with Stolford.

She even teased him by saying archly, "For you must know you have spared me the humiliation of a public trial for I was intent upon making use of my weapon."

His smile was crooked. "You may speak lightly of it if you wish, but I believe I know you sufficiently by now to understand quite to perfection you would not have hesitated in using it."

She smiled in return. "Then you begin to understand me."

"There is one more thing," he said, his voice dropping to a murmur as he overlaid their joined hands with his remaining hand. "I treated you very badly in the orchard and I do apologize. I merely, that is, I think I became overwhelmed. I do not understand what is happening between us and I am not at liberty, nor would it be of any use, that is . . . the devil take it . . . I have no answer for you but I do apologize."

She smiled for her heart was feeling very full again. "I think I understand. I accept your apology."

His gaze caught and held as it so frequently did when she was in his company. She was struck anew by how handsome he was, the summer sunlight glinting on his blond locks. She did not know just how much time actually passed before she realized she was still holding his hand. The extended farewell bordered on impropriety. She withdrew her hand at last, offered a small curtsy and bid him good-day.

Kelthorne watched her join Mrs. Ash and Shelly. Judith took Shelly into her arms and gave the child a warm hug and began speaking with her in the sweet, lively manner she always used with the child. He could just make out her words. "You saw the bear?" she cried. "And was it very big? Were you not frightened?" Shelly's eyes grew wide as she responded, "Bigger than even Mrs. Marnhull's wagon or even . . ." The rest was lost to him since the ladies moved away.

He turned in the direction of Miss Currivard and Laurence who appeared to be deep in conversation. Miss Currivard even seemed a little sad. When he approached them, fully intent upon doing the pretty with Miss Currivard, he heard her say, "I am come to believe it is a hopeless case." Surprisingly, it appeared at the same time as though she brushed a tear from her cheek.

"What is a hopeless case?" he asked, joining them.

Miss Currivard blushed and stammered. Her eyes, indeed, were dewy. "Well, we were just speaking . . . that is, I am not certain . . . I suppose it hardly matters . . ."

When she broke off completely, Laurence added quickly, "We were speaking of Miss Lovington and her desire to purchase a cottage one day. I fear Miss Currivard has such a tender heart that she has become increasingly saddened by Miss Lovington's circumstances."

"Ah," he murmured. Miss Currivard did, indeed, have a good heart.

"Yes," Miss Currivard added, drawing in a deep breath. "We both believe it has become a rather hopeless case for her unless . . . well, unless she receives assistance from those who care about her."

"Quite so," Laurence said, nodding vigorously. "Friends like Miss Currivard and myself. We both mean to be of use to her."

"Yes, that is what we mean to do." She breathed a rather

strange sigh of relief. "And we hope you will be willing to be of use as well."

"Of course I should like to," he responded. "But do you truly believe 'tis so necessary?"

Miss Currivard regarded him for a long moment, then said, "Though I believe with all my heart in Miss Lovington's fine character, this life will wear on her as the years pass and when her choices become even more restricted, she will undoubtedly cave to such material pressures. I know I would."

Kelthorne was startled by such an admission. "How can you speak so?"

"You forget, my lord. My experience of the world is different from the majority of the ladies of your class. Of course I comprehend fully what a great privilege and comfort it is to be, shall we say, 'well-shod.' But I have also seen the sufferings, and not just in England, of impoverished women in my travels with my father. I think it a rare thing in a culture when a woman has as many opportunities as a man. If driven to poverty, a man may labor in the fields or in the mines or on sailing ships, but what can a lady do when cast from her home whatever the reason? I promise you I am in awe of what Miss Lovington has achieved. I want to help her as much as I can. I am determined to do it."

"As am I," Laurence cried.

Kelthorne knew they did not understand just how badly they were tormenting him. He desired to be of use to Judith as well but the more he was in her company, the more he could feel his heart becoming deeply attached to her and there was no purpose to it! She was a songstress, of no small merit to be sure, but traveling with an acting troupe! How could that ever make her a fit companion for him?

Yet, the more he was with her, the more his thoughts became constricted with a need to keep her close to his side forever. Short of wedding her, he could only make her his mistress, a thought which had been crossing his mind with greater and greater frequency. However, he could hardly do so with his prospective bride-to-be in residence beneath his roof and he would certainly not do so were he to enter into an engagement.

In truth, he did not know what to do. He did not know how to thwart the present philanthropic direction of the conversation without appearing heartless, even cruel.

"You both mean well, but I am not convinced it will serve."

At that, Laurence laughed. "Well, I fear you have no choice in the matter. Miss Currivard and I are determined to help her. You may partake of our schemes or absent yourself, it will not matter."

"Indeed, I am quite in agreement with Laurence," Miss Currivard said.

He was surprised she made use of his friend's Christian name but he could see that Laurence was quite pleased. He even crossed his arms over his chest and smirked at Kelthorne as though daring him to contest Miss Currivard on any score.

"Very well," he said, acquiescing. "You may rely upon me, but I hope you will not be disappointed if your plans do not reap the rewards you are seeking."

"That will be an impossibility," Miss Currivard cried, smiling broadly, "for the Gypsy promised me that I was to accomplish great things and so I mean to begin now. What do you say, Laurence, to a benefit concert for Miss Lovington?"

"An excellent notion only how shall we manage it?"

As the trio walked back to the castle, the entire trip was spent deciding just how the task could be accomplished while including the troupe at the same time. Kelthorne was rather surprised at the vigor with which the pair entered into their scheme. God knows he was not indifferent, not by half, but given his tendency to single Miss Lovington out whether he wished to or not, he thought it wise to keep silent and let Miss Currivard make her plans.

Later that afternoon, Judith sat beside Margaret as the whole troupe discussed quite heatedly the proposal laid be-

fore John and Margaret, in private, not a half hour earlier, by
Miss Currivard and Mr. Doulting. It would seem their intention was to host a benefit concert for the troupe and for
Judith jointly. The concert, if agreed to, would include the
best seats by invitation and requiring a minimum donation
of ten pounds—an enormous amount by any standard—per
person. Lesser seats would be at the usual prices, and those
who wished could attend for free making use of the grass,
blankets and the hillside. They had made it clear that the pri-
mary motivation was to help Miss Lovington secure her future and the secondary to be of use to Mr. Ash in his object
of seeing the troupe engaged in London. The proceeds
would be split in half just as the performance at the concert
would be split, Miss Lovington performing for one hour,
with Miss Currivard accompanying her, and the troupe, in
whatever manner appealed to the actors, for a second hour,
the arrangement of which would be entirely at Mr. Ash's dis-
cretion.

Judith could feel the resentment. She could not comprehend how Miss Currivard and Mr. Doulting could have been
so baconbrained in making such an offer. "Of course this is
nonsense," Judith cried. "I will not hear of such a thing. I
shall be happy to perform for an hour but the proceeds must
belong to the troupe and disbursed as is usual. A private musi-
cale is one thing, but this ridiculous scheme of theirs is quite
another."

"I see ye mean to show some sense!" Charles cried hotly.
He paced up and down between the fire ring and the tables.

"This is not a matter of sense, Charles, but of what is
right."

"What is right!" he cried, turning upon her sharply. "How
dare ye speak of what is right! Every time the troupe must
discuss *yer ladyship*, and whether some gentleman or other
has gone beyond the pale and the whole troupe must therefore pull up stakes and leave the countryside just to protect
ye—by God, were ye a man, I should plant ye a facer fer yer

audacity! Ye sing well enough, but ye have not a particle of the actress about ye. Of what use are ye to an acting troupe anyway?"

John moved toward him swiftly and caught his arm. "That be enough, Charlie. Judy has brought the crowds when all our recitings of *Richard*, *Henry* and *Hamlet* have failed to excite the smallest interest. So, I'll not have ye crowing in this manner. As fer the offer, I'll not see it refused fer I'll wager that it means a hefty addition to our purse and that must satisfy us all—fair or not!"

"She's bewitched ye as she has the castle ladies! Do none of ye see that she is more trouble than she is worth?" His voice was powerful and he threw his arms about in his practiced manner so that several members of the troupe began to mutter.

Judith had never liked Charles but in this moment, she had never quite understood the depths of his hatred for her. She knew he was justified in his complaints but she did not think that the level of his rage was reasonable. "I am willing to compromise and Miss Currivard need not know of my decision."

"Oh, but she will," Charles cried bitterly.

"I vow I would never say anything!" she cried defensively.

"'Tis not the problem, Judy," Margaret said. "It would seem Miss Currivard suspected either that the troupe would demand as much from ye or that ye would offer as ye have. She said the proceeds would go directly into an account to be held fer ye until ye was ready to purchase yer cottage."

Charles slapped his hand hard against his thigh. "'Tis not right!" he shouted. "'Tis a mockery of the troupe."

"Aye, it is!" Betty cried. The rest joined in soundly.

"I quite agree," Judith returned rising from her seat and addressing them all. "This is not as I would wish it to be. I beg you will believe me. I think there must be only one solution—there should not be such a concert!"

"Aye, aye," the troupe responded strongly.

But John, ever with an eye to the troupe's economies, said, "Ye must think, all of ye, carefully on this. There is not just the money to be thought of. Miss Currivard is a great heiress. Cook at the castle says her dowry alone is eighty thousand pounds." Several low whistles went round the group. "And she has a love of the theater, which she told me herself. I do not like the idea of offending a lady who might take it into her head one day to help us, to be a patroness."

These words brought a stunning silence to the troupe.

He pressed on. "Sometimes 'tis best to give up a little to get a lot. Fer whatever reason, Miss Currivard has taken a fancy to our Judy and I believe we ought to let her have her way in this. Nay, Judy, do not argue. I am begging the troupe to make a wise, if quite frustrating, decision, with an eye to the future. Think on it."

"This is humbug, the lot of it!" Charles cried. He threw up his arms and stomped away. The rest of the troupe began to disperse as well.

Judith tried to speak again with John, but he would have none of it. "The troupe must decide now. Let it be. There is nought ye can do now."

"But I have never seen Charles so angry."

"Charles," John murmured scathingly. He drew her aside and said, "Do ye think fer one minute, m'dear, that were the same arrangement offered to the likes of him, that he would be so gracious as to refuse fifty per cent?" He laughed harshly. "He would cut off his nose first and feed it to the goat, that he would!"

Judith could not help but laugh yet she knew John spoke the truth. Charles had but one interest, his own future.

"I just wish that Miss Currivard had been more generous to the troupe." She then shuddered. "I wish we had not come to Portislow. I have never had so much trouble as during my time here."

"Well, ye may be easy, Judith, fer I shall tell ye something that I have not told the others. The manager of the fair says they are to travel into Devonshire in a few days and we are to go with them."

Judith stared at him, feeling a horrible sense of panic seize her heart. "How many days?" she inquired, strange tears welling up in her eyes.

"Four or five. If the attendance dwindles by the third day, we will leave the next."

"I see. Does Miss Currivard know that she has but a handful of days?"

"Aye. The concert will be in three—if the troupe agrees."

"Very well. I beg you will excuse me, John. I . . . I have some sewing I must attend to immediately." Before he could comment, she turned and walked briskly in the direction of her tent.

Once within, she began to weep in the most ridiculous manner. Four days. She had but four days left in this beautiful valley, amongst those who had been so kind to her, who had included her in drawing room life and who, for a brief moment, had made her feel as though her existence was not so wretched as it was.

The truth, however, poured through her that when she had run away from Stolford so many years ago and at such a tender age, she had resigned every possibility, every hope that her place in society could ever be returned to her.

TWELVE

In the end, the troupe agreed to Miss Currivard's schemes. The concert was held beneath the stars, with a makeshift stage and with row upon row of chairs contributed by the castle and by the local theater. Beyond the chairs were twice as many rows of hard wooden benches. Past the benches, a multitude had gathered perched on the hillside on blankets. Children ran to and fro, and the declining sun cradled the narrow valley in a glow.

Judith stood in the wings but Miss Currivard, to a great deal of applause, had already taken her seat at the piano-forte. The hills formed a crescent in front of the stage and would return the actors' voices as well as her own so that all could be heard. A wild juggling act performed by Henry and Freddy had already enlivened the audience. So it was, that when she took the stage, nodded to Miss Currivard, and the first notes of the ballad, "The Poor Hindoo Girl," struck the night air, Judith gave herself completely to every note and nuance of the song.

Upon the fading of the last note, the crowd shouted their approval and applauded at the same time. So began the concert which Judith knew was likely to change her life.

In the middle of her second song, "The Lucky Escape,"

Judith became aware of Stolford. He was seated to her left, positioned between Kelthorne's sisters. His smile was as lascivious as she had known it so many years ago. How she detested him.

She chose, however, to ignore him entirely. She was no longer an unprotected child of fourteen to be intimidated by him. She had endured a great deal in eight years, and as she made her way through the verses of the song, she became more and more determined to make certain he understood she was not a halfling still green behind the ears. Kelthorne may have disrupted his assault but only just before she would have made use of her dagger, something about which she was profoundly certain Stolford was entirely unaware. She realized as she finished the song that she wished he would misbehave that she might prove her mettle.

With that, she met his gaze, cast him a wholly challenging stare, then, on a flourish of the shawl wrapped about her elbows, swept from the stage.

Charles followed soon after mesmerizing the audience with his selections from *Hamlet,* after which Margaret, John, Betty and Lydia acted an uproarious farce.

During her next song, Judith brought Shelly on stage and as they had practiced for three days, the little girl sat on a stool beside her smiling and moving her shoulders back and forth to the beat of the music. The ladies of the audience were heard to coo and sigh for there was nothing sweeter than Shelly with a wreath of buttercups in her hair, a smile on her lips, and swaying to the rhythms as Miss Currivard played the pianoforte. The brilliant applause that followed, increasing as Shelly took her bow, prompted the little girl to move downstage and take three more bows until her mother finally carried her screaming off the stage.

"Heaven help us now," Margaret said, smiling broadly, "fer I do believe we have just seen an actress born."

Since the audience was still applauding, Margaret allowed Shelly to take one more bow, tempting her back with the promise of one of Mrs. Marnhull's sweetmeats if she would be a good girl. The prize worked and Judith once more took the stage.

This time, she sang "Captivity," a very moving ballad, which Marie Antoinette was supposed to have sung during her imprisonment. Her heart always warmed to the words and melody. Perhaps for that reason, when her gaze found Kelthorne, her song swelled and a sigh passed around the audience. A breeze swept down the hill and since the ballad was a favorite, she motioned for the audience to join her. How sweet was the sound of so many voices returning to her, blending with her voice, balancing the pianoforte and so enriching the moment that scarcely an eye was left without a tear.

When she left the stage, Betty, Kitty and Angelique performed a carefully choreographed dance to a Mozart sonata, which Margaret played for them. The playful dance proved to be precisely what was needed to follow the melancholy aspect of her song. This was John's gift, a talent for arrangement that kept the flow of the night's performance moving strongly forward.

The climax was a final number in which the entire cast sang the tune, "How Sweet in the Woodlands." So powerful and moving was the result that the audience was on its feet before the last note had faded against the hills.

The concert was crowned by three encores, one performed by Judith and the others by the ensemble.

Only then did the evening draw to a close.

The cast remained near the stage to greet those who would praise their efforts.

Stolford approached Judith but she met him with her shoulders squared. Perhaps because of her countenance or because he had Lady Radsbury on one arm and Mrs. Newnott on the other, he did nothing more than praise her quite fulsomely. Kelthorne's sisters did as well, but their appreciation was expressed in a cool manner. Judith believed she understood why.

As she left the concert, she realized the only person she

had not seen afterwards was Kelthorne. A very deep disappointment settled over her heart. Did he not know, not understand that in little more than a day, she would be leaving Portislow?

Kelthorne knew he was being ridiculous skulking in the shadows as he was, but he had to see Judith one last time, alone.

As the crowds streamed away from the stage, he stole into the wooded growth at the edge of the hill and watched and waited. He had seen her address his sisters and Stolford. How proud he was that she had met the marquess so confidently. He had smiled thinking of her dagger and to a degree wished that Stolford would provoke her that he might feel the sting of her blade.

He watched her leave the concert area at last and as she began making her way westward back to the camp, he kept track with her progress holding to the shrubby growth of the hillside. She kept glancing all about her as though looking for someone.

He heard Miss Currivard's voice and saw that she and Laurence were calling to Judith. How animated Miss Currivard was gesticulating with her hands in a manner that reminded him of an excited bird. How much she enjoyed performing with Judith. How guilty he felt about her presence in his home when his desire was all for Judith. Still, he waited.

At last, Laurence and Miss Currivard moved on. Laurence politely offered his arm and Miss Currivard took it. How good Laurence was to have tended to her when he had not. He would have to thank Laurence later.

Now, however, he must speak with Judith, he must say good-bye in the only manner that would ease his heart. He must hold her in his arms, only how to reach her with so many people around, though fewer by the minute. She dawdled. She spoke with those who passed her. What was she waiting for? Why did she not turn toward camp? Worse, still, how was he to keep her from doing so?

Once Laurence and Miss Currivard were well out of sight, he stepped from the woods and waved to her. The hour was late and the light very dim. She saw him and did not hesitate but picked up her skirts and began to run.

When she reached him, he drew her deep into the shadows.

"I am leaving very soon," she said a little out-of-breath.

"I know. I had to see you one last time."

"I wished to say good-bye as well so I kept looking for you. When I could not find you, I was desolate. But here you are."

He could barely see her face. "I am here. Judith, my darling, whatever am I to do when you are gone?"

She touched his face gently. "I was never happier than when I was with you," she said quietly, her thumb stroking his cheek.

"Oh, God," he breathed, taking her strongly in his arms. He kissed her forcefully and to his great delight she wrapped her arms about his neck. A powerful desperation existed between them in that moment. Was she really leaving? Would he not see her again? How could he bear such separation? How would Judith fare without him?

Judith felt her tears begin to seep from her eyes and roll down her face and along her neck. She could not seem to stop them. She realized now that she loved him. That all which had transpired between them was more than just a transient *tendre*. She loved him. Her heart belonged to him and always would.

She drew back and swiped at her tears. "I fear I have become a watering pot, but dear Lord Kelthorne, I am going to miss you, quite dreadfully."

"I . . . I love you," he proclaimed suddenly, taking her once more into his arms. He kissed her forehead, her cheek, her chin. "I love you, Judith. With all my heart, with all my being! You have become as necessary to me as the sun to the moon, the tides to the sea, the day to night. Would there be any beauty in my life without you, any perfection, any completion? Judith, I wish you to. . . ."

"Aubrey!"

Judith released him and turned to stare into the field beyond. She saw that both Kelthorne's sisters were not fifteen feet away.

Kelthorne took her hand and led her from the woods. "You begin to frighten me," he called to them. "Surely we could not be seen?"

Lady Radsbury shook her head. "We saw Miss Lovington running toward the woods and became concerned for her."

"And how fortunate," Mrs. Newnott said, "that 'twas we who saw her. Good God, Aubrey, what were you thinking?"

Judith was deeply embarrassed on so many score.

Kelthorne drew her close to his side. "I am in love with her," he stated sharply. "I mean to marry her."

His sisters' mouths fell agape in unison. Judith might otherwise have been amused but the situation was rife with every possible pain. She turned toward him and withdrew her arm. "You cannot be serious," she cried, so much so that he turned to her with a shocked expression.

"I was never more so. Do you not wish to be my wife?"

"What I wish I forsook eight years ago! I have never been ignorant of that nor should you. The things you said to me in the orchard, these are precisely what will always be thought and believed of me. How could I ever assume the role of your wife without feeling the disapproval of everyone who is important to you for so long as I lived?"

"I do not give a fig for that!"

"For the comfort of your family, of your sisters, of your children? Good God, Kelthorne, you have not thought the situation through in the least."

"She is right," Lady Radsbury said, but so gently that Judith turned to her. She saw much to her surprise that Kelthorne's eldest sister was weeping. "You are very good, Miss Lovington. I did not expect to hear these words of sense from you and for that I beg you will forgive me. All the while you were in my brother's drawing room I felt as though you belonged among us but we all know 'tis impossible, utterly impossible!"

"But I love her," Kelthorne said.

Judith heard the break in his voice, but pressed him by saying, "Your children deserve better. You know what people are, you know the gossip will never die, you know my reputation was ruined the day I took up with the troupe."

"*My* reputation is a thousand times worse."

"You will always be forgiven because you are a man and now I must go. Indeed, I must."

"You cannot!" he cried, trying to take her arm, but she slipped behind Lady Radsbury.

"Prevent him," she whispered. "Speak to him, reason with him, remind him a hundredfold of these truths." With that, she ran away.

For the next hour or so, Judith shed her tears. Eventually, however, she realized no amount of weeping would suffice to relieve the deep suffering of her heart. How odd to think that just a few short weeks before she had arrived in Portislow fairly content in her life, certainly resigned to her fate, and building, however slowly, to retirement in a cottage, hopefully in Devonshire. But in that space of time, she had tumbled violently in love with a man she could never possess. Even as sweet as the times were that she had shared with Kelthorne, she would have wished her love for him undone for the pain that troubled her now.

There was nothing left to be done now, however, except to begin packing. On the morrow, the camp would pull up its stakes and begin the slow process of moving south into Devonshire where a new audience would be found, where there would be more shillings to earn and precious memories to forget.

From the bottom of her wardrobe, she drew a satchel and settled it on the bed, drawing it wide open. Slowly and carefully, as she had done a hundred times before, she began to pack her most treasured belongings.

"So, ye had thought to get yerself a lord."

Judith turned, startled by the sound of Charles's voice. "I did not hear you scratch," she stated, lifting her chin. He could mean no good by coming to her tent at so late an hour. Her knee twitched where the bottom of the sheath and dagger rested against her leg. She did not think she would have need of it, but there could be no two opinions on the subject that Charles Hemyock despised her.

"I never entertained such a hope," she stated calmly, turning her back to him and removing the sampler, which she had brought from her home in Sussex, from the wall of her tent.

He snorted his disbelief. "Did not ye just!" he cried bitterly. "Always thinkin' yerself above yer company, better than the rest with yer accent so prim, so genteel."

She turned back to face him. "What do you want? Why are you here? If you mean to tell me again how greatly you detest me, there is no need for you have never kept that opinion to yourself."

He lowered his lids, glaring at her through a squint. "I made a new friend tonight. The Marquess of Stolford. He knows talent and he sees it in me. He means to do great things fer me."

"Everyone sees that in you, Charles. You are the most gifted actor I have ever seen."

He shook his head and snorted again. "Do ye mean to flatter me now? To what purpose?"

"To no purpose. I merely offered my opinion. As to your character, I only think it unfortunate that it does not match your abilities, for then you would be a truly great man, worthy of every success and attainment. As it is now, you will astonish me if you achieve even a mediocre career for all your profound persuasiveness of gesture and speech."

He stood up very straight. "I knew it would come to this. Ye are jealous of me. Ye always have been and for that reason ye've stood in my way but fer the last time. The last time, I tell ye, so be warned, my pretty Judy. Be warned."

With that he laughed harshly and quit her tent.

Judith sat down on her bed, carefully as always lest the corner give way yet again. She did not take his threats seriously. She had the loyalty and protection of the troupe. What could he do to her?

Kelthorne stood outside the conservatory, the summer night cool on his face. He could hear Miss Currivard's laughter coming from the music room as well as Laurence's voice. He smiled, if sadly. Laurence certainly had the ability to make Miss Currivard laugh, which, given his circumstances and the fact that Laurence was his dearest friend, he was gratified that she enjoyed his company. Once they were wed, she would often find him in their house. Still he delayed opening the door. He felt certain in doing so he was sealing his fate.

The hour was near midnight by his calculation. After he had escorted his sisters back to the castle, he left them at the front door and walked about his grounds for a very long time. He pondered all that Judith had said as well as the arguments his sisters had presented against wedding her.

In the end he had felt he had no choice but to agree with all of them. Judith was an actress. She was tainted. She would never be viewed as anything more by the society in which he moved.

She had been right about one thing, no matter how questionable his own conduct over the past ten years, his escapades would be entirely overlooked. Hers, real or imagined, would not. Even their children would suffer the insults about her past, about having lived and labored for so many years as part of an acting troupe.

Having come to an acceptance of his situation, that Judith could never be the Countess of Kelthorne and that Miss Currivard was in every respect an appropriate bride for him, he finally resolved to do his duty, which had brought him to the door of the conservatory where he now stood. If he must leave Judith behind, if he must go forward with Miss Currivard, then he would begin tonight. He would ask her to become his wife even now.

He opened the door and with a steadiness if grimness of purpose, he walked to the music room where the door was half-closed. He was surprised that he could hear neither Laurence telling one of his amusing anecdotes nor Miss Currivard's attending laughter. He pushed the door open and, much to his great astonishment, he found Miss Currivard locked in Laurence's arms.

"What the deuce!" he cried. "What is the meaning of this? Laurence, I cannot believe you would use me so badly?"

They had drawn apart sharply and now stared at him. Laurence appeared conscious but Miss Currivard seemed rather amused. "I beg your pardon?" she responded, her lips twitching.

"W-well, why are you kissing my friend? Are you not here to become betrothed to me?" The ill usage he felt was powerful in the extreme.

For some reason, she began to laugh. "I only wish you could see the self-righteousness in your expression of this moment!" she exclaimed.

"Abigail—Miss Currivard," Laurence began softly. "Do but consider . . ."

She took his hand. "I have considered. I have considered for days, even weeks now, even from the beginning. He never loved me, not even in the slightest degree, and you did."

"Y-you love her?" Kelthorne asked, stunned.

"Aye," he murmured, his expression haunted.

"But I do not understand. When did this happen? How?"

Miss Currivard looked at him as though he were a complete simpleton. "It happened every time your friend felt obligated to atone for your truly odious conduct or did you think me oblivious to your feelings for Miss Lovington or to your quite dogged pursuit of her?"

"I . . . that is . . . I never meant . . . it was a mistake . . . it should never have happened. I would not have hurt you for the world. I esteem you greatly. I admire you."

Miss Currivard looked away from him, her expression growing momentarily somber. When she met his gaze anew, she said, "Did I not comprehend your character so much as I do, that you are truly a fine man, I would not hesitate to say that I have never been so humiliated as I have been these several weeks beneath your roof. But it will be an even greater insult to me to hear you deny that you have behaved wretchedly."

Kelthorne threw himself into a chair by the pianoforte. "Good God, so I have," he murmured. "I have been so lost in my own struggles, trying desperately not to love Judith, that is, Miss Lovington, that I did not even see you." He looked up at her. "My dear Miss Currivard, how will you ever forgive me? I have been a perfect cretin."

"That is much better," she cried, smiling once more. "But you are forgiven, you know. For had you offered for me at the outset, I should have accepted you. And had I done so, I should have doomed myself to the greatest unhappiness imaginable."

He felt obliged to protest. "I would have tended to your happiness. I can promise you that. I would not have done you injury. I beg you will believe me!"

"I do, but do you not see how very sad that would have been for both of us, that you would have *dutifully* striven to make me happy? But you must understand, my lord, that is not to what I am referring at present." She released Laurence's hand and slipped her arm about his very tightly, drawing close to him. "Had I accepted of your offer"—here she turned to look at Laurence—"I should never have discovered until too late that a better man for me was right beneath my nose."

Kelthorne glanced from one to the other and complete enlightenment dawned. "You love him and he loves you!" he cried, jumping to his feet. "By Jove, this is the best news you could have given me. You are wealthy and now Laurence may write his poetry."

"Precisely," she stated.

"Nothing could make me happier."

"Are you certain?" Laurence asked. "For I will admit to you that I made every use of the numerous opportunities you provided to win her affections."

"Is this so?" Miss Currivard asked, obviously stunned.

Laurence sighed. "I suppose there is nothing for it but to confess the truth," he said. "Abigail, the moment I laid eyes on you I was lost. Even then, I might have been able to forget you save that you kept laughing at all my jokes."

Miss Currivard smiled warmly. "You are the dearest man."

"You loved her from the beginning, indeed?" Kelthorne queried.

"Hopelessly," he admitted.

He shook his head. "I wish you had said something to me. I would have stepped aside, you must have known I would."

"I was never assured of Abigail's sentiments until now. I truly believed it possible that the pair of you might have one day formed an attachment."

"What altered that opinion?"

Laurence and Miss Currivard exchanged a glance. Miss Currivard sighed and turned back to Kelthorne. "Because of the way you could not release Miss Lovington's hand after the day of the fair. Do you remember? I realized *'twas a hopeless case.*"

"Of course. I see now what you were about."

"I will admit to having had a *tendre* for you but after that day, most surprisingly, I did not feel particularly sad. Only then was it borne in on me how much I had come to depend upon Laurence's society for my contentment, very deeply so."

"I cannot tell you how happy I am," Kelthorne said. "This has ended just as it should have." He laughed suddenly. "Only tell me, have you heard a little of Laurence's poetry?"

"While you were *dallying* with Miss Lovington," Miss Currivard did not hesitate to explain, "Laurence was reading me all of his poems."

"*All?*" he inquired.

"Well, there were a few he said he felt obliged to burn."

"I imagine there were."

"But we intend never to speak of his former *interests*."

"A wise decision." He thought for a moment then addressed Miss Currivard. "There is one thing I should like to know—if you knew that I had feelings for Miss Lovington, why were you constantly forcing us to be together—Cheddar Gorge, the soiree? I always felt you had some design in mind, but what could it possibly have been?"

She smiled. "I needed to know to a certainty precisely how you did feel about her and whether, given the opportunity, you would fall so passionately in love with her that nothing else mattered. From the first I had my suspicions and they were proved wholly true. I never meant to torment you but since I was risking my happiness, I felt obligated to understand the truth as best I could. Do you blame me?"

He shook his head. "Again, I believe you made another wise decision."

On the following morning, Kelthorne stared at his eldest sister. "What do you mean, you intend to introduce me to Bath society?"

"I believe I have spoken plainly enough only perhaps you wish to understand my motives better. I am sorry for you, for this tragedy that has occurred during these weeks here in Somerset. I thought Bath might provide a helpful diversion.

There are always people to be met in the Pump Room and parties at least once a week. You will not be dull and I did have several young ladies who I wished to make known to you quite apart from Miss Currivard, each of whom would be quite acceptable to the *beau monde* in general."

"I, too, think you will be content in Bath," Amy said, reaching a hand across the breakfast table to give his arm a gentle squeeze. "At least I would wish it so for I vow, Aubrey, neither of us have seen you so blue-devilled."

He rose abruptly but spoke in a softened voice to his sisters. "I know you mean only kindness, but you have to understand that I have given up my soul in relinquishing Judith and I do not believe I shall recover it in Bath. I mean to go to London."

"No!" Amy cried, rising sharply to her feet as well so that her chair rocked alarmingly. "Aubrey, you cannot! You have been doing so well in Portislow!"

"Pray, Aubrey," Mary cried, her eyes filling with tears. "Do not do this, I beg of you."

"I wish I could feel remorse for what I mean to do, but I cannot." With that, he quit the breakfast room.

He returned to his bedchamber and dressed in riding gear. A hard push to London was what was needed and he would do so at once. He could not bear remaining behind knowing that Judith would very soon leave Somerset. Besides, the tenderness now in constant attendance between Miss Currivard—now a very dear Abigail—and Laurence, served painfully to remind him of what he had lost.

No, he must leave Portislow and soothe his unhappiness in the varied, if debauched, delights of London.

THIRTEEN

"Then we are not leaving today?" Judith asked. She had been washing dishes and now stood wiping her hands. She was relieved by the interruption since the water was far too hot.

"John says we must wait," Margaret said. "Charles must see a doctor."

"But does anyone know what is the matter with him? Even the smallest guess?" She felt uneasy. Charles was never sick.

"Nay. Even Mrs. Marnhull has seen ought like it. He thrashes about, complains of a pain in his stomach and will let no one touch him."

"Has he a fever?"

"Nay." She paused and frowned.

"What is it, Margaret? What are you not telling me?"

"He says he were poisoned at the castle when he returned the bread baskets this morning. Cook gave him a sweetmeat but why would anyone want to hurt him, that's what I'd like to know. Sounds havey-cavey to me." She lowered her voice to a whisper. "I am inclined to believe he is play-acting."

"But to what purpose? Of everyone present, he has been the most anxious to leave."

"Aye," she agreed, but she frowned anew. "La, but there is Shelly teasing poor Horace." She hurried away calling her daughter's name.

Judith was left to plunge her hands once more into the scalding water and continued washing the dishes. She tried to feel even a small portion of compassion toward Charles but found she could not. He was little better than a weasel and even then, she thought the epithet unkind to the countryside creature.

She spent her day, therefore, relaxing in her tent or taking walks about the countryside. At two o'clock the doctor arrived and pronounced that Charles was suffering from an unknown ailment and gave him a dose of laudanum that put him in a stupor for the rest of the day. The doctor would call on his patient in the morning and only then would John determine if the troupe was to finally leave Portislow.

Judith was grateful for the delay if for no other reason than that during her walks, she chose to memorize the entire vicinity, especially the areas around the castle and the orchard, which held such dear memories for her. If a constant and quite painful longing traipsed behind her, she took great care to remind herself of the various truths that had already served to separate her forever from Kelthorne. She knew only too well just how even proper gentlemen treated ladies of the stage. There would be no end to the innuendos and gossip were she to step from her present world and enter Kelthorne's. Had she been risking only her own peace of mind, she rather believed she might have agreed to wed him but as soon as there were children, she understood quite to perfection just how cruel their playmates could be.

There was another question, however, that needed to be answered. Now that Stolford knew of her whereabouts and that she no longer feared him, she did not need to stay hidden with the troupe. She was free to leave if she wished to do so. Yet, where would she go? That was the question. She even thought of seeking out her uncle in Kent, but would he want her once he learned what she had been doing for eight years?

The thought so saddened her that she decided she would not try to make any such determination, at least not yet, at least not until the troupe had left Somerset and she could become more accustomed to her life without Kelthorne. Time enough to make changes. For the present, she had an obligation to the troupe to continue performing.

As the night drew close around the camp and fatigue settled into every tent, she prepared for bed. She brushed out her hair and had just begun to set a braid, when she heard a faint scuffling just beyond her tent. The hour was past eleven so she was a little concerned that someone would be abroad, particularly before a day of travel. She rose and would have investigated further, but silence returned and she resumed her seat and continued plaiting her hair.

Once her hair was in a neat braid, she rose to her feet and was about to lift the skirt of her nightdress in order to untie the sheath holding her dagger to her leg, when another scuffle alerted her. By that, however, it was too late. She turned and saw a large, masked man holding a club. His eyes were as dark as night. The club rushed toward her. She was falling before she could comprehend what was happening.

Kelthorne had been sitting for a very long time, several hours in fact, in a parlor on the first floor of an inn just on the border between Somerset and Wiltshire. He had arrived there earlier in the day and had meant to push on to the metropolis but he could not seem to depart his home county for one simple reason—the very thought of leaving Judith behind had become so severe an ache in his heart that he had been unable to move since half past three.

The hour was now much advanced though not yet midnight. He was finishing his third brandy when he suddenly cried out into the empty parlor, "The devil take it! I will marry the chit no matter what anyone says!"

He rose hastily and called for the landlord who came to him sleepy-eyed.

"There's a good fellow," he said, "and I do beg your pardon, but I believe I must pay the shot and take my leave. I will pay for the room of course."

At these words, the landlord nodded quite agreeably. "Wery good, me lord. Wery good." A clattering in the cobbled yard drew him to the window. "Wat's this now? A coach so late? Does anyone know there be murderers and thieves abroad at night and good men need their rest?"

Kelthorne moved to the window as well and was properly shocked to find his sisters descending a hired post-chaise. He went to them at once. "What is amiss?" he asked, drawing them into the taproom. "Has something happened?"

The ladies regarded one another. "Not precisely," Mary said. "That is, we left everyone at Portislow in good health. But we have learned something of import that has led us to believe we have made a very great mistake."

"I hope you have not come to tell me you have just learned there is another heiress of trade in Bath."

"No, no!" Amy cried. "We have no intention of preventing you from staying on your course to London, if that is what you truly wish. But we had to tell you."

He saw their sincerity and gestured to the stairs. "I have a parlor on the first floor." Searching in his pocket he tossed a sovereign to the landlord. "Will you tend to the horses, feed the postboy and send tea up for the ladies?"

He bowed happily more than once, thumbing the fine coin in his hand. "Yes, me lord. With pleasure."

Kelthorne followed quickly in his sisters' wake. They looked fatigued, which they should since they had been traveling no doubt most of the evening. "Will you not sit down?"

"Yes, of course," Mary said.

Once they had arranged their skirts and exchanged a troubled glance, he broke their silence. "What the deuce is going forward? Mary, for God's sake, what is wrong?"

"It is concerning Miss Lovington," she said. "No, no, she is perfectly well. As it happens, Stolford came to call on us earlier this afternoon and when he left on foot, I had decided myself to walk into town for there was a particular bonnet in one of the shop windows I had admired and which I thought I might purchase. But as I descended the hill, I heard voices and recognized Stolford's laugh. I would have made my presence known but I heard him speak Miss Lovington's name and I simply had to know what he would say of her. What I learned rather shocked me for he said, 'That is not her real name, Mr. Hemyock. She is Judith Pensbury of Sussex.' Aubrey, she must be the daughter of Sir Christopher Pensbury for I remember it most particularly that there had been rumors his daughter had disappeared but later her uncle put it about that she had died."

Kelthorne stared at his sister. "Good God, but are you certain? However, she once told me that her home had been in Sussex so it must be true." Sir Christopher in his time, before ill health removed him from London, had been a prominent London figure, a friend to the Regent and well known in the First Circles. His second wife was said to have had associations with the Marquess of Stolford, which would further confirm his sisters' news.

"Only, Aubrey, why did she leave home? What could have prompted her to such imprudence?"

Amy looked at Mary and gasped. Kelthorne could see that she had just guessed at the truth. "Do you think it possible Stolford was involved?" she asked.

Mary drew in a sharp breath as well. "You must have the right of it, for I now recall that Lady Pensbury became Stolford's mistress after Sir Christopher died, if she was not already. Aubrey, you probably did not know of her dealings with Stolford for you were very engaged in your own concerns that many years ago. But this was the gossip of the time and having met Miss Pensbury, I can see now that it must all have been true."

"Do you remember how nervous she was when she first met him in the church in Portislow?" Amy asked. "I had never seen her so distressed."

"I do, indeed, for I know I thought it odd at the time."

Mary pressed her hand to her mouth and shook her head. "Stolford must have made improper advances when she was but a schoolgirl—"

Amy finished her thought, "And she ran from him and took up with the troupe."

Mary turned to Kelthorne. "What do you think, brother?"

"I believe you have discovered the truth. I most certainly do."

Amy said, "But I know that Sir Christopher's daughter had been well-dowered, some fifteen thousand pounds by recollection. Miss Lovington—that is, Miss Pensbury's future is thereby secured. Yet, she seems to be wholly ignorant of it."

"There can be no doubt she does not know. But it is perfectly understandable since she was so young at the time."

Mary rose suddenly and took Kelthorne's hands in her own. "I am so sorry that I pressed you to marry Miss Currivard, to marry at all. It was very wrong of me and I apologize."

He was gratified by her remorse. "Thank you," he said sincerely. "I believe I needed to hear you say as much."

"Pray do not go to London," Amy said. "We wish to make things right. Now that we know who Miss Lovington really is, there can be no objection to such a marriage now."

"You must understand one thing," he said forcefully. "I had meant to return to Somerset this very night and had Judith been the daughter of a beggar I would still have taken her to wife. Nothing—I vow—nothing would have prevented me. These revelations will make the future together a trifle easier for us both but that is all. She is the woman for me. She was from the beginning and I do not wish to live without her."

Amy rose as well, drew close and petted his arm. "We know. Indeed, when we saw you together, besides being alarmed, I think Mary and I were both struck by how much you did love her and how much not only does Miss Lov—

that is—Miss Pensbury love you but how honorable her character is that she would so sacrifice her happiness for your sake, indeed, even for ours."

"She is wholly good," he stated.

The landlord arrived bearing a tray of tea and toast, even slices of cheese and red apples.

Amy pressed her hand to her stomach. "How grateful I am!" she cried, smiling at the man. "Thank you, for we have not eaten in hours."

Though Kelthorne was anxious now to be going, to pursue Judith into Devonshire if necessary, he took up a seat opposite his sisters and even shared the tea and toast. The return journey would require many more hours and a little sustenance was quite necessary.

The more he thought about just where the troupe might be, that it was possible they were already in Devonshire, he realized he should take a more southerly route by which he hoped to intercept Judith more quickly.

When he said as much, Amy said, "Oh, but the troupe did not leave Somerset today. One of the members, Mr. Hemyock—the very one Stolford told of Miss Pensbury's identity—took ill. The doctor was summoned. It was believed he suffered from some poisoning or other."

"Might they have left after you departed?"

"Unlikely because your servants had it on good authority that the doctor was due to tend the patient in the morning as well."

"Then we are for Somerset," he said.

Judith awoke very slowly. Her head ached severely though cushioned, but in what manner she knew not, against the occasional jolting of what she grew to realize was the bouncing of a coach along a road.

A rather deep rut lifted her head from its safe place then set it down hard again. She moaned softly. A hand slid down her arm and squeezed her at the joint of the elbow, quite tenderly. For the barest moment she felt safe and breathed deeply.

"Are you beginning to awaken, my dear?"

Her body stiffened and a low laugh followed.

"I see that you are and that you apparently know me by my voice."

Stolford.

Prior events rushed back to her, recalling a partially masked man and a club. Oh, how her head ached. For some reason she remembered as well being but fourteen and how the marquess had cornered her in a darkened hall, covered her mouth and pressed himself against her. His words spoken hotly into her ear so many years ago resounded now in her head. *You are mine, little Judy. Mine.*

She would never be his. She had resolved as much then and she resolved as much now whatever he thought, whatever his plans so tidy as they appeared to be. She had escaped him once when she was so young and powerless. Did he think her less capable now? Now, when she had lived at the edge of civilization in a traveling troupe?

She felt the leather sheath against her thigh. What a fool he was if he thought she was unprotected merely because she was alone. Indeed, she relied on his prejudice against helpless females upon whom he had preyed for so many years. Tonight, she would succeed. Tonight, the tide would turn against him.

She chose not to speak but moaned again faintly, pretending to be very ill. She even feigned weeping.

"Yes, yes, have your cry out, my dear. You will feel much better."

Her soul smiled. Better and better.

When the coach began to slow, she whispered as pitifully as she could manage, "Wh-where are we, my lord? My head hurts. How I wish for laudanum or brandy perhaps." Having watched Betty and the others for so many years, she knew how to deliver a line. How odd to think that her time with the troupe would serve her in this manner.

She pretended to try to lift herself then flopped down on what she realized was his cape serving as a pillow on his lap. She felt ill at the knowledge that she was reclining against him but there was nothing she could do, not if she hoped to succeed.

He thumped his cane on the roof of the carriage and called to his coachman. "We will rest here for the night." He patted her arm then lifted her abruptly. "I beg you will right yourself, my dear. I have no doubt you can walk. You have suffered only a little bump on the head, after all. I have a long cloak for you to wear."

She lifted herself up and with as much drama as would have caused her fellow actors to complain vigorously about her ham-handed performance, she threw herself against the squabs and moaned again. "I know I can walk," she whispered mournfully. She then slumped to her right and sought the blade.

"Judith," he whispered, leaning close. "How long I have waited for just this moment." She felt his breath on her neck and then his lips. "And you have grown into such a beautiful young woman."

She was having difficulty reaching the sheath, which had somehow become turned on her leg. She could feel the bulk of the blade beneath her. He kissed her again. "No," she murmured, keeping to her weak accents.

"Yes," he returned, his hand now pulling her nightdress from her shoulder.

She realized she would have to turn into him in order to retrieve the dagger, an act that would encourage him in his wretched conduct, but there was nothing for it, the blade would not be wrested from her in this position. She turned abruptly and faced him thinking that his triumphant expression would last but a second more.

The dagger fell into her hand. She cleared the edge of her

nightdress and plunged the blade deeply. A long painful scream filled the coach.

The return journey in the company of his sisters tried Kelthorne's soul. Of course two pairs of horses certainly traversed the miles in a goodly time, but now that he had made the decision to take Judith to wife, he could not get back to her quickly enough. The hours wore on. He wondered vaguely if the roads and coach making would ever improve sufficiently to allow for faster travel. On such a night as this every rut the coach hit set his nerves on fire.

By the time the vehicle neared Portislow, his sisters slumbered against his shoulders, one on either side of him. He cradled them in his arms, appreciative for this quite wonderful gesture in pursuing him with apologies and the rather stunning news of Judith's true identity.

Thoughts of Judith reminded him of Sir Christopher Pensbury. He tried to recall what he knew of him. So many years ago he would have been engulfed in his own riotous pursuits and certainly not interested in rumors concerning Sir Christopher or Stolford's relationship to him.

And Judith had run away from Stolford when her father had been ill to the point of dying. How much he had grown to despise the marquess.

"Aubrey, you are crushing my arm," Amy whispered looking up at him.

"I beg your pardon, dearest," he whispered. "Forgive me."

"Are you all right?" she whispered. "The lamplight may be very faint by I know that expression. What is amiss?"

"Is Stolford still at the George in Portislow?" He had begun to think he might just call upon him.

"No," she murmured snuggling once more against his arm and yawning. "He is returned to his home. He took his leave of us this afternoon, just before I heard him speaking with that actor."

"What were his reasons?"

"He said he remembered an engagement in Bath, which I must say I thought a rather inadequate excuse for leave-taking, but he seemed anxious even happy to be going. I only wonder now that Mary and I had come to think him an agreeable sort of man."

"He does not lack for abilities," Kelthorne said.

"Of what are you speaking?" Mary said, coming out of her slumbers.

"Of Stolford's leave-taking."

She shuddered against him.

Kelthorne pondered the fact that Stolford had bothered to have a conversation with Charles Hemyock in the first place. And why would Stolford have been speaking to Charles about Judith?

Kelthorne knew the truth before it could be in any manner confirmed. He fairly pushed Mary aside as he lowered the window and called out to the postboy, issuing a string of brisk orders. "There will be two sovereigns for you if you will agree to it."

The experienced horseman smiled back at him, an expression evident in the rising dawn. "As ye wish!" he shouted.

"Whyever are we going to the camp now?" Mary asked. "Miss Pensbury will be asleep."

"By God I hope she is! Indeed, I hope with all my heart she is!"

Before the wheels of Kelthorne's coach ceased rolling, he had leapt from the vehicle, calling out Judith's name, hurrying in the direction of her tent.

Within a few seconds, the camp had come to life, figures emerging from tent after tent, protesting the commotion and desiring to know what drunkard was shouting Judith's name.

Kelthorne had just moved past Mrs. Ash, even hearing her address him by name, when he found Judith's tent and brushed open the canvas flap. His heart sank. The tent was empty and the bed still in a tidy state. Judith was nowhere to be seen.

John and Margaret both entered the tent. "What has happened, m'lord?" she asked.

"Where the devil is she?" he cried, turning on them both. "Where is my Judith? What has happened to her?"

Margaret's eyes, upon seeing the empty bed, grew wide and disbelieving. "I . . . I do not know. I saw her before bed, but that were ten o'clock."

Mr. Ash seemed equally dumbfounded. He turned around and posed the question to the growing crowd, "Who last saw Judy? Anyone? Tell us!"

Several answered but the response was similar to Mrs. Ash's, Judith had been seen near the bathing tent or near Mrs. Marnhull's wagon or carrying Shelly about, all before half past nine.

He felt a tug on his sleeve. He glanced to his right. Mary appeared quite overset. "We should ask Mr. Hemyock, do you not think so, Aubrey?"

"Charles?" Mr. Ash cried. "He won't be of any use. He's been sick all day and into the night."

"He was last seen at the castle conversing with the Marquess of Stolford and I do not believe I must tell you that he is no man of honor!"

"Ye think some mischief is afoot?" Mr. Ash asked.

"Aye."

"Charles it be then. This way."

By now, the entire camp moved in their wake and then gasped suddenly as one for Charles suddenly appeared before them, emerging from his tent fully dressed and bearing a satchel in his hands. "I feel better now and I am leaving!" he cried in his powerful voice.

Kelthorne understood the trick and was not in the least humbugged. "Where is Judith?"

"I don't know wat ye mean," he said.

"He's lying!" Henry cried. Nothing more needed to be said. Henry, Horace and Freddy threw themselves upon Charles and pinned him to the ground.

Kelthorne moved to stand over him. "What the devil have you done?"

"I don't know wat ye mean," he said, but he could not meet Kelthorne's gaze.

"Gentlemen," Kelthorne said, glancing at the three men holding Charles in check, "would you be so good as to lift Mr. Hemyock to his feet that I might *encourage* him to speak."

"Aye! With pleasure!" Henry cried.

"Aye!"

In one swift movement, they lifted Charles to his feet.

A moment later, Kelthorne stepped quite close to him. "It would seem you have a choice. You may tell us all now just what mischief you have accomplished or I can plant you the first of what I promise will be as many facers as needed to get the truth from you."

Charles recoiled. "Not my face!" he cried. "Anything but my face!"

Kelthorne could have laughed for his vanity, save that the situation was so desperate. "Then you will have to speak for I think I shall begin with your nose, which I believe more than one lady has said is possibly your best feature. What do you say? Shall I break your nose or perhaps even better, smash it into a thousand little pieces?"

"No!" Charles shrieked, his voice elevating.

"Mama," little Shelley said, rubbing her eyes. "Why does Charlie sound like a girl?"

"Oh, dear," Mrs. Ash cried. "There, there, m'darlin'. Come back to bed. Charlie is practicing a new play is all. Come now."

"I thought 'twere Betty squealing."

The laughter that rolled about the troupe did little to allay the trembling that had taken hold of Charles.

Kelthorne pressed his point home not by speaking but by forming a fist, setting it level with Charles' nose and then drawing his arm back.

"I'll tell ye wat ye want to know!" Charles squealed again.

"By God, Betty," Mrs. Marnhull cried. "He does sound like ye."

The story that spilled quickly from him was as appalling as it was frightening. He had made an arrangement with the Marquess of Stolford, in exchange for his patronage, to help him abduct Judith from her tent, something that had been accomplished quite to perfection near eleven o'clock when the camp was asleep. Stolford, it would seem, had several gentlemen in his employ, which he used for just such nefarious deeds as the one that had taken place that very evening.

"You sold Judith to Stolford for his patronage?" Kelthorne asked, horrified.

"He means to establish me in Drury Lane. I shall be the next Keane."

Kelthorne laughed and shook his head. "I should like to see him attempt to do anything of the sort. Not that you are without talent, Mr. Hemyock, but the point in fact is that, if memory serves, Stolford violated one of the daughters of the owner, or was it two of them, and risks life and limb should he come near the premises. Yes, I should like to see him try to establish you or anyone at Drury Lane."

"Two of his daughters?" he asked, dumbfounded.

"I fear it is so. Might I suggest that the next time you desire to garner the support of a nobleman, you choose a man who has even the smallest intention of honoring his word?"

The expression on Charles's face brought any merriment dropping sharply away. He had been humbugged in the worst possible way. His shoulders fell. "If this be true—" he began, lifting his gaze, but waiting.

"'Tis true, horribly and wretchedly."

"Then I must speak."

"There is more?"

"If caught, I were supposed to tell ye that he is gone to Bristol where he has a yacht."

"Where has he taken Judith?"

"He would not tell me but I made it my business to know. I followed the man wat carried Judy. He walked over a mile with her in his arms, he were that strong, and not puffing mind, carried her like a babe. I kept to the shrubs and saw him put her in Stolford's coach then take up the reins."

"How did you know it was Stolford's coach?"

"The coat of arms painted on the side."

"The arrogance," Kelthorne muttered. "Which direction?"

"He drove south."

"Exeter?" Kelthorne asked.

"P'rhaps."

"He's lying again!" Bobby cried out.

"No, he is not," Kelthorne stated firmly.

"How can ye be so certain?" Horace asked. "He is a man of great ability on the stage and is this not a stage?"

"That is a very wise thing for you to say, Horace, indeed, it is. But Charles is speaking the truth to me because he knows that if he is not and my precious Judith comes to even a mite of harm, even the smallest scratch, I shall spend the rest of my days searching out his hiding place and then I shall require a pound of flesh and then another until he is properly deceased."

Charles once more began to tremble. Tears even flooded his eyes. "I swear 'tis the truth and if ye mean to follow, I shall come with ye to make certain ye find Judy."

"You shall, indeed," Kelthorne said jovially. As he guided Charles to the post-chaise, he was feeling far from content. Perhaps he knew which direction to go but the thought that Judith had been in Stolford's power for such a long time filled him with the worst dread.

"My lord," John called to him strongly. "Will ye not wait that we might accompany ye?"

"I cannot, but make haste, Mr. Ash. Take my sisters to the

castle. Mary, have my head groom arrange all the necessary transport. Mr. Ash, see that riders are sent ahead to search out the path I follow. I will leave word at each hamlet of the proper direction to travel in order to speed your progress, just check at each inn or tavern. Do not worry! I will find her!"

With that, he hastened the postillion on.

FOURTEEN

Kelthorne was agreeably surprised in at least one thing—he had not the smallest difficulty in discovering the precise direction Stolford had taken his prey. So confident was the marquess in his abilities that he had used the Stolford coach by which to abduct Judith, a vehicle that was quite overgrown and sported, as Charles had said, his coat of arms emblazoned on both sides. Such a coach was highly recognizable and at nearly every village or town through which they passed, someone had been about, even during the middle of the night, who admitted to having seen the vehicle. He offered a shilling to any stableboy who would await the succession of vehicles to follow. He had no difficulty in acquiring the help he needed.

Arriving at the town of Langport in nearly the center of Somerset, he called to the landlord who stood near the door of his taproom.

"I wish to know if the Marquess of Stolford's coach passed this way last night," Kelthorne asked.

"Nay," the landlord called back but he was smiling.

Kelthorne thought there was something odd about his expression. "You did not see the coach? For I have been given to understand he was traveling in this direction and I was hopeful of finding him very soon."

"Oh, I saw the coach, but it did not pass."

Kelthorne frowned. "Why do you speak to me in riddles? If you saw the coach how did it not pass?"

The landlord looked past Kelthorne into the street where a collection of coaches and wagons began drawing near and stopping. "What be all this?" he asked.

Kelthorne glanced back. His scheme had worked. "These are friends of mine. Now, answer me, sir!" Kelthorne cried sharply. "How did the coach not pass but yet you saw it?"

The landlord returned his attention fully to Kelthorne. "Because 'tis in the courtyard with his lordship's horses."

Kelthorne took each word as though he was being struck a series of light blows to his face. "And the inmates have rested here?" he shouted, leaving his coach and running toward him. "They are here? Even now and there is a lady among them?" He swallowed hard.

"Aye, in the bedchamber."

He felt the blood first rush from his face and then reenter with such force of feeling that the landlord's eyes grew very wide and he took a prudent step backward and then another. "Which . . . chamber?" Kelthorne asked, his jaw tight.

The color had now left the landlord's face. He lifted his arm gesturing toward the staircase. "First floor, third door on left, facing the street."

"Thank you."

Kelthorne heard rather than saw the crowd flow into the taproom as he bounded up the stairs two by two, then counted the doors as he ran by. Third on the left, the door was ajar and voices could be heard within, one of them Judith's of that he was certain. He pushed the door wide ready to do battle with the infamous rogue. He lifted his fists. He called out, "I will protect you, my darling!" Only to find a very odd scene before him. "What the deuce?"

"Kelthorne!" Judith cried. "You have come! How . . . how very sweet of you!"

She was holding a bowl of very red water in which numerous bloody rags were lumped together. Two servants were at either end of the bed restraining Stolford who lay with his eyes closed and in obvious discomfort, his complexion deathly pale. A man, clearly a surgeon by occupation, sat in a chair by the bed, his spectacles sitting at the end of his nose as he concentrated on the task before him.

"What happened?" Kelthorne asked, moving to stand beside Judith.

The crowd that had entered the taproom shortly on his heels, had also pounded up the stairs, and now began to push its way into the bedchamber.

"John," Judith cried, "Lady Radsbury, Mrs. Newnott, Betty! I do not understand. Have you all come?"

"Of course," Amy said. She drew up beside Kelthorne and slipped her arm through his, but looked down at the patient. "Oh, dear. What are you doing, doctor?"

"I am setting a very deep row of stitches in this man's arm and after I am done, I intend to close this hideous wound with another set. However, I first mean to do this." He poured brandy in the wound and the Marquess of Stolford moaned pitifully. He was obviously dosed quite heavily with laudanum but there was some pain that the opiate simply did not obliterate. Every stitch, for instance, brought his body convulsing and if one stableboy had not been holding him firmly by the shoulders and arms, and another by the legs, the doctor could have done nothing for him.

"I am feeling rather ill," Amy said. "Forgive me, Aubrey, but I believe I shall retire. Mary, give me your arm."

The sisters left and John was not long in encouraging the troupe members to follow in their wake. He was about to leave as well, but he turned back to Judith and said, "Well done, Judy."

"Thank you, John. You realize you probably saved my life this evening with your help and instructions."

He nodded beaming with no small degree of pride. Nudging Kelthorne once, he quit the chamber.

Kelthorne stood for some time assessing the situation before him. He met Judith's gaze and smiled if but a little. "I am so relieved to find you well. You have no idea."

"But how did you come to be here?" she asked.

"In part, because of my sisters, Miss *Pensbury*."

At the use of her Christian name, her color faded and she weaved slightly on her feet. "Who told you?" she asked. "And how did anyone know or learn of it?"

"Stolford made mention of it to Mr. Hemyock and Amy chanced to overhear it. I had made my way almost to Wiltshire earlier—well, it would be yesterday now—then stayed my journey. I had meant to go to London and forget my sadness—" another forceful moan disrupted his explanation but only for a moment. "I could not go to London, Judith. I cannot resume that life, that barren place of chasing after such transient pleasures that have no meaning and never any real love. But I realized I cannot live without you either, my darling." From the corner of his eye, he could see that the good doctor had ceased his clever sewing and was smiling broadly.

The surgeon said, "Pray do not let either myself or my helpers stop you for if I do not much mistake the matter, the lady needs to hear what you have to say."

"As well I know it," Kelthorne responded. To Judith he continued, "I was a fool to allow you and my sisters to persuade me against marrying you."

Judith had tears in her eyes. "But, Kelthorne, nothing is changed . . ."

"Nothing is changed?" he cried, laughing, but seeing that she was overset, he took the bowl of noxious water and held it in her stead. "I find you here at an inn, in a situation I can only describe as peculiar in the extreme, I address you by what is believed to be your rightful name and you have just now confirmed the very important truth that you are the daughter of Sir Christopher Pensbury."

"Is that the right of it?" the doctor cried, craning his head around to stare at Judith. "The missing Pensbury daughter?"

Judith nodded. "Aye," she stated simply.

"By Jove, this has been a night of miracles," the surgeon cried. "A lady finally bests this worthless blackguard—" He poured another dose of brandy in the wound, causing Stolford to moan loudly in his stupor and to once more try to wrest himself from the strong stablehand's arms. The surgeon continued, "and then I find the lady is none other than Sir Christopher's daughter. Do you know I once met your father, miss," he stated proudly. "What a fine man he was. But why have you been absent all these years? And, sir, you may put the bowl on the table. I will not have need of it now. I bled him earlier, but 'tis enough. Although, if I bled him a little more he might not recover, and I promise you I am sorely tempted to do so!"

Kelthorne chuckled. "You tempt me as well, but you had best continue your stitching." He placed the bowl on the table near the wall then resumed his place beside Judith. He addressed her, "The good doctor has asked the most essential question possible," he said. "Tell him, Judith, why you have been absent for the past eight years. I wish to hear it from your lips as well."

Judith lifted her arm and pointed at the marquess. Her hand trembled and her eyes suddenly flooded with tears. "I have been hiding from him."

Kelthorne did not hesitate but took her fully in his arms and held her tightly. "Did he hurt you this night? Did he hurt you, my love? Tell me. Please, tell me."

At that, she gave a watery laugh. "He did not have the chance, for I used every trick I had learned among the troupe and led him to believe I was weak and ill and all the while I was securing the dagger, which, as you know, John taught me how to use. When I turned into him, while in the coach, he thought—well, I suppose it does not matter now what he thought—but I cut him instead, deeply on the arm as you see now. I . . . I confess I almost hurt him further once I saw that I had incapacitated him. He does not like to be in pain."

Seeing her distress, he held her more closely still. "Do not think on it," he said softly. "You are uninjured and that is all that matters."

"Give me the word," the surgeon said, his expression now grim. "And I shall bleed him until there be no blood left."

Kelthorne placed his hand firmly on the doctor's shoulder. "Keep stitching, my good man, though I think we shall leave you to it."

He drew Judith away from the bed. "There is so much I must tell you. For one thing, and this is most important, you have a dowry awaiting you. My sister, who recalled rumors of your disappearance so many years ago, believes it to be some fifteen thousand pounds."

"What?" she cried.

"I am not surprised you did not know."

"I was so very young," she said, frowning. "My step-mother led me to believe I was penniless."

"I also think it possible your father may have left you more. Such a large dowry indicates wealth and a possible inheritance. You are no longer poor as you imagined yourself to be."

"Is it possible?" she queried, tears once more brimming in her eyes.

"Aye," he said softly, smiling at her.

She placed a hand on his cheek. "Thank you again for coming to find me. I am so very grateful, you have no idea."

He held her tightly once more and even if there was an audience, he kissed her warmly and deeply. How thankful he was that she was unharmed. How much he loved her.

The moment could not last, not with any degree of modesty and her nightdress withheld little from his imagination so that very soon he drew back from her and cleared his throat. "Perhaps we should join the troupe," he said.

"I should like that very much."

When they turned toward the door, he felt obligated to warn her. "Charles is here," he said quietly.

"Indeed? Did he, as I suspect, arrange the matter with Stolford?"

"He did. We are not yet certain what to do with him." With that, he escorted her from the chamber. By now a veritable riot of noise was in progress. Betty had even taken to singing, which was not her strongest ability. The taproom had come alive and at the top of the stairs an old man in his nightcap and gown shouted at them.

Kelthorne addressed him. "It will be of no use. They are a quite an incorrigible troupe of actors. However, if you wish for a brandy or perhaps a cup of rum punch, I shall be honored to have you as my guest."

"And who be ye?" he cried hotly, turning back to him.

"The Earl of Kelthorne," he stated, "at your service."

"What humbug! Kelthorne is quite old, by Jove and . . . well, by all that's wonderful, did that old ferret finally stick his spoon in the wall?"

"Aye," Kelthorne responded, laughing.

"Well, then! A cup of punch it shall be for he was the worst nipcheese I ever knew. I am an architect by trade and once built a cottage for one of his tenants and what it cost me . . . !" The man ground his teeth. "But this is all in the past now." He began moving down the stairs. Kelthorne followed behind with Judith. The man called out to the landlord, "Punch, if ye please and since the lady," here he winked at Kelthorne, "and since the lady is also in her nightdress, I shall not demure another moment. Actors, you say, and *actresses*?"

"Aye," Judith said, laughing.

The man hurried down the remainder of the stairs but Kelthorne held Judith back. "It was a terrible insult," he whispered. "I am sorry. Do you wish to retire? I shall provide a bedchamber for you if you so desire."

Judith looked up at him and smiled if crookedly. "Have you forgotten already that I, too, am a member of this troupe? Do you think there is even one of the men who has not seen me in my robe and nightdress, in my cap and with my hair tied up in rags?"

Kelthorne stared at her feeling oddly aghast. "I suppose it never occurred to me."

"Of course not, for you are being ridiculously naïve about me."

"Are you certain you do not wish for a private parlor?" he asked again.

At that he knew he had erred for a cool light entered her eye. "Not by half," she stated and then began a quick running descent of the stairs in what he realized were her bare feet.

"Judy!" Henry called to her.

Kelthorne followed slowly after and watched as one after the other, everyone in the troupe, save Charles, embraced her. He felt a profound degree of jealousy that was not in the least fair given the truly wretched circumstances of the night's events. Yet, she was the woman he loved, the woman he fully intended to make his wife and she was being passed from man to man just like any of the ladies.

When he reached the bottom step, his sister Mary approached him. "They are certainly a lively group," she said. "I could only wish that Judith were not so indelicately clad. 'Tis quite disconcerting."

He glanced at his sister. "She has been through a terrifying and difficult ordeal," he snapped. "Would you fault her for this?" He was being quite irrational since his own recent thoughts had been of a similar nature.

"I do beg your pardon," she said hastily. "I mean to do better and it was unforgivable that I should complain of her attire."

"Just so," he returned piously but his conscience smote him.

After Judith had regaled the troupe of just how she had come to do a fearful injury to the Marquess of Stolford, all eyes suddenly turned to Charles who was hunched in a corner.

Judith stepped toward him. "I knew you were many things, Mr. Hemyock, but not this. I knew you disliked me but to wish to see me ruined at Stolford's hands? I would not have thought you so cruel."

He glared at her. Not the smallest amount of remorse appeared in his eyes. "Ye never belonged in the troupe. Always above yer company, walking about with yer nose in the air, all yer ladylike manners, so smug and all the time laughing at us all."

"There you are greatly mistaken, Charles. Do you truly believe that I did not respect John and Margaret, Betty, Henry and the rest?"

"Of course not! Who would when Margaret came from the East End and worked as all girls worked or any of them wat give themselves to the gentlemen."

"Ye've said enough," John cried hotly, intervening by grabbing Charles by the arm and jerking him to his feet. "Now, get out and do not let me see yer face again for as all these good people are my witness I'll not leave a shred of skin on yer pretty face if ever I see ye. Leave, I say!" He threw him toward the door. Charles turned back as if to speak, but John said, "Ye've forfeited everything by wat ye've done this night. Yer things I'll give to the poor." He reached into his pocket, withdrew a small purse and flung it at him. "Twenty pounds and not a tuppence more."

Charles, always unable to resist a dramatic finish, flourished a grand bow, lifted his head high, turned on his heel, flung open the door and passed through. Dawn had passed and morning was bright on the horizon.

Judith felt the cold morning upon her skin. She shivered and at once felt Margaret's arm about her.

"Kelthorne," John suddenly called out. "Will ye not have a cup of punch? 'Tis a fine bowl the landlord makes."

Judith turned to watch him and saw his hesitation. His sisters flanked him, each of whom seemed to have grown uncomfortable. Her heart sank. Here was the truth that she already knew, which she understood a thousand times better than Kelthorne ever would. He might have spent much of his career dallying amongst the ladies of the theater but with his sisters to protect and his responsibilities as the Earl of Kelthorne, he could not easily cross the boundaries dictated by their society.

"I think it time to go," he said, meeting Judith's gaze.

Margaret turned to Judith. "Indeed, it is, Judy. Time fer ye to go."

"But I have not had a cup of punch yet," she stated firmly, holding Kelthorne's gaze. "I should like a cup, perhaps even two."

Lady Radsbury and Mrs. Newnott looked up at their brother. Kelthorne took a step away from them and toward Judith but there was nothing conciliatory in his expression. He extended his hand to her. "We should all go. 'Tis time my sisters returned to Portislow."

"Of course it is," Judith said. "I bid you all a safe journey." She dipped a curtsy, bowing her head, but afterward moved swiftly in the direction of the steaming bowl of punch, which sat on the bar. "A cup if you please, landlord."

An awful silence reigned behind her. Even the landlord was uncertain what he ought to do. "A cup please. You were so kind to me this evening and I will always be grateful."

His expression relaxed and he ladled a cup and handed it to her. She took a sip and then another. Margaret approached her. "Judy," she whispered close to her ear. "Do but think wat ye are doing. Such a man will not like to have his will thwarted."

Judith relaxed suddenly and turned and kissed her cheek. She then slid her arm about Margaret's waist and turned her toward Kelthorne. "This is my family, my lord," she said. "Mrs. Ash is as dear to me as a sister could ever be. Here my loyalties lie and perhaps always shall. I beg you will take your sisters home."

His expression was wholly grave. "And you will not attend us?" he inquired, a sad light entering his eye.

"Nay."

"But Judy—" John began, drawing nigh as well.

She smiled up at him. "You are more my family, Mr. John Ash, than I have ever known."

There were sudden tears in his eyes. "This is wat ye wish?"

"Aye," she responded.

"Come," Kelthorne said, taking his elder sister's arm. "We should leave."

"But Aubrey—" Mary protested.

"Yes, Aubrey, this cannot be right."

"All will be well," he said, but he did not look at Judith again.

She watched him go and sipped her punch at the same time for fear that the ache in her throat would soon force a flood of tears to her eyes and that would never do. She knew she was doing what was right, especially after he kicked up such a dust about her nightdress. She believed only in that moment had he truly come to understand just what manner of life she had been living for eight years.

Still, her throat ached. She drank deeply, again and again.

So it was that on the following morning, she awoke in her tent without the faintest idea how she had come to be there. The camp was alive with the peculiar shouting that occurred when the tents were being struck and the wagons loaded. How her head ached, though she was not certain to which cause she could ascribe the pain she was presently feeling. After all, she had been struck over the head little more than thirty hours past, but then she had never imbibed so much rum punch in her life!

Sitting on the edge of her bed and wondering as she always did if the corner would hold, she lowered her head gently into her hands and moaned softly. She determined never to become foxed again. Indeed, she could not help but wonder who would ever repeat such an experience as this.

Events of the night before flooded her mind. She did not want to think about anything that had happened, yet the memories rolled through her head one after the other like a tide that could not be turned. Only one thought snagged her, that she had a dowry and a very great one at that. Even her cousins had only had five thousand each. When she had left her home at fourteen, she had taken so very little with her and she had been just young enough that she had not known what she would bring to a contract of marriage.

She had a dowry and perhaps an inheritance. She would probably be able to do what she pleased and go where she desired. How was that possible? She truly did not know what to do.

A soft scratching sounded on her canvas door. "'Tis I," Margaret said.

Judith lifted her head. "Come," she whispered, but even then the sound of her voice was like a trumpet to her own ears. She winced and moaned anew.

Margaret entered bearing a cup of tea. "'Tis very weak. John always takes a cup after such a night."

Judith took it in trembling hands. She noted that the cup was but half full and nicely warm to the touch. "Thank you," she murmured.

Margaret sat on the small stool by the doorway. "Be ye feeling better?"

Judith smiled. "Better than what? Better than a lady whose head is being clamped in a vise? The answer must be no."

Margaret chuckled. 'Oh, Judy, how I am going to miss ye! I can hardly bear to think on it, I am that sad."

Judith sipped the tea. "Of what are you speaking? I am continuing on with the troupe." She knew at least this much, that she had a responsibility to the troupe and would not think of abandoning them now, particularly since their principal actor was gone. "I thought I made myself very clear on that subject last night."

Margaret shook her head and sighed. "I were hoping ye discovered by now how wrong ye were. Ye should have gone with Kelthorne and his sisters. They were willing."

"But I was not, not under such circumstances. Can you

not understand as much?" She wished they were not discussing the matter now. Her stomach felt queasy even with the warm tea.

"Nay, I do not understand. Ye love him and he loves ye. Wat more is there to consider, I ask ye?"

"Only the future. If he could not even bear to pass an hour or two in the company of all of you, how will he ever properly manage how I have lived since I was fourteen? No, Margaret, in this I know I am right and his conduct proved it to me last night. I am for Devonshire."

Margaret frowned as though trying to make her out. "Very well. I see that ye are not to be moved. John wished me to tell ye that the wagons will be ready in no more than an hour."

Judith nodded and surrounded the cup with both her hands, sipping deeply once more. As Margaret rose and turned to go, Judith said, "Thank you, Margaret."

"Fer the tea? O' course."

Judith shook her head. "Not for the tea, though I am grateful for that, but for your friendship and kindness to me. No sweeter soul exists on earth than yours."

Margaret smiled a watery smile. "And thank ye fer believing in me. 'Tis changed m'life, as ye very well know." She quit the tent but Judith had one last glimpse of her swiping at a damp cheek just before she called out to her daughter, "Shelly! Get off Horace's back! He's trying to tie up the goat!"

"'Tis my fault!" Mary cried.

"No, dearest, 'tis all mine!" Amy countered. "I am to blame. I should have insisted upon a cup of punch! And did not the bowl smell heavenly? But that is quite beside the point!"

Mary pouted and scowled at him. As Kelthorne watched her in some amusement, he thought she appeared to be about twelve instead of five and thirty, the wife of a peer and the mother of eight hopeful children. He found he was rather astonished by both his sisters, something he rarely was. "Well," she continued, "we are at least settled on this, Amy, that you and I both should have accepted so civil an offer of rum punch!"

"I think you are both being ridiculous," Kelthorne countered. Rufus looked up at him. He was seated beside his master, his head draped over the toe of his boot. Kelthorne leaned down to rub his ears.

They were seated in the drawing room, only the three of them present. Lord Radsbury had gone to London on business as was expected of him and Mr. Newnott and Mr. Emborough were off hunting. Miss Banwell and Miss Upton were practicing a new ballad in the small music room while Miss Currivard and Laurence had taken, as was their habit, to walking about on the hilltop garden. Mr. Currivard was due to arrive in a fortnight's time to meet his prospective son-in-law. Laurence was understandably nervous about the forthcoming encounter, but he had never been happier. How odd to think that love had found them both in Somerset.

A sennight had passed since the troupe had quit Portislow. The vale had begun to slumber once more. The apples in the orchard grew riper with each passing day. Every once in a while sunlight sparkled on the leaves in just such a manner as to hint of autumn.

For his part, Kelthorne had never known such lowness of spirit in his entire life. The night of Stolford's injury, he had needed Judith to choose yet he still did not comprehend why. He had forced the matter and that just following a time when she had barely recovered from the abduction. He wondered, as he had several times since, what would have happened had he not pressed the issue, had he—as his sisters were so markedly regretting—taken a cup of punch with the acting troupe.

Yet, he could not shake the wretched feeling of ill-usage and a piercing jealousy, which had attacked him in that moment, upon seeing her while clothed in but her nightdress being embraced by every man of the troupe.

"Aubrey," Mary said suddenly, sitting up very straight. "You are not fearful of her innocence, are you?"

He met her gaze and shook his head. "No," he stated simply.

"Then what is it?"

He rose abruptly and began pacing the chamber. "She was in her nightdress for everyone to see!" he cried sharply, throwing an arm wide. "And this was to be my wife?"

When he turned to face his sisters, he saw that they were staring at each other in consternation. He thought they understood now why he had been, and continued to be, so adamant about not following after Judith, begging her forgiveness for his snobbery, and bringing her back to Portislow. However, they soon began to smile and then to laugh. Finally, they were in such hysterics that he grew angry.

"What the deuce is so very funny about that! She was in her nightdress and all the men of the troupe were gawking at her as well as the servants in the inn. And you expect me to marry such a female?" His words, however, merely served to cause them both to laugh harder still until tears flowed down Amy's cheeks and Mary's face had turned a violent shade of red.

He was mightily offended that his sufferings had become such a source of amusement to his dear family.

He sat down again, feeling injured and more ill-used than ever. He refused to even look at them.

They continued to laugh for some time throwing out incomprehensible phrases to one another that would set them off once more at various intervals, things such as, "Imagine . . ." or "he complains . . ." or "what great irony."

When at last their amusement had abated, they moved to stand side-by-side in front of him. Mary made her case quite simple. "What a sapskull you are to think you deserve someone so precious as Judith Pensbury when, given your quite sordid career, you would complain of Miss Pensbury in her nightdress. You are a hypocrite, Aubrey, and I wash my hands of you."

"As do I," Amy said. "I could bear all the gossip about your adventures in great part because you never pretended to be something you were not. Perhaps I did not always like what you did, but neither did you hold to a moral place in society as Stolford was wont to do. I could not agree more with Mary. You do not deserve her, not by half."

With that, his sisters retired from the chamber intent on resting before dinner.

Kelthorne stared at the empty doorway for a very long time. He, a hypocrite? How utterly absurd! Judith should have chosen him and not the troupe.

The simple question "Why?" posed itself in his mind. He rose from his seat and moved to stare out the window, at the empty vale below. Clouds had moved in from the west and only a faint line of blue deep on the horizon showed how fair the weather had been. A rumbling in the distance bespoke rain.

He tried to imagine the camp and how resistant the tents were to rain, how difficult the daily routines would quickly become, how Mrs. Marnhull would have Horace set up an awning to protect her precious bread and, at this hour, the meal she was undoubtedly preparing. He wondered what Judith was doing, sewing in her tent or perhaps teaching Shelly her letters or practicing a new ballad with Mrs. Ash.

He sighed heavily. So, why was it she should have come with him?

Lightning flashed and with it came an odd understanding of what had really happened a sennight past. He had been frightened of her past, afraid that she might actually have been right, that once they were married, there would be endless gossip about her years with the troupe, and he truly did not know whether he could have born the relentless gabble-mongering. Good God, he had been the worst of cowards in that moment. Instead of standing by her, he had all but told her that she was unworthy to be his wife.

He felt sick with remorse. His sisters had been right to laugh at him and to wash their hands of him. In his fear, he had wanted her to prove, quite irrationally, that she was worthy of him by doing what? By abandoning a group of people, especially John and Margaret Ash, who had taken her in, given her a home and protected her for so many years.

Mary had been right. He had been a sapskull!

The wind began to whip the countryside, the usual frenzy just before a hard rain. A moment more, the first raindrops tapped on the window.

He stared into the countryside, in a southerly direction toward Devonshire. He had no intention of letting such absurd fears have command of him. He determined in this moment to spend the rest of his life, if need be, proving that he had been very wrong to have so deserted her.

His gaze traveled to the west and in an instant, he knew precisely what he wanted to do to begin atoning for his misdeeds.

FIFTEEN

Judith stared at Kelthorne thinking she must be seeing a ghost. A full fortnight had passed since he had left her at the inn in Langport. He stood in the doorway of her tent, an odd light in his eye. She could hardly catch her breath. What did he mean by coming? She thought she had made her intentions, her loyalties perfectly clear.

"Why have you come?" she asked. "No, do not give me answer. I do not wish to hear anything you have to say! Besides, I cannot speak with you for I am to perform very shortly!" If only he did not appear to such extreme advantage in his coat of blue superfine and his shirt points angled across his fine cheeks just so. She experienced the strongest most inexplicable urge to touch his hair, which just barely brushed the collar of his coat. She gave herself a shake. "Indeed, I cannot imagine why you have done so and I do wish you would leave my tent on the instant!"

"I shan't do so and you know very well why I have come."

"I do not!" she exclaimed.

He crossed the very small space separating them and took her in his arms quite roughly, forcing all the air from her lungs. Drawing air in proved wretchedly difficult since he was looking at her in such a way. She placed her hands on his shoulders and pushed, but he did not give way. "You should desist at once," she said, but her accents were pathetically weak. How would he ever believe her if she did not address him with greater spirit?

He shook his head and then he kissed her.

Judith withheld the enjoyment of the experience for about half a minute and then it was as though her body were made of butter and she simply melted against him. He kissed her quite deeply in response which served to remove any sensation whatsoever from the bottom of her feet. Her arms, quite traitorously, encircled his neck and she became lost. Even more profoundly, however, was that the dull stone that had become her heart since she had sipped the rum punch over a fortnight past had become quite instantly replaced with a feather.

How she loved him.

He drew back. "My darling, you must come back to Portislow with me. I need you so."

"But you left me in Langport."

"I was a fool. I should have had punch with you, my sisters as well. They have told me repeatedly how they should have pressed me to do so and now I have come to you to beg your forgiveness."

"This is madness," she said, but she was clinging to him now as though her life depended upon remaining within the circle of his embrace.

"The most beautiful sort of madness."

"Oh, do not say such wicked things to me. Do you know how you tempt my heart?"

"I wish to tempt much more than your heart, my darling."

"What a scandalous thing to say!" she cried. How she delighted in him.

"Ah, but you have mistook my meaning, dearest, though now that I think on it, I rather like your interpretation. However, I was thinking more of your place beside me in my home and in London. I intend to take my responsibilities seriously in the House of Lords and I will need an accomplished bride beside me, a songstress in this case to charm my enemies in our drawing room."

"You are being abominably absurd," she whispered. She kissed him. She loved what he was saying to her, giving her a hope that was not a hope at all.

"Marry me," he said softly against her lips then kissed her anew.

After a very long moment, indeed, she said, "I cannot. You know I cannot."

"Are you very certain, indeed?"

"Aye," she whispered.

He drew back. "Well, I thought you would say as much, so I have brought someone with me who I hope will persuade you."

Judith sighed as he released her. She could well withstand his sisters or even Miss Currivard and Mr. Doulting. However, when an entirely new face appeared at the opening of her tent, one that seemed both familiar yet not, she gasped. "Uncle!" she cried.

He had tears in his eyes and spread his arms wide. "Why did you not come to me! All these years, my dearest niece! I could have protected you!"

Judith found herself in a strong embrace and tears she had withheld for a very long time flooded her face. She held him fast, entirely overcome with so many thoughts and feelings that for a very long time she could not speak. She met Kelthorne's gaze over her uncle's shoulder and murmured her thanks. He stepped from the tent and let the canvas door fall for privacy.

When at last Judith was able to draw away from him, she sought her kerchief, mopped her face and blew her nose soundly. She realized that she was not the only one making serious use of a kerchief.

"Oh dear, oh dear," her Uncle Pensbury said. "To think I am looking at you now. Kelthorne told me of Stolford but why did you run away? I could have protected you."

She shook her head. "You do not understand how determined he was. I made my way to your house but Stolford had anticipated me. His coach was in your drive. I waited for days, but there was always one of his servants about. I knew I was not safe. Everyone underestimated his determination except my governess. She knew what he was. She helped me to escape my father's house and then she took a ship to the colonies."

Her uncle seemed unbearably sad. "I wish that I could dispute you, but when I recall that first year of your disappearance, Stolford was never far from my home. Perhaps you are right, but this existence for my poor niece—!"

"You must never think of it in that manner, uncle. I have been safe and beloved in the care of John and Margaret Ash."

"They have cared for you well, then?"

"Sacrificing for me innumerable times."

"Only, Judith, pray tell me what is this nonsense of your having refused the Earl of Kelthorne when he is persuaded you are very much in love with him?"

"'Tis not nonsense. My absence for so many years in polite society will promote nothing but the worst gossip and it will soon be widely known where I have been. How can such a questionable existence ever allow Kelthorne, or any children we might have, a proper place in society."

"There is only one proper place in society," her uncle said. "Safely within the confidence and trust of one's friends. Beyond that, 'tis social squabbling and ill will, which I promise you has always existed and probably always shall no matter how innocent the circumstances. No, Judith, I am persuaded you are being something of a coward in not facing these problems."

She did not like hearing such words but she sighed heavily nonetheless. She had already begun to see that her remaining with the troupe, when her identity as Judith Pensbury would very soon come to light, was becoming both unnecessary and ridiculous as each day passed especially given the manner in which Stolford had been vanquished at last.

Still, she felt unable to leave what had been her home for so many years and her responsibility to those who had become dear to her through their care and concern. "I beg you will not press me, uncle. You cannot know what these people have come to mean to me."

"I have met Mr. Ash and his good wife besides having been informed of their kindness to you by Kelthorne. I, therefore, cannot argue with you. I will say only this, 'tis time to come home, dearest Judith, and claim that which is rightfully yours both by birth and by your remarkable courage in evading your enemy for eight years and more. You have earned what has come to you and that very rightly so, my dear. You will make a very fine countess and your experiences among these exceptional people will only add to your ability to do justice to that post."

Judith looked into his warm, loving eyes and remembered that this was what she had always loved best about her Uncle Pensbury—the sincere manner in which he was used to address her, even as a child, and how she had always felt safe in his company. "I am still not persuaded, uncle. I beg you will give me time."

"As much time as you require, my pet. There is something I do wish you to know. Stolford will not bother you again. Kelthorne and I consulted a solicitor and then had a rather lengthy conversation with the marquess. We did not feel pressing the matter in a court of law would be of much use to anyone so we suggested an extended tour of the Continent lasting no less than ten years would be appropriate."

Judith was pleased. "What did he say?"

"That he had been desirous of residing in Paris anyway."

"He is a wretched creature."

Her uncle stared at her for a moment then asked with a half-smile, "Did you truly cut him with a dagger?"

"Yes," she stated, but she was smiling as well.

"No less than the beast deserved!"

At that moment, Margaret called to her, "Judy! Come and be quick about it for ye will not believe what has happened!"

Judith rarely heard Margaret in such a state and rushed from her tent, bidding her uncle to follow her. She saw Margaret waving her forward in the direction of the stage.

"'Tis frightful!" Margaret called to her, all the while urging her forward hurriedly. The troupe had once again set up their makeshift stage in a field.

Judith picked up her skirts and ran. She could hear the audience booing and hissing and making a terrible fuss. She had never heard such disapproval of anyone in the troupe in all these many years.

"Good heavens, Margaret," she cried in a hushed whisper as she reached her at the wings of the stage. "What has happened?"

"Ye must see fer yerself." She then held the curtain back if slightly.

Judith clamped a hand over her mouth to keep from crying out and laughing at one and the same time. Kelthorne had taken the stage with a book of poetry, Shakespeare, as it were, and was reading with the most awful cadence possible. At the same time in what appeared to be a completely random manner, he would cast a hand dramatically in the air.

The audience, aware they were being cheated of their pennies, grew louder still and finally a cabbage hit the earl on the foot. He looked up and pretended his shock. "Are you not delighted with my performance!" he called out to the jeering crowd.

Judith began to smile and then to laugh. Her heart blossomed like a rose beneath sunshine. She ventured quickly upon the stage and joined him addressing the audience, "You must forgive the latest addition to our troupe. He has not practiced quite long enough but if you will be so good as to resume your seats and quiet your displeasure, I shall sing for you."

A rolling sigh passed around the audience like a breeze

soughing through the treetops. She glanced to the wings and gestured for Margaret to join her. She took Kelthorne's hand and drew him with her to the center of the stage. She did not let his hand go but rather smiled at him and as she had before, began to sing, "Captivity."

She sang for him and to him, though occasionally sharing her love with the audience. She came to a quiet understanding that this would be her very last performance in a professional troupe, making each note a trifle more poignant than might otherwise have been expected in a small market town in Devonshire.

Afterward, John, Henry and Freddy pretended to attack Kelthorne and drag him off the stage much to the great amusement of the audience. John then encouraged her to sing as did the rest of the troupe. She sang for an hour and then two, the audience with her until the very last note. Resounding applause shook the makeshift stage. She sang three encores.

After the final one, Kelthorne took the stage once more begging the indulgence of the audience. A hush fell over the crowd. He turned to her. "Will you marry me, Judith, or will I have to bear these cabbages every night for the rest of my life, for I promise you, until you do agree, I shall take up residence in a tent next to yours and travel England until one or the other of us is dead and buried. 'Tis your choice but I believe the audience would rather you said 'aye' than 'nay.' " He turned and asked the audience, "What say *ye?*"

One man, holding a cabbage in his hand, cried out, "Marry 'im, else I will throw this beauty!"

"Am I to be forced into accepting you?" she cried playfully.

"I will have you however I can get you, make no mistake."

She sighed yet again. "Then I suppose I must acquiesce." With that he thoroughly delighted the audience by giving expression to his sentiments by kissing her soundly.

Happily, there were no cabbages on this occasion only applause, a shouting of huzzas, and numerous whistles.

"How can you suggest such a thing in the midst of our betrothal ball?" Judith complained, but her heart was far from insistent. "We cannot leave when it is barely just begun."

He held her hand firmly and tugged her along the path that descended the side of the hill from the point of the conservatory. "We will only be absent for a little while and since I have every confidence that our guests mean to stay until the small hours of the morning, no one will feel slighted."

"Oh, very well, but it most improper," she chided yet she was smiling.

He drew to a sudden halt. "I will take you back if you truly wish for it."

Her breath caught as it so very often did as she met his gaze, the warmth of his expression, the liveliness of his eye. "Well," she mused. "We are halfway to the orchard now. I suppose it will do no harm, but only for a few minutes, mind."

He smiled, kissed her fully on the lips and just as she was hoping for more, he drew back and once more began tugging her almost anxiously down the hill.

Nor could she coax him to speak. He was oddly silent, yet smiling all the while as though he had some great secret. "What is it?" she asked, when they were but twenty yards or so from orchard.

"I shan't tell you just yet. I must find the exact spot where I first met you. Come."

She shook her head in some amusement. She now felt certain he had some notion in his head.

When at last they were agreed that this was the precise location where he had first kissed her, he took her hands firmly in his. "My darling Judith," he began.

Judith squeezed his hands and smiled. Her heart had

begun to race, but out of the corner of her eye, she saw a blur and turning cried out, "No!" A moment later, she was lying flat on her back, and Rufus was licking her face. Pushing him back, she glared at Kelthorne who had begun to laugh. "Was this your idea?" she cried. "Did you actually arrange to have him knock me down as he did that first night?"

He pulled Rufus away by his collar and at the same time, slid his hand beneath Judith's arm. "On no account! I am not so ham-handed at lovemaking as this!"

"I think it very odd," she said, but her fingers found a favorite spot on Rufus's left ear and began soothing him.

"I have noticed that he never likes being separated from you for very long," Kelthorne said. "In that, he and I share a similar doting affection. Although I am persuaded that however much he might be fond of you, he is not as passionate toward you as I am."

She let go of Rufus and slipped her arms about his neck. "And you are passionate," she stated, her heart swelling with love. "My favorite thing, I must confess."

He groaned faintly as he caressed her cheek. "I am growing impatient with all this waiting."

"We have only a fortnight more," she said, laughing at him, "until the banns are properly read.

"It might as well be a century in my opinion."

He kissed her again, much as he had on the hill drawing back far too soon. She whimpered her displeasure. But he held her at bay.

"Now, I have something I wish to give you," he said. From the pocket of his coat he withdrew what appeared to be a letter and held it for her.

The light was very dim through the leafy apple trees. She had to turn the paper several different angles in order to catch enough moonlight by which to read it. After a few lines, she gasped, "Why, this is from the owner of Drury Lane," she cried. "And 'tis addressed to John." She gasped anew and met what was now his beaming gaze. "You secured an engagement for them?"

"Aye," he responded. "So I did."

"Oh, Aubrey, I could not have asked for anything better. Only, how did you manage it?"

He suddenly appeared rather conscious. "As it happens, I have numerous connections with people of the theater."

She began to laugh. "Of course, you wicked fellow."

He held her gaze seriously for a moment. "But those days are finished. You must believe me in that."

"I do," she said, sliding her arms about his neck. "Thank you, Aubrey. You have changed my life in every beautiful manner possible."

"As you have mine," he responded sincerely. "I love you, Judith, with all my heart."

More Regency Romance
From Zebra

More Historical Romance From
Jo Ann Ferguson

Available Wherever Books Are Sold!

Visit our website at **www.kensingtonbooks.com.**